"She can stay."

O'Rourke pointed toward Chandra before focusing his attention on the crying infant. He touched the infant tenderly, as he gently rolled the screaming baby from front to back, fingers expertly examining the child. It was all Chandra could do to keep from cradling the baby herself, holding the infant close and rocking him.

This has got to stop, Chandra, she told herself, *he's not yours—he's not!* If she had any brains at all, she would walk out of Riverbend Hospital and never look back. Let the proper authorities take care of the child. If they could locate the parents, so be it. If not, the social-services agencies would see that he was placed with a carefully screened couple who desperately wanted a child....

But she stayed, compelled by the child and fascinated by the doctor examining him. Why she felt a special bond with the child and the doctor she didn't know, yet she felt as if they, all three, were already inextricably bound to each other.

D0974869

Dear Reader,

Welcome to Silhouette **Special Edition** . . . welcome to romance. Each month, Silhouette **Special Edition** publishes six novels with you in mind—stories of love and life, tales that you can identify with—romance with that little "something special" added in.

May has some wonderful stories blossoming for you. Don't miss Debbie Macomber's continuing series, THOSE MANNING MEN. This month, we're pleased to present *Stand-in Wife,* Paul and Leah's story. And starting this month is Myrna Temte's new series, COWBOY COUNTRY. *For Pete's Sake* is set in Wyoming and should delight anyone who enjoys the classic ranch story.

Rounding out this month are more stories by some of your favorite authors: Lisa Jackson, Ruth Wind, Andrea Edwards. And say hello to Kari Sutherland. Her debut book, *Wish on the Moon,* is also coming your way this month.

In each Silhouette **Special Edition** novel, we're dedicated to bringing you the romances that you dream about—stories that will delight as well as bring a tear to the eye. And that's what Silhouette **Special Edition** is all about—special books by special authors for special readers!

I hope you enjoy this book and all of the stories to come!

Sincerely,

Tara Gavin
Senior Editor
Silhouette Books

LISA JACKSON
Million Dollar Baby

Silhouette Special Edition

Published by Silhouette Books New York

America's Publisher of Contemporary Romance

SILHOUETTE BOOKS
300 East 42nd St., New York, N.Y. 10017

MILLION DOLLAR BABY

ISBN: 0-373-09743-3

First Silhouette Books printing May 1992

Printed in the U.S.A.

Books by Lisa Jackson

LISA JACKSON

was raised in Molalla, Oregon, and now lives with her husband, Mark, and her two sons in a suburb of Portland, Oregon. Lisa and her sister, Natalie Bishop, who is also a Silhouette author, live within earshot of each other.

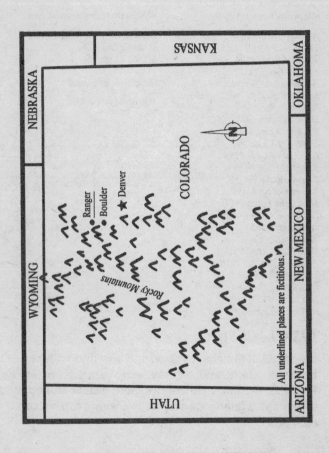

NEBRASKA

KANSAS

WYOMING

COLORADO

UTAH

ARIZONA

NEW MEXICO

OKLAHOMA

Ranger
Boulder
★ Denver

Rocky Mountains

All underlined places are fictitious.

N

Chapter One

The dog stuck his wet nose in Chandra's face. He whined and nuzzled her jaw.

"Go 'way," Chandra grumbled, squeezing her eyes shut. She burrowed deeper into the pillows, hoping Sam would get the message, but Sam didn't give up. The persistent retriever clawed at her covers and barked loudly enough to wake the neighbors ten miles down the road. "Knock it off, Sam!" Irritated, she yanked a pillow over her head and rolled over. But she was awake now and couldn't ignore Sam's whining and pacing along the rail of the loft; the metal licenses hanging from his collar rattled noisily.

When she didn't respond, he snorted loudly and padded quickly down the stairs, whereupon he barked again.

So he had to go out. "You should've thought of this earlier." Reluctantly, Chandra pulled herself into a sitting position and shoved a handful of hair from her eyes. She shivered a little and, yawning, rubbed her arms.

Sam barked excitedly, and she considered letting him out and leaving him on the porch. As Indian summer faded into autumn, the nighttime temperature in the Rocky Mountain foothills had begun to dip toward freezing. "It would serve you right," she said ungraciously as she glanced at the clock on the table near the bed. One forty-three. Still plenty of time to fall asleep again before the alarm clock was set to go off.

Grumbling under her breath, she had leaned over and was reaching under the bed, feeling around for her boots, when she heard it: the sound that had filtered through her dreams and pierced her subconscious over Sam's insistent barking. The noise, a distant wail, reminded Chandra of the hungry cry of a baby or the noise a Siamese cat would make if it were in pain. Chandra's skin crawled.

You're imagining things! she told herself. She was miles from civilization....

The cry, distant and muffled, broke the silence again. Chandra sat bolt upright in bed. Her heart knocked crazily. Clutching the quilt around her shoulders, she swung her feet to the floor and crossed the worn wood planks to the railing, where she could look down and survey the first floor of the cabin.

Moonlight streamed through the windows, and a few embers glowed behind the glass doors of the wood stove. Otherwise the cabin was cloaked in the darkness that night brought to this isolated stretch of woods.

She could barely see Sam. His whiskey-colored coat blended into the shadows as he paced beside the door, alternately whining and growling as he scratched on the threshold.

"So now you're Lassie, is that it?" she asked. "Telling me that there's something out there."

He yelped back.

"This is nuts. Hush, Sam," Chandra commanded, her skin prickling as her eyes adjusted to the shadows. Straining to listen, she reached for the pair of old jeans she'd tossed carelessly across the foot of the bed hours earlier. The familiar noises in this little cabin in the foothills hadn't changed. From the ticking of the grandfather clock to the murmur of the wind rushing through the boughs of the pine and aspen that surrounded the cabin, the sounds of the Colorado night were as comforting as they had always been. The wind chimes on her porch tinkled softly, and the leaky faucet in the bathroom dripped a steady tattoo.

The cry came again. A chill raced up Chandra's spine. Was it a baby? No way. Not up here in these steep hills. Her mind was playing tricks on her. Most likely some small beast had been wounded and was in pain—a cat who had strayed or a wounded raccoon... maybe even a bear cub separated from its mother....

Snarling, Sam started back up the stairs toward her.

"Hold on, hold on." Chandra yanked on her jeans and stuffed the end of her flannel nightshirt into the waistband. She slid her feet into wool socks and, after another quick search under the bed, crammed her feet into her boots.

Her father's old .22 was tucked into a corner of the closet. She hesitated, grabbed her down jacket, then curled her fingers over the barrel of the Winchester. Better safe than sorry. Maybe the beast was too far gone and she'd have to put it out of its misery. Maybe it was rabid.

And maybe it's not a beast at all.

By the time she and the retriever crept back downstairs, Sam was nearly out of his mind, barking and growling, ready to take on the world. "Slow down," Chandra ordered, reaching into the pocket of her jacket, feeling the smooth shells for her .22. She slipped two cartridges into the rifle's cold chamber.

"Okay, now don't do anything stupid," she said to the dog. She considered leaving Sam in the house, for fear that he might be hurt by the wounded, desperate beast, but then again, she felt better with the old dog by her side. If she did stumble upon a lost bear cub, the mother might not be far away or in the best of moods.

As she opened the door, a blast of cool mountain air rushed into the room, billowing curtains and causing the fire to glow brightly. The night wind seemed to have forgotten the warm breath of summer that still lingered during the days.

Clouds drifted across the moon like solitary ghosts, casting shadows on the darkened landscape. The crying hadn't let up. Punctuated by gasps or hiccups, it grew louder as Chandra marched across the gravel and ignored the fear that stiffened her spine. She headed straight for the barn, to the source of the noise.

The wailing sounded human. But that was insane. She hadn't heard a baby cry in years... and there were no children for miles. Her dreams must have confused her... and yet...

She opened the latch, slid the barn door open and followed an anxious Sam inside. A horse whinnied, and the smells of dust and saddle soap and dry hay filled her nostrils. Snapping on the lights with one hand, she clutched the barrel of the gun with the other.

The horses were nervous. They rustled the straw on the floor of their boxes, snorting and pawing, tossing their dark heads and rolling their eyes as if they, too, were spooked. "It's all right," Chandra told them, though she knew that something in the barn was very, very wrong. The crying became louder and fiercer.

Her throat dry, her rifle held ready, Chandra walked carefully to the end stall, the only empty box. "What the devil...?" Chandra whispered as she spied a shock of black fur—no, *hair*—a baby's downy cap of hair! Chandra's heart nearly stopped, but she flew into action, laying down the gun, unlatching the stall and kneeling beside the small, swaddled bundle of newborn infant.

The tiny child was bound in a ratty yellow blanket and covered by a tattered army jacket. "Oh, God," Chandra whispered, picking up the small bundle only to have the piercing screams resume at a higher pitch. Blue-black eyes blinked at the harsh overhead lights, and the infant's little face was contorted and red from crying. One little fist had been freed from the blankets and now waved in agitation near its cheek. "Oh, God, oh, God." The baby, all lungs from the sound of it, squealed loudly.

"Oh, sweetheart, don't cry," Chandra murmured, plucking pieces of straw from the child's hair and holding him close to her breast, trying to be soothing. She scanned the rest of the barn, searching for the mother. "Hey—is anyone here?" Her sweat seemed to freeze on her skin as she listened for a response. "Hey? Anyone? Please, answer me!"

The only noises in the barn were the horses snorting, the baby hiccupping and crying, Sam's intermittent growls and Chandra's own thudding heart. "Shh . . . shh . . ." she said, as if the tiny infant could understand her. "We'll fix you up."

A mouse scurried across the floor, slipping into a crack in the barn wall, and Chandra, already nervous, had to bite back her own scream. "Come on," she whispered to the baby, as she realized the child had probably been abandoned. But who would leave this precious baby all alone? The infant howled more loudly as Chandra tucked it close to her. "Oh, baby, baby," Chandra murmured. Maternal emotions spurred her to kiss the downy little head while she secretly cursed the woman who had left this beautiful child alone and forsaken. "Who are you?" she whispered against the baby's dark crown. "And where's your mama?"

Wrapping the infant in her own jacket, she glanced around the dusty corners of the barn again, eyeing the hayloft, kicking open the door to the tack room, scanning the corners behind the feed barrels, searching for any signs of the mother. Sam, yelping and jumping at the baby, was no help in locating the woman's trail. "Hello? Are you here?'' she called to anyone listening, but her own voice echoed back from the rafters.

"Look, if you're here, come on into the house. Don't be afraid. Just come in and we'll talk, okay?''

No answer.

"Please, if you can hear me, please come inside!''

Again, nothing. Just the sigh of the wind outside.

Great. Well, she'd tried. Whoever had brought the child here was on his or her own. Right now, the most pressing problem was taking proper care of the baby; anything else would have to wait. "Come on, you,'' she whispered to the infant again, tightening her hold on the squirming bundle. Ignoring the fretting horses, she slapped off the lights and closed the barn door behind her.

Once she was back in the cabin, Chandra cradled the child against her while she tossed fresh logs into the wood stove. "We'll get you warm,'' she promised, reaching for the phone and holding the receiver to her ear with her shoulder. She dialed 911, praying that the call would be answered quickly.

"Emergency,'' a dispatcher answered.

"Yes, this is Chandra Hill, I live on Flaming Moss Road,'' she said quickly, then rattled off her address over the baby's cries. "I discovered an infant in my barn. Newborn, dehydrated possibly, certainly hungry, with a chance of exposure. I—I don't know who it belongs to... or why it's here.''

"We can send an ambulance.''

"I live twenty miles from town. It'll be quicker if I meet the ambulance at Alder's Corner, where the highway intersects Flaming Moss.''

"Just a minute.'' The dispatcher mumbled something to someone else and then was back on the line. "That's fine. The ambulance will meet you there.''

"Good. Now, please contact the emergency room of the hospital....'' Mechanically, she began to move and think in a way she hadn't done in years. Placing the child on the couch next to her, she carefully unwrapped the howling infant. Furious and hungry, the baby cried more loudly, his skinny little legs kicking. "It's a boy...probably two or three days old," she said, noticing the stump of the umbilical cord. How many infants so like this one had she examined during her short career as a physician? Hundreds. Refusing to let her mind wander into that forbidden territory, she concentrated on the wriggling child and carefully ran her fingers over his thin body. "He's Caucasian, very hungry, with no visible marks...." Her hands moved expertly over the smooth skin of the newborn, checking muscles and bones, small fingers and toes, legs, neck, spine, buttocks, head.... "Wait a minute..." She flipped the switch of a brighter light and noticed the yellow pallor of the whites of the baby's eyes. "He appears jaundiced and—" she touched the downy hair again, carefully prodding "—there's some swelling on the back of his head. Maybe caput succedaneum or cephalhematoma...yes, there's a slight bleeding from the scalp, and it appears only on the right side of his head. I don't think it's serious. The swelling isn't too large, but you'd better have a pediatrician look him over the minute he gets there." She continued to examine the infant as if he were her patient, her gaze practiced and sure. "I can't find anything else, at least not here without medical equipment. Did you get everything?"

"Every word," the dispatcher replied. "You're being recorded."

"Good." Chandra shone her flashlight in the baby's eyes, and he blinked and twisted his head away from the light. "Notify the sheriff's office that apparently the child's been abandoned."

"You don't know the mother?" the dispatcher questioned.

Chandra shook her head, though the woman on the other end of the line couldn't see her. "No. I have no idea whom this guy belongs to. So someone from the sheriff's office should come out here and look through my barn again and check the woods. I called out and looked around for the mother, but I didn't have much time. I was more concerned with the child." She glanced to the windows and the cold night beyond. "My guess is she isn't far off. You've got the address."

Chandra didn't wait for a response, but hung up. She pulled a blanket from her closet and rewrapped the tiny newborn. He was beautiful, she thought, with a shock of downy black hair that stood straight off his scalp and a voice that would wake the dead. But why had he been abandoned? Had the mother, perhaps homeless, left him in the relative comfort of the barn as she searched for food? But why not stop at the cabin? Why leave him in the barn where there was a chance he would go unnoticed, maybe even die? Chandra shuddered at the thought. No, any responsible mother would have knocked on the door and would never, *never* have abandoned her child. "Come on, you," she said to the baby, "we've got work to do. You can't just lie there and scream."

But scream he did until she swaddled him more tightly and held him in her arms again. Only then did his cries become pitiful little mews. Chandra clutched him even tighter; the sooner she got him to the hospital the better.

Sam was sitting at attention near the couch. She looked in his direction, and the big dog swept the floor with his tail. "You," she said, motioning to the retriever, "stick around. In case the mother wanders back or the police show up."

As if the dog could do anything, she thought with a wry smile.

She found more blankets and tucked the child into a wicker laundry basket which, along with several bungee cords and the baby, she carried to her suburban. After securing the basket by the safety belt in the back seat, she crisscrossed the bungee cords over the baby, hoping to hold him as tightly and safely as possible.

"Hang on," she said to the infant as she hauled herself into the driver's seat, slammed the door shut and switched on the ignition. She rammed the monstrous rig into gear. The beams of the headlights washed across the side of the barn, and Chandra half expected a woman to come running from the shadows. But no one appeared, and Chandra tromped on the accelerator, spewing gravel.

"Dr. O'Rourke. Dr. Dallas O'Rourke. Please call E.R."

Dallas O'Rourke was writing out instructions for a third-floor patient named William Aimes when the page sounded. He scowled menacingly, then strode to the nearest house phone and punched out the number for the main desk of Riverbend Hospital. Checking the clock at the nurse's station, he realized he'd been on duty for the past twenty-two hours. His back ached and his shoulders were stiff, and he felt gritty from lack of sleep. He probably looked worse than he felt, he thought grimly as the receiver of the phone rubbed against the stubble of beard on his chin.

A voice answered, and he cut in. "This is Dr. O'Rourke. I was just paged."

"That's right. I'll connect you to E.R."

The telephone clicked and a familiar voice answered quickly. "Emergency. Nurse Pratt."

"O'Rourke." Leaning a stiff shoulder against the wall, he scribbled his signature across Aimes's chart, then rubbed his burning eyes. How long had it been since he'd eaten? Six hours? Seven?

"You'd better hustle your bones down here," Shannon Pratt advised. "We're swamped, and we've got a live one coming in. The switchboard just took the call. Something about an abandoned baby, a newborn with possible exposure, dehydration, jaundice and cephalhematoma."

Dallas scowled to himself. What was the old saying? Something about no rest for the wicked? The adage seemed to apply. "I'll be down in a few minutes." God, what he wouldn't do for a hot shower, hotter cup of coffee, and about ten hours in the rack.

He only took the time to leave the chart in the patient's room and give the third-floor nurses' station some instructions about Bill Aimes's medication. "And make sure he takes it," Dallas warned. "It seems Mr. Aimes thinks he can self-diagnose."

"He won't fool us," Lenore Newell replied, and Dallas was satisfied. Lenore had twenty years of nursing experience under her belt, and she'd seen it all. If anyone could get Bill Aimes to swallow his medication, Dallas decided, Nurse Newell could.

Unwilling to wait for the elevator, he took the stairs to the first floor and shoved open the door. The bright lights and frenetic activity of the emergency room greeted him. Several doctors were treating patients, and there was a crowd in the waiting room.

Shannon Pratt, a slim, dark-haired woman and, in Dallas's opinion, the most efficient nurse on staff, gave the doctor a quick smile. "They're on their way. Mike just called. They'll be here in about five minutes."

Mike Rodgers was one of the regular paramedics who drove ambulance for Riverbend Hospital.

"How's the patient?"

Shannon glanced at the notes she'd attached to a clipboard that she cradled with one arm. "Looks like the information we received from the first call was right on. The paramedics confirmed what the woman who called in already told us. The baby—only a couple of days old—has some signs of exposure as well as possible jaundice and slight swelling on one side of the head—the, uh, right," she said, rechecking her notes. "No other visible problems. Vital signs are within the normal range."

"Good. Order a bilirubin and get the child under U.V. as soon as I finish examining him. Also, I want as much information from the mother as possible, especially her RH factor. If she doesn't know it, we'll take blood from her—"

Shannon touched Dallas lightly on the arm. "Hold on a minute, Doctor. The mother's not involved."

Dallas stopped. He glanced swiftly at Nurse Pratt—to see if she was putting him on. She wasn't. Her face was as stone sober as it always was in an emergency. "Not involved? Then how the hell—"

Pratt held up a hand. "The woman who found the child—"

"The woman who *found* the child?" Dallas repeated as they passed the admitting desk, where Nurse Lindquist, a drill sergeant of a woman, presided. Over the noise of rattling gurneys and wheelchairs, conversation, paging and computer terminals humming, Dallas heard the distant wail of a siren.

Pratt continued, "The mother isn't bringing him in. This is a case of abandonment, or so the woman who called—" she glanced down at her notes on her clipboard again "—Chandra Hill, claims. Apparently she's saying that she discovered the baby in her barn."

"Her *barn?*"

"Mmm. Doesn't know how he got there." Shannon rolled her large brown eyes and lifted one slim shoulder. "I guess we'll find out soon enough."

Dallas swore silently. "If she's not the mother, how can we do anything with—"

"We're already working on consent forms," Pratt cut in, ahead of him, as she usually was in a case like this. "The police are involved, and someone's looking up a judge to sign the waiver so we can admit the kid as a Baby John Doe."

"Wonderful," Dallas growled under his breath. With his luck, the kid's mother would show up, demand custody and file a complaint against the hospital. Or worse yet, not show up at all, and the child would have to be cared for by the state. "Just damned wonderful." What a way to end a shift!

The siren's wail increased to a glass-shattering scream that drowned out all conversation. Lights flashing, the white-and-orange rig ground to a stop near the double glass doors of the emergency room. Two men Dallas recognized hopped out of the cab and raced to the back of the emergency van.

"Okay, listen up," Dallas ordered Pratt. "I'll need that bilirubin A.S.A.P., and we'll need to test the child—drugs, HIV, white count, everything," he said, thinking of all the reasons a person might abandon a child. Maybe the woman couldn't afford proper medical attention for herself and the baby; maybe the child needed expensive care. "And get ready with an IV or a bottle..." God, what a mess!

The paramedics shoved open the back doors of the ambulance. Pulling out a small stretcher and carrying it between them, Mike Rodgers and Joe Klinger ran across the short covered span near the doors. A tiny baby, insulated by a thermal blanket, was strapped to the stretcher and was screaming bloody murder.

"Okay, Doc, looks like it's show time," Shannon observed as Dallas caught a glimpse of another vehicle, a huge red van of some sort, as it sped into the lot and skidded into a parking space.

The doors to the emergency room flew open. The paramedics, carrying the small stretcher, strode quickly inside.

"Room two," Nurse Pratt ordered.

Under the glare of fluorescent lights, Mike, a burly redheaded man with serious, oversize features and thick glasses, nodded curtly and headed down the hall without breaking stride. "As I said, it looks like exposure and dehydration, heart rate and b.p. are okay, but—"

Mike rattled off the child's vital signs as Joe unstrapped the child and placed him on the examining table. Dallas was listening, but had already reached for his penlight and snapped his stethoscope around his neck. He touched the child carefully. The right side of the infant's head was a little bit swollen, but there wasn't much evidence of bleeding. A good sign. The tiny boy's skin was tinged yellow, but again, not extremely noticeable. Whoever the woman was who found the child, she knew more than a little about medicine.

Dallas glanced over at the paramedic. "This woman who called in—Ms. Hill?—I want to talk to her. Do you have her number?"

"Don't need to," Mike said. "She followed us here. Drove that damned red van like a bat outta hell...."

The red van. Of course. Good. Dallas wasn't convinced that she wasn't the mother just trying to get some free medical attention for her child. So how did she know about the child's condition? Either she'd diagnosed the baby herself or someone else had... someone who understood pediatric medicine. One way or another, Dallas thought, flashing the beam of his penlight into the baby's dark eyes, he needed to talk to Ms. Hill.

"When she shows up," he said, glancing at Nurse Pratt, "I want to see her."

Riverbend Hospital sprawled across five acres of hills. The building was either five floors, four or three, depending upon the terrain. Painted stark white, it seemed to grow from the very ground on which it was built.

It resembled a hundred other hospitals on the outside and inside, Chandra thought; it was a nondescript medical institution. She'd been here before, but now, as she got the runaround from a heavyset nurse at the emergency room desk, Chandra was rapidly losing her temper. "But I have to see the child, I'm the one who found him!" she said, with as much patience as she could muster.

The admitting nurse, whose name tag read Alma Lindquist, R.N., didn't budge. An expression of authority that brooked no argument was fixed on features too small for her fleshy face.

Chandra refused to be put off by Nurse Lindquist. She'd dealt with more than her share of authority figures in her lifetime—especially those in the medical profession. One more wouldn't stop her, though Nurse Lindquist did seem to guard the admittance gate to the emergency room of Riverbend Hospital as if it were the portal to heaven itself and Chandra was a sinner intent on sneaking past.

"If you're not the mother or the nearest living relative," Nurse Lindquist was saying in patient, long-suffering tones, "then you cannot be allowed—"

"I'm the responsible party." Chandra, barely holding on to her patience, leaned across the desk. She offered the woman a professional smile. "I found the boy. There's a chance I can help."

"Humph," the heavyset nurse snorted, obviously unconvinced that the staff needed Chandra's help, or opinion for that matter. Alma Lindquist lifted her reddish brows imperiously and turned back to the stack of admittance forms beside a humming computer terminal. "I'm sure Dr. O'Rourke will come out and let you know how the infant's doing as soon as the baby has been examined. Now, if you'll just take a chair in the waiting area..." She motioned a plump hand toward an alcove where olive green couches were grouped around Formica tables strewn with worn magazines. Lamps offered pools of light over the dogeared copies of *Hunter's Digest, Women's Daily, Your Health,* and the like.

Chandra wasn't interested in the lounge or hospital routine or the precious domain of a woman on an authority trip. Not until she was satisfied that everything humanly possible was being done for the baby. "If you don't mind, I think I'll just see for myself," she said swiftly. Lifting her chin and creating her own aura of authority, Chandra marched through the gate separating the examining area from the waiting room as if she'd done it a million times.

"Hey! Hey—you can't go in there!" the nurse called after her, surprised that anyone would dare disregard her rules. "It's against all procedure! Hey, ma'am! Ms. Hill!" When Chandra's steps didn't falter, Nurse Lindquist shouted, "Stop that woman!"

"Hang procedure," Chandra muttered under her breath. She'd been in enough emergency rooms to know her way around. She quickly walked past prescription carts, the X-ray lab and a patient in a wheelchair, hurrying down the tiled corridors toward the distinctive sound of a baby's cry. She recognized another voice as well, the deep baritone belonging to the redheaded paramedic who had hustled the baby into the ambulance, Mike something-or-other.

She nearly ran into the paramedics as they left the examination room. "Is he all right?" she asked anxiously. "The baby?"

"He will be." Mike touched her lightly on the shoulder, as a kindly father would touch a worried child. "Believe me, he's in the best hands around these parts. Dr. O'Rourke'll take care of the boy."

The other paramedic—Joe—nodded and offered a gap-toothed smile. "Don't you worry none."

But she was worried. About a child she'd never seen before tonight, a child she felt responsible for, a child who, because she'd found him, had become, at least temporarily, a part of her life. Abandoned by his own mother, this baby needed someone championing his cause.

The baby's cries drifted through the partially opened door. Without a thought to "procedure," Chandra slipped into the room and watched as a scruffy-looking doctor bent over a table where the tiny infant lay.

The physician was a tall, lanky man in a rumpled lab coat. A stethoscope swung from his neck as he listened to the baby's heartbeat. Chandra guessed his age as being somewhere between thirty-five and forty. His black hair was cut long and looked as if it hadn't seen a comb in some time, his jaw was shaded with more than a day's growth of beard, and the whites of his eyes were close to bloodshot.

The man is dead on his feet. This was the doctor on whom she was supposed to depend? she thought angrily as her maternal instincts took charge of her emotions. He had no right to be examining the baby. Yet he touched the child gently, despite his gruff looks. Chandra took a step forward as he said to the nurse, "I want him on an IV immediately, and get that bilirubin. We'll need a pediatrician— Dr. Williams, if you can reach him." The physician's gaze centered on the squirming child. "In the meantime, have a special crib made up for him in the pediatric ward, but keep him isolated and under ultraviolet. We don't know much about him. See if he'll take some water from a bottle, but keep track of the intake. He could have anything. I want blood work and an urinalysis."

"A catheter?" Nurse Pratt asked.

"No!" Chandra said emphatically, though she understood the nurse's reasoning. But somehow it seemed cruel to subject this tiny lump of unwanted human flesh, this small person, to the rigors of twentieth-century hospital technology. *But that's why you brought him here, isn't it? So that he could get the best medical attention available?* Belatedly, she held her tongue.

But not before the doctor's head whipped around and Chandra was suddenly caught in the uncompromising glare of Dr. Dallas O'Rourke. She felt trapped, like a specimen under a microscope, and fought against the uncharacteristic need to swallow against a suddenly dry throat.

His eyes were harsh and cold, a vibrant shade of angry blue, his black eyebrows bushy and arched, his skin swarthy and tanned as it stretched tight across the harsh angles of his cheekbones and a nose that hooked slightly. Black Irish, she thought silently.

"You are . . . ?" he demanded.

"Chandra Hill." She tilted her chin and unconsciously squared her shoulders, as she'd done a hundred times before in a hospital not unlike this one.

"The woman who found the child." Dr. O'Rourke crossed his arms over his chest, his lab coat stretching at the shoulder seams, his lips compressed into a line as thin as paper, his stethoscope momentarily forgotten. "Ms. Hill, I'm glad you're here. I want to talk to you—"

Before he could finish, the door to the examining room flew open and banged against the wall. Chandra jumped, the baby squealed and O'Rourke swore under his breath.

Nurse Lindquist, red-faced and huffing, marched stiffly into the room. Her furious gaze landed on Chandra. "I knew it!" Turning her attention to the doctor, she said, "Dr. O'Rourke, I'm sorry. This woman—" she shook an accusing finger in Chandra's face "—refused to listen to me. I told her you'd talk to her after examining the child, but she barged in with complete disregard to hospital rules."

"I just wanted to see that the baby was safe and taken care of," Chandra interceded, facing O'Rourke squarely. "As I explained to the nurse, I've had medical training. I could help."

"Are you a doctor licensed in Colorado?"

"No, but I've worked at—"

"I knew it!" Nurse Lindquist cut in, her tiny mouth pursing even further.

"It's all right, Alma," O'Rourke replied over the baby's cries. "I'll handle Ms. Hill. Right now, we have a patient to deal with."

Nurse Lindquist's mouth dropped open, then snapped shut. Though her normal pallor had returned, two high spots of color remained on her cheeks. She shot Chandra a furious glare before striding, stiff backed, out of the room.

"You're not making any points here," the doctor stated, his hard jaw sliding to the side a little, as if he were actually amused at the display.

"That's not why I'm here." *Arrogant bastard,* Chandra thought. She'd seen the type before. Men of medicine who thought they were gods here on earth. Well, if Dr.

O'Rourke thought he could dismiss her, he had another think coming. But to her surprise, he didn't ask her to leave. Instead, he turned his attention back to the baby and ran experienced hands over the infant's skin. "Okay, that should do it."

Chandra didn't wait. She picked up the tiny little boy, soothing the child as best she could, rocking him gently.

"Let's get him up to pediatrics," Dr. O'Rourke ordered.

"I'll take him." Nurse Pratt, after sending Chandra a quizzical glance, took the child from Chandra's unwilling arms and bustled out of the room.

The doctor waited until they were alone, then leaned a hip against the examining table. Closing his eyes for a second, he rubbed his temples, as if warding off a headache. Long, dark lashes swept his cheek for just an instant before his eyelids opened again. "Why don't you tell me everything you know about the baby," he suggested.

"I have," Chandra said simply. "I woke up and found him in my barn."

"Alone?"

"*I* was alone, and as far as I could tell, the baby was left."

He rubbed the back of his neck and winced, but some of the tension left his face. He almost smiled. "Come on, let's go down to the cafeteria. I'll buy you a cup of coffee. God knows I could use one."

Chandra was taken aback. Though his voice was gentle, practiced, his eyes were still harsh and assessing. "Why?"

"Why what?"

"The coffee. I don't think—"

"Humor me, Ms. Hill. I just have a few questions for you."

With a shrug, she agreed. After all, she only wanted what was best for the child. And, for the time being, this hard-edged doctor was her link to the baby. He held the door open for her, and she started instinctively toward the elevators. She glanced down a hallway, hoping to catch a glimpse of Nurse Pratt and the child.

Dr. O'Rourke, as if reading her mind, said, "The pediatric wing is on two and the nursery is on the other side, in maternity."

They reached the elevators and he pushed the call button. Crossing his arms over his chest and leaning a shoulder against the wall, he said, his voice slightly kinder, "Let's get back to the baby. You don't know whom he belongs to, right?"

"That's right."

"So he wasn't left by a relative or friend, someone who wasn't interested in keeping him?"

"No." Chandra felt a tide of color wash up her cheeks. "Look, Dr. O'Rourke, I've told you everything I know about him. My only concern is for the child. I'd like to stay here with him as long as possible."

"Why?" The doctor's gaze had lost its hard edge, but there were a thousand questions in his eyes. He was a handsome man, she realized, surprised that she noticed. And had it not been for the hours of sleeplessness that honed his features, he might even be appealing. But not to her, she reminded herself.

The elevator bell chimed softly and the doors whispered open. "You've done your duty—"

"It's more than duty, okay?" she cut in, unable to sever the fragile connection between her and the baby. Her feelings were pointless, she knew, but she couldn't just drive away from the hospital, leaving that small, abandoned infant. Not yet. Not until she was assured the child would be cared for. Dr. O'Rourke was holding the door open, so she stepped into the elevator.

"Dr. O'Rourke. Dr. Dallas O'Rourke..."

The doctor's shoulders slumped at the sound of the page. "I guess we'll have to take a rain check on the coffee." He seemed as if he were actually disappointed, but that was ridiculous. Though, to be honest, he looked as though he could use a quart of coffee.

As for Chandra, she was relieved that she didn't have to deal with him right now. He was unsettling somehow, and she'd already suffered through a very unsettling night. Pressing the Door Open button so that an elderly man could enter, she watched O'Rourke stride down the hall. She was grateful to be away from his hard, assessing gaze, though she suspected he wasn't as harsh as he outwardly appeared. She wondered if his sharp tongue was practiced, his guarded looks calculated. . . .

"There she is! In there! Stop! Hold the elevator!"

Chandra felt a sinking sensation as she recognized the distinctive whine of Nurse Lindquist's voice. No doubt she'd called security and was going to have Chandra thrown off the hospital grounds. Footsteps clattered down the hall. Chandra glanced back to O'Rourke, whom she suddenly viewed as her savior, but he'd already disappeared around the corner at the far end of the corridor. As she looked in the other direction, she found the huge nurse, flanked by two deputies from the Sheriff's Department, moving with surprising speed toward her. Chandra's hand froze on the elevator's Door Open button, although her every instinct told her to flee.

One of the deputies, the shorter one with a flat face and salt-and-pepper hair, was staring straight at her. He didn't bother with a smile. "Chandra Hill?"

"Yes?"

He stiff-armed the elevator, holding the doors open, as if to ensure that she wouldn't escape. "I'm Deputy Bodine, and this is Deputy White." He motioned with his head toward the other man in uniform. "If you don't mind, we'd like to ask you a few questions about the child you found on your property."

Chapter Two

"So I followed the ambulance here," Chandra said, finishing her story as the two officers listened, alternately exchanging glances and sipping their coffee as she explained how she discovered the abandoned child.

Deputy Stan Bodine, the man who was asking the questions, slid his cafeteria chair closer to the table. "And you have no idea who the mother might be?"

"Not a clue," Chandra replied, tired of repeatedly answering the same questions. "I know it's strange, but that's what happened. Someone just left the baby in my barn." What was it about everyone in the hospital? Why were they so damned disbelieving? Aware of the curious glances cast her way by a few members of the staff who had come down to the cafeteria for their breaks, Chandra leaned across the table and met the deputy's direct gaze. "Why would I lie?"

"We didn't say—"

"I know, but I can tell you don't believe me."

Deputy White, the younger of the two, stopped writing in his notepad. With thin blond hair, narrow features and a slight build, he wasn't the least bit intimidating. In fact, he seemed almost friendly. Here, at least, was one man who seemed to trust that she was telling the truth.

Deputy Bodine was another story. As bulky as the younger man was slim, Bodine carried with him a cynical attitude honed by years with the Sheriff's Department. His expression was cautiously neutral, but suspicion radiated from him in invisible waves. As he swilled the bitter coffee and chewed on a day-old Danish he'd purchased at the counter, Chandra squirmed in her chair.

"No one said we didn't believe you," Bodine answered patiently. "But it's kind of an outrageous story, don't you think?"

"It's the truth."

"And we've seen lots of cases where someone has... changed the facts a little to protect someone."

"I'm *not* protecting anyone!" Chandra's patience hung by a fragile thread. She'd brought the baby to the hospital to get the poor child medical attention, and this cynic from the Sheriff's Department, as well as the good Dr. O'Rourke, were acting as if she were some kind of criminal. Only Deputy White seemed to trust her. "Look, if you don't believe me, you're welcome to check out all my acquaintances and relatives. I just found the baby. That's all. Someone apparently left him in the barn. I don't know why. There was no trace of the mother—or anyone else for that matter." To keep her hands busy, she rolled her cup in her fingers, and a thought struck her. "The only clue as to who the child might be could come from his swaddling. He was wrapped in a blanket—not the one I brought him here in—and an old army jacket."

Bodine perked up a bit. "Where's the jacket?"

"Back at my cabin."

"We'll pick it up in the morning. And don't disturb anything in that stall where you found the kid...or the rest of the barn for that matter." He took another bite of his Danish and washed it down with a swallow of coffee. Several crumbs fell onto the white table. He crumpled his cup. Without getting up from his chair, he tossed the wadded cup high into the air and watched as it bounced off the rim of a trash container.

The younger man clucked his tongue and tucked his notepad into his pocket. "I don't think the Nuggets will be drafting you this season," he joked. He shoved out his chair and picked up the discarded cup to arc it perfectly into the trash can.

"Lucky shot," Bodine grumbled.

Chandra was just grateful they were leaving. As Bodine scraped his chair back, Dr. O'Rourke strode into the room. He was as rumpled as before, though obviously his shift was over. His lab coat was missing, and he was wearing worn jeans, an off-white flannel shirt and a sheepskin jacket.

"Just the man we wanted to see," Bodine said, settling back in his chair. Chandra's hopes died. She wanted this interrogation over with.

"So I heard." O'Rourke paid for a cup of coffee and joined the group. "Nurse Pratt said you needed some information on Baby Doe. I've left a copy of the admittance forms at the E.R. desk, and I'll send you a complete physical description of the child, as well as that of his condition, as soon as it's transcribed, probably by the afternoon. I can mail it or—"

"We'll pick it up," Bodine cut in, kicking back his chair a little so that he could view both Chandra and O'Rourke in one glance. "Save us all some time. Anything specific we should know right now?"

"Just that the baby is jaundiced, with a swelling on the right side of his head, probably from a difficult birth. Other than that, he looks pretty healthy. We're keeping him isolated, and we're still running tests, but he's eating and giving all the nurses a bad time."

Chandra swallowed a smile. So O'Rourke did have a sense of humor after all.

The doctor continued. "A pediatrician will examine him as soon as he gets here, and we'll give you a full report."

"Anything else?" White asked, scribbling quickly in his notepad again. He was standing now, but writing as quickly as before.

"Just one thing," O'Rourke replied, his gaze sliding to Chandra before returning to the two deputies. "The umbilical cord wasn't severed neatly or clamped properly."

Bodine dusted his hands. "Meaning?"

"Meaning that the baby probably wasn't born in a hospital. I'd guess that the child was delivered without any medical expertise at all. The mother probably just went into labor about three days ago, experienced some difficulty, and when the baby finally arrived, used a pair of scissors or a dull knife to cut the cord."

Chandra sucked in her breath and O'Rourke's gaze swung to her. She cringed at the thought of the baby being born in anything less than sterile surroundings, though, of course, she knew it happened often enough.

"What do you think?" O'Rourke asked, blue eyes drilling into hers.

"I don't know. I didn't really look at the cord, only to see that it wasn't bleeding." Why would he ask her opinion?

"You examined the infant, didn't you?"

Chandra's response died on her tongue. Dr. O'Rourke didn't know anything about her, she assumed, especially her past, and she intended to keep it that way. She'd come to this part of the country for the express purpose of burying her past, and she wasn't about to unearth it now. She fiddled with her coffee cup. "Yes, I examined him."

"And you were right on with your diagnosis."

No reason to explain. Not here. The Sheriff's Department and Dr. O'Rourke—and the rest of the world, for that matter—might find out all about her eventually, but not tonight. "I've had medical training," she replied, the wheels turning in her mind. "I work as a white-water and camping guide. We're required to know basic first aid, and I figure the more I know, the better I can handle any situation. So, yes, I've taken every medical course I could."

O'Rourke seemed satisfied; his gaze seemed less suspicious and his eyes turned a warmer shade of blue.

Bodine stood and hiked up his pants. "Well, even if you don't think the baby was delivered in a hospital, it won't hurt to check and find out if anyone's missing a boy."

"Missing from a hospital?" Chandra asked.

O'Rourke lifted a dark eyebrow. "What better place to steal a newborn?"

"Steal?" she repeated.

Squaring his hat on his head, Deputy Bodine said, "The black-market baby business is booming these days."

"You think someone *stole* this baby then left him in my barn? That's crazy—"

Bodine smiled his first genuine smile of the night. "Sounds a little farfetched, I admit, but we have to consider every angle. Could be that whoever took Baby Doe could have holed up in your barn for the night and something went wrong. Or they left him there while they went searching for food or more permanent shelter."

"Or you could've scared 'em off," Deputy White added.

Chandra shook her head. "There was no one in the barn. And I live nearly ten miles from the nearest store."

"We'll check out all the possibilities in the morning," Bodine assured her. Turning his gaze to O'Rourke, he said, "Thanks, Doctor. Ms. Hill."

The deputies left, and Chandra, not even realizing how tense she'd become, felt her shoulders slowly relax.

"So how's he doing?" she asked, surprised at her own anxiety, as if she and that tiny baby were somehow connected, though they weren't, of course. The child belonged to someone else. And probably, within the next few hours, Bodine and White would discover the true identity of Baby Doe and to whom he belonged. Chandra only hoped that the parents had one hell of an explanation for abandoning their child.

"The boy'll be fine," O'Rourke predicted, stretching his long legs in front of him. He sipped from his cup, scowled at the bitter taste and set the cup on the table, content to let the steam rise to his face in a dissipating cloud. Chandra noticed the lines of strain around the edges of his mouth, the droop at the corners of his eyelids.

"Can I see him?" she asked.

"In the morning."

"It *is* the morning."

His gaze locked with hers and the warmth she'd noticed earlier suddenly fled. "Look, Ms. Hill, I think you and the kid both need some rest. I know *I* do." As if to drive home his point, he rubbed a kink from his shoulders. "You can see him around ten."

"But he *is* eating." She'd heard him say so before, of course, but she couldn't stem the question or the concern she felt for the child.

A whisper of a smile crossed the doctor's thin lips. "Nurse Pratt can barely keep up with him." O'Rourke took another swallow of his coffee, his unsettling eyes regarding Chandra over the rim of his cup. She felt nervous and flustered, though she forced herself to remain outwardly calm. "So who do you think left him in your barn?" he asked.

"I don't know."

"No pregnant friends who needed help?"

Her lips twisted wryly. "I already told the deputies, if I had friends who needed help, I wouldn't suggest they use one of my stalls as a birthing room. They could've come into the house or I would've driven them to the hospital. I think, somehow, we would've found 'room at the inn,' so to speak."

O'Rourke arched a thick eyebrow, and his lips twitched as if he were suppressing a smile. "Look, there's no reason to get defensive. I'm just looking for some answers."

"I gave all of mine to the deputies," she replied, tired of the unspoken innuendoes. She leaned forward, and her hair fell in front of her shoulders. "Now *you* look, *Doctor* O'Rourke, if I knew anything about that baby—anything at all—I'd pass that information along."

He didn't speak, but his relentless stare continued to bother her. The man was so damn intimidating, used to getting his way—a handsome, arrogant son of a gun who was used to calling the shots. She could see he was tired, irritated, but a little amused at her quick temper. "You know," she said, "I expected the third degree from the police, but not from you."

He lifted a shoulder. "The more I know about the child, the better able I am to take care of him. I just don't want to make any mistakes."

She was about to retort, but the words didn't pass her lips. Chandra knew far too well about making mistakes as a physician. Her throat closed at the sudden burst of memories, and it was all she could do to keep her hands from shaking. She took a quick drink of coffee, then licked her lips. When she looked up at O'Rourke again, she found him staring at her so intently that she was certain he could see past the web of lies she'd so carefully woven around her life here in Ranger, Colorado. Did he know? Could he guess that she, too, had once been a physician?

But no one knew about her past, and that's the way she intended to keep it.

The silence stretched between them, and she shuffled her feet as if to rise. It was late, and she wanted to get some sleep before she returned later in the morning, and yet there was something mesmerizing about Dr. O'Rourke that kept her glued to her chair. He was good-looking in a sensual way that unnerved her, but she'd been around lots of good-looking men, none of whom had gotten under her skin the way O'Rourke had. Maybe it was because he was a doctor, or maybe it was because she was anxious about the baby, or maybe he was just so damned irresistible that even she, a woman who'd sworn off men, and most specifically men with medical degrees, was fascinated. She nearly choked on her coffee.

As if sensing she was about to flee, he finished his coffee and cleared his throat. "You know," he said, tenting his hands under his chin, "you'd better get used to answering questions, because the minute the press gets wind of this story, you're going to be asked to explain a helluva lot more than you have tonight."

The press. Her heart dropped like a stone and memories rushed over her—painful memories of dealing with reporters, photographers, cameramen. Oh, God, she couldn't face them again. She wasn't ready for the press. What if some hotshot reporter saw fit to dig into her background, through her personal life? Her hands grew suddenly damp. She slid her arms through the sleeves of the jacket she'd tossed over the back of her chair. "I think I can handle a few reporters," she lied, hoping she sounded far more confident than she felt.

"It'll be more than a few. Think about it. This could be the story of the year. Christmas is only a few months away, and the press just loves this kind of gut-wrenching drama."

"You could be wrong."

O'Rourke shook his head and stifled a yawn. "Nope. An abandoned baby, a complicated, unexplained birth, perhaps a missing mother, the mystery child swaddled only in an old army jacket—could it be the father's?—it all makes interesting copy." Rubbing a hand around his neck, he added, "You'll have a couple of reporters from the *Banner,* maybe someone from Denver. Not to mention the local television stations. My guess is that this story will go regional at least." He lifted his eyebrows speculatively, as if he believed he were far more informed than she. Typical. "And once the story hits the news services, I'll bet that neither one of us is gonna get a moment's rest." He crossed one battered running shoe over the other and rested his heels on the seat of the chair Deputy White had recently vacated.

"Are you trying to scare me?" Chandra asked.

"Just preparing you for the inevitable."

"I can handle it," she assured him, while wondering what it was about this man that made her bristle. One minute she wanted to argue with him, the next she wanted to trust him with her very life. Good Lord, she must be more tired than she'd guessed. She'd instinctively come to depend on him because he was a doctor—the one man who could keep her in contact with the baby. After all, he could stop her from seeing the child.

Deep down, though, she knew her anger wasn't really directed at Dr. O'Rourke specifically. In fact, her wrath wasn't really aimed at doctors in general; just at a few doctors she'd known in her past, especially a particularly egotistical plastic surgeon to whom she'd once been married: Douglas Patrick Pendleton, M.D., P.C., and all-around jerk.

Now she couldn't afford to have Dr. O'Rourke against her. Not only was he her link to the child, there was a chance he might help her with the press and the Sheriff's Department—not that she needed any help, she reminded herself. But Dr. O'Rourke did seem fair and was probably sometimes kind, even though he appeared ragged and cynical around the edges.

"I guess I am tired," she finally said, as half an apology. Dr. O'Rourke wasn't the least bit like Doug. No, this man with his rugged good looks, beat-up running shoes and worn jacket looked more like a mountain climber than an emergency-room physician. She couldn't imagine him reading medical journals or prescribing blood-pressure medicine or attending medical conferences in Chicago or New York.

And yet it did seem possible that he could care for an abandoned infant. On that score, Chandra was comfortable. O'Rourke, she sensed, was a good doctor, the kind of man who had dedicated himself to people in need rather than to the almighty dollar. Unless the unshaven jaw, worn clothes and fatigue were all part of an act.

She didn't think so. His gaze was too honest. Cutting, yes. Intense, certainly. But honest.

Scraping back her chair, she stood and thrust her hand across the table. "Thanks for all the help."

He clasped her palm with his big hand, and she forced a smile, though Dr. O'Rourke didn't return the favor. As his fingers surrounded hers, the doctor stared at her with those electric blue eyes that could look straight into her soul, and her face suddenly felt hot.

Quickly, Chandra yanked back her hand and stuffed it into the pocket of her jeans. Her voice nearly failed her. "I'll be back later," she assured him as she turned and marched out of the cafeteria, hoping he didn't guess that she'd reacted to his touch. She was tired, that was all. Tired and nervous about the infant. God, what a night!

Dallas watched Chandra Hill retreat. A fascinating woman, he thought grudgingly as he swirled the dregs of coffee in his cup. There was something about her that didn't quite click, an attitude that didn't fit with the rest of her.

Still, she intrigued him. The feel of her hand in his had caused his heart to race a second, and she'd reacted, too— he'd seen the startled look in her eyes as she'd drawn back. He laughed inwardly. If she only knew how safe she was with him. He'd sworn off beautiful women long ago, and despite her uncombed hair, hastily donned clothes and face devoid of makeup, Chandra Hill was gorgeous.

And trouble. One hundred fifteen pounds of trouble packed onto a lithe frame. She obviously bucked authority: Nurse Lindquist would testify to that. At the thought of Alma Lindquist's agitated expression, Dallas grinned. Yes, he imagined Chandra with her sharp tongue and high-handed attitude could get under anyone's skin.

Fortunately, Dallas didn't have time for a woman in his profession. Not any woman. And especially not a firecracker like Ms. Hill. He rubbed his eyes and blinked several times, trying to dispel her image.

He was off duty. One last look at the Baby John Doe and then he'd go home and sleep for twelve hours. Maybe longer. But first, he might stop by the sheriff's office and listen to the recording of Chandra Hill's call to the emergency dispatcher. If he heard the tape, perhaps he'd get a better perspective on what condition the child was in when she found him. Oh, hell, it probably wouldn't do any good. In fact, he decided, he was just curious about the lady. And he hadn't been curious about a woman in a long, long time.

Squashing his cup with one hand, he shoved himself upright and glanced at the corridor down which Chandra had disappeared.

Who was this tiny woman with her unlikely knowledge of medicine? Jaundice was one thing, the layman could spot that. And a lay person might notice the swelling on the baby's head. But to come up with the medical term after a few first aid courses? Unlikely.

Nope. For some reason, Chandra Hill was deliberately holding back. His eyes narrowed at the thought.

Obviously the child wasn't hers. He'd checked out her trim figure and quick step. No, she wasn't the least bit postpartum, and she was far too young to have a daughter who'd gotten pregnant. But a sister? Or a friend?

Could the baby be stolen? Could Chandra have taken the child from its home, then realized it needed medical attention, concocted this story and brought him in? Dallas didn't think so. A dozen questions about Chandra Hill swam through his tired mind, but he couldn't come up with an answer.

Drawing in a long breath, he was surprised that the scent of her—a clean soapy scent unaffected by perfume—lingered in the stale air of the cafeteria, a fresh breeze in this desert of white walls, polished chrome, chipped Formica and the ever-present smell of antiseptic.

She was definitely a mystery, he decided as he shoved back his chair, but a mystery he was too damned tired to unravel.

Chapter Three

Sam was waiting for Chandra. As she opened the door, he jumped up, yipping excitedly, his tail wagging with unbridled enthusiasm. "Oh, come off it," Chandra said, smiling despite the yawn that crept up on her. "I wasn't gone that long."

But the big dog couldn't get enough attention. He bounded back and forth from his empty dish to her as she started for the stairs. "Don't get too anxious, Sam. Breakfast isn't for another three hours." In the loft, she nudged off one boot with the toe of the other. "What a night! Do you believe it? The police and even the doctor seem to think I had something to do with stealing the baby or kidnapping the kid or God only knows what! And that Dr. O'Rourke, you should meet him . . ." She shook her head, as if she could physically shake out her own thoughts of the doctor. Handsome, arrogant and sexy, he was a man to steer well clear of. But she couldn't. Not if she wanted to see the baby again. "Believe me, this is one mess," she told the dog, who was still pacing in the kitchen.

She thought about checking the barn one last time, but was too exhausted. Tossing off her jacket, she dropped onto the unmade bed, discarded her jeans and sought solace under the eiderdown quilt she'd inherited from her grandmother.

With a disgruntled sigh, Sam swept up the stairs and parked in his favorite spot on the floor near the end of the bed. Chandra heard his toes click on the old pine boards as he circled three times before dropping to the floor. She sighed to herself and hoped sleep would quickly overcome her weary body as it seemed to have done for the old dog.

Three days after moving into this place a couple of years before, Chandra had discovered Sam, so thin his ribs showed beneath his matted, dusty coat, his eyes without spark and a wound that stretched from one end of his belly to the other. He'd snarled at her approach, his white teeth flashing defensively as she'd tried to touch him. But she'd brought him water and food, and the listless dog had slowly begun to trust her. She'd eventually cleaned the wound, the mark of a cornered wild animal, she'd guessed, and brought Sam into the house. He'd been with her ever since, a permanent and loving fixture in her life.

But a far cry from a man or a child.

She smiled sadly and pulled the covers closer around her neck. Just because she'd found an abandoned infant was no reason to start dreaming old dreams that she'd discarded long ago. But though her body was fatigued, her mind was spinning with images of the wailing, red-faced infant, the sterile hospital room and the unsettling visage of Dr. Dallas O'Rourke. Even with her eyes closed, she could picture him—jet black hair, eyes as blue as a mountain lake and lips that could thin in anger or gentle into the hint of a smile.

Good Lord, what was wrong with her? In frustration, she pounded her pillow with her fist. In less than four hours, she had to get up and lead a white-water expedition of inexperienced rafters down the south fork of the Rattle-snake River. She didn't have time for complications, especially complications involving a man.

She glared at the clock one more second before squeezing her eyes closed and thinking how she would dearly love someday to have a baby of her very own.

Dallas washed the grit from his eyes and let the spray of the shower pour over him. He leaned one arm against the slippery tiles of the stall and closed his eyes as the jets of hot water soothed the ache of overly tired muscles.

The past thirty-six hours had been rough, one case after another. A twelve-year-old with a broken arm, a messy automobile accident with one fatality and two critically injured passengers flown by helicopter to Denver, a drug overdose, two severe strep cases, an elderly woman who had fallen and not only broken her hip, but fractured her pelvis, and, of course, the abandoned baby.

And it was the thoughts of the infant and the woman who'd found him that continued to rattle around in Dallas's tired mind. Probably because he was overworked. Overly tired. His emotions already strung tight because of the phone call....

He twisted off the faucets and pulled down a towel from the top of the glass shower doors, rubbing his body dry, hoping to infuse a little energy through his bloodstream.

He should eat, but he couldn't face an empty refrigerator. The joys of being a bachelor, he thought fatalistically, because he knew, from the experience of a brief, painful marriage, that he would never tie himself down to one woman again. No, medicine was his mistress, and a demanding mistress she was. She exacted far more attention than any woman would. Even the woman to whom he'd been married, Jennifer Smythe O'Rourke Duncan.

The bitch. He still couldn't think of her without the bitter taste of her betrayal rising like bile in his throat. How could he have been duped by her, when all along, she'd been more of a slave to her precious profession than he had to his?

He didn't bother shaving, that he could do in the morning, but walked through the connecting door to the bedroom and flopped, stark naked, onto the king-size bed. He dropped the towel onto the floor. He'd pick up it and his discarded clothes in the morning.

Muttering oaths he saved for the memory of his marriage, he noticed the red light flashing on his phone recorder, though he hadn't been paged. A personal call. Great. He didn't have to guess who the caller was. He rewound the tape and, settling back on the pillows, listened as his half brother's voice filled the room.

"Hey, Dal. How's it goin'? I just thought I'd touch base before I drop by tomorrow. You remember, don't ya?"

How could he forget, Dallas thought grimly. His half brother, Brian, was here in the waning weeks before college started, not because he was working, but because he'd spent the summer camping and rafting in the wilderness. Only now, with less than two weeks until he left for school, did Brian think about the more practical side of education.

"Hey, man, I really hate to bug you about this and I'll pay you back every dime, you know I will, but I just need a little something to keep me goin' until my money gets here."

Right. Brian's money was scholarship dollars and not nearly enough of them to pay for the tuition, books and a carefree life-style.

The machine clicked off, and Dallas scowled. He shouldn't loan Brian another nickel. Already the kid was into him for nearly ten thousand. But his mother's other children, Brian, Brian's twin sister, Brenda, and their older sister, Joanna, were the only family Dallas had ever known.

However, the loans to Brian were starting to bother Dallas, and he wondered, not for the first time, if he should be writing checks directly to University of Southern California rather than to the kid himself.

He'd find out this afternoon. After he felt refreshed and after he made rounds at the hospital, checking on his patients. The image of the newborn flitted through his mind again, and Dallas wondered if he'd run into Chandra Hill. Now there was a woman who was interesting, a woman who knew her own mind, a woman with a presence of authority that was uncommon, a woman who, even in old boots, jeans and a nightshirt, her hair wild, her face free of makeup, was the most attractive woman he'd seen in a long, long time.

He rolled under the covers, switched off the light and decided, as he drifted off, that chances were he might just see her again. And that thought wasn't all that unpleasant.

Chandra pulled her hair into a ponytail when she heard the hum of an engine and the crunch of tires against the gravel drive. She pulled back the curtains to discover a tan cruiser from the Sheriff's Department rolling to a stop near the barn. Sam, vigilant as ever, began to bark and growl.

"You haven't had this much excitement in a long while, have you?" Chandra asked the retriever as she yanked open the door. Two deputies, the same men she'd met in the hospital, climbed out of the car.

She met them on the porch.

"Sorry to bother you so early," Deputy White apologized, "but we're about to go off duty and would like to check over the barn and house."

"Just to see if there's anything you might have missed," Bodine added.

"I hope there is," Chandra replied, feeling more gracious this morning than she had last night. She thought again, as she had for the past four hours, of the dark-haired infant. She'd called the hospital the minute she'd awakened, but had been unable to prod much information from the nurse who had taken her call. "Doing as well as can be expected. Resting comfortably...in no apparent distress...."

When Chandra had mentioned that she'd brought the baby in, the nurse had warmed a bit. "Oh, Miss Hill, yes. Dr. O'Rourke said you'd probably call." Chandra's heart had nearly stopped. "But there's nothing new on the baby's condition."

So Chandra had been given stock answers that told her nothing. *Nothing!* Except that O'Rourke had had the decency to advise the staff that she would be inquiring. Surprised that he'd bothered at all, she again decided she'd have to make a friend of O'Rourke, even if it killed her.

She hadn't been this frustrated since she'd lived in Tennessee.... With a start, she pulled herself away from the painful thought of her past and her short-lived marriage, noticing that the deputies looked beyond fatigued. "How about a cup of coffee before you get started?" she asked, and the weary men, seeming much less belligerent in the soft morning light, smiled in response.

"I wouldn't want to trouble you," White said.

"No trouble at all. I was just about to pour myself a cup."

"In that case, you're on," Bodine cut in, obviously not wanting the younger man to talk them out of a quick break.

They followed her inside. Sam, ever watchful, growled deep in his throat as they crossed the threshold, but the men seemed unintimidated by the old retriever.

Chandra reached for two mugs from the shelf near the kitchen window and couldn't help asking, "Have you learned anything else?"

"About the baby?" Bodine asked, and taking off his hat, he shook his head. "Not yet. We thought maybe we could find something here. You got that jacket?"

"The what...? Oh! Just a minute." She poured them each a mug of coffee from the glass pot warming on the burner of the coffee maker. From the closet, she retrieved the ratty old army jacket and tattered blanket that had swaddled the newborn. Smudges of dirt, a few wisps of straw and several patches of a dark, dried substance that looked like blood discolored the dull green jacket. Faded black letters stated: U S ARMY, but no other lettering was visible.

"Anyone could pick up something like this in a local G.I. surplus store," Bodine grumbled to himself as he searched the jacket's pockets and discovered nothing more exciting than lint. He focused his attention on the blanket. It offered few clues to the identity of the newborn, fewer than the jacket. Frowning, he pulled a couple of plastic bags from his pocket and wrapped the blanket and jacket separately, then accepted a cup of coffee. Motioning toward his plastic-encased bundles, he added, "We'll see if the lab can come up with any clues from these."

"But don't hold your breath," White added. "Despite what Sheriff Newell thinks, the lab guys aren't gods. There's just not too much here to go on." He flashed a hint of a smile as Chandra handed him a steaming cup. "Thanks."

"Our best hope is for someone to step forward and claim the kid."

"Is it?" Chandra asked, surprised by her own sense of dread of some relative appearing. "But what if whoever tries to claim the child is a fraud?"

"We won't let that happen." Nonetheless, Bodine's eyebrows drew together and a deep cleft appeared on his forehead. He was worried. He studied the hot black liquid in his mug, as if he could find the answers he was searching for in the coffee. "Why don't you go over your story one more time." He held up a couple of fingers when he caught Chandra's look of distress. "Since we're here, talk us through it again and show us what you did last night."

Chandra wasn't all that eager to repeat the story, but she knew that was the only way to gain the deputies' confidence. And after all, they were all on the same side, weren't they? Didn't Chandra, the police and the hospital staff only want what was best for the tiny, motherless infant?

"Okay," she said with a forced smile. "It's just exactly what I said last night." As they sipped their coffee, Chandra pointed to the loft. "I was sleeping up there when Sam—" the big dog perked up his ears and his tail dusted the floor at the sound of his name "—started barking his fool head off. Wouldn't let up. And that's when I heard the sound."

"The baby crying," White cut in.

"Yes, but I didn't know that it was a baby at first." She continued while they finished their coffee, then led them back outside as Sam tagged along.

The sun was climbing across the morning sky, but frost still glazed the gravel of the parking lot. Sam nosed around the base of a blue spruce where, hidden in the thick needles, a squirrel scolded him. Deputy White tossed the jacket and blanket onto the front seat of the car.

"The noise was coming from the barn." Chandra followed her footsteps of the night before and shoved open the barn door. Shafts of sunlight pierced the dark interior, and the warm smell of horses and musty hay greeted her. The horses nickered softly as dust motes swirled in the air, reflecting the morning light.

"The baby was in the end stall." She pointed to the far wall while petting two velvety noses thrust over the stall doors.

As the officers began their search, Chandra winked at Cayenne, her favorite gelding. "I bet you want to go out," she said, patting his sleek neck. In response, the sorrel tossed his head and stamped. "I'll take that as a yes." Cayenne shoved his big head against her blouse and she chuckled. "Grouchy after you missed a night's sleep, aren't you?" She walked through the first stall and yanked open the back door. One by one, she opened the connecting gates of the other stalls and the horses trotted eagerly outside to kick up their heels and run, bucking and rearing, their tails unfurling like silky banners behind them.

Chandra couldn't help but smile at the small herd as she stood in the doorway. Life had become so uncomplicated since she'd moved to Ranger, and she loved her new existence. Well, life had been uncomplicated until last night. She rubbed her hand against the rough wood of the door and considered the baby, who only a few hours before had woken her and, no doubt, changed the course of her quiet life forever.

Inside the barn, Deputy Bodine examined the end stall while Deputy White poked and prodded the barrels of oats and mash, checked the bridles and tack hanging from the ceiling and then clambered up the ladder to the hayloft. A mouse scurried into a crack in the wall, and cobwebs, undisturbed for years, hung heavy with dust.

"This yours?" Bodine asked, holding up Chandra's father's .22, which she'd left in the barn upon discovering the infant.

Heat crept up her neck. "I must've dropped it here when I found the baby. I was so concerned about him, I didn't think of much else."

Bodine grunted as he checked the chamber.

"Nothing up here," Deputy White called down from the loft.

"I could've guessed," Bodine muttered under his breath as he turned his attention back to the stall, instructing Chandra to reconstruct the scene. She pointed out the position of the baby and answered all the questions he asked. Deputy White climbed down the ladder from the loft and, after observing the stall, asked a few more questions that Chandra couldn't answer.

The deputies didn't say as much, but Chandra read in their expressions that they'd come up against a dead end. Outside, they walked through the paddocks and fields, and even followed a couple of trails into the nearby woods. But they found nothing.

"Well, that's about all we can do for now," Bodine said as they walked across the yard. He brushed the dust from his hands.

"What about the baby?" Chandra asked, hoping for just a little more information on the infant. "What happens to him?"

"Don't worry about him. He's in good hands at the hospital. The way I hear it, Dr. O'Rourke is the best E.R. doctor in the county, and he'll link the kid up to a good pediatrician."

"I see."

Bodine actually offered her a smile. "I'm sure O'Rourke will let you look in on the kid, if you want. In the meantime, we'll keep looking for the baby's ma." He opened the passenger side of the cruiser while Deputy White slid behind the wheel. "If we find her, she's got a whole lotta questions to answer before she gets her kid back."

"And if you don't find her?"

"The baby becomes a ward of the state until we can locate a parent, grandparent or other relative."

Chandra's heart wrenched at the thought. "He'll be put in an institution?"

"Probably a foster home—whatever Social Services decides. But we'll cross that bridge when we come to it. Right now, we have to find the mother or next of kin. We'll keep you posted," he said, as if reading the worry in her eyes for the very first time.

Bodine slid into his seat, and Deputy White put the car into gear. Chandra waited until the car had disappeared around the bend in the drive before returning to the house with the rifle.

So what happens next? she wondered. If nothing else, the baby was certainly a part of her life.

As she walked into the house, she heard the phone ringing. She dashed to the kitchen. "Hello?"

"Miss Hill?"

She froze as she recognized Dr. O'Rourke's voice. "Hello, doctor," she said automatically, though her throat was dry. Something was wrong with the baby. Why else would he phone her?

"I thought you'd like to know that the baby's doing well," he said, and her knees nearly gave out on her. Tears of relief sprang to her eyes. O'Rourke chuckled, and the sound was throaty. "He's got the nurses working double time, but he's eating, and his vital signs are normal."

"Thank God."

"Anytime you want to check on him, just call," Dallas said.

"Thanks for calling."

There was a long pause before O'Rourke replied. "You seemed concerned last night and...since the boy has no family that we know of..."

"I appreciate the call."

As Dallas hung up the phone in his office at the hospital, he wondered what the devil had gotten into him. Calling Chandra Hill? All night long he'd remembered the worry in her eyes and, though he wasn't scheduled to work for hours, he'd gotten up and gone directly to the hospital, where he'd examined the baby again.

There was something about the boy that touched a part of him he'd thought was long buried, though he assumed his emotions were tangled up in the circumstances. The baby had been abandoned. Dallas's emotional reaction to the infant was because he knew that baby had no one to love him. No wonder he had felt the unlikely tug on his heartstrings when he'd examined the baby and the infant had blinked up at him with trusting eyes.

"This is crazy," Dallas muttered, and headed back to the parking lot. He would drive over to the club and swim out his frustrations before grabbing some breakfast.

Riverbend Hospital appeared larger in daylight. The whitewashed walls sprawled upward and outward, seeming to grow along the hillside, spawning several clinics connected by wide breezeways. The Rocky Mountains towered behind one facility, and below it, within view, flowed the Rattlesnake River. The town of Ranger was three miles away.

Chandra parked her truck in the visitors lot and prepared herself for a confrontation with another nurse on an authority trip. She wouldn't have to pass anywhere near the emergency room, so in all probability, she wouldn't run into Nurse Lindquist again. Or Dr. O'Rourke. He'd appeared dead on his feet last night, surely by now he was sleeping the morning away.

Probably with his wife.

Chandra's eyebrows pulled together, and above her nose a groove deepened—the worry line, Doug used to call it. The thought that Dr. O'Rourke was married shouldn't have been unpleasant. Good Lord, he deserved a normal life with a wife and kids ... yet ...

"Oh, stop it!" she grumbled, walking under the flat roof of a breezeway leading to the main entrance of the hospital. The doors opened automatically and she walked through.

The reception area was carpeted in an industrial-strength weave of forest green. The walls were gray-white and adorned with framed wildlife posters hung exactly ten feet apart.

A pert nurse with a cap of dark curls, a dash of freckles strewn upon an upturned nose and a genuine smile greeted Chandra from behind the information desk. "May I help you?"

Chandra returned the woman's infectious grin. "I hope so. I'm Chandra Hill. I brought in the baby—"

The nurse, Jane Winthrop, laughed. "I *heard* about you and the baby," she said, her dark eyes flashing merrily. "I guess I should transfer to the night shift in E.R. That's where all the action is."

"Is it?" Chandra replied.

"Oh, yeah. But a lot of it's not too pretty, y'know. Car accidents—there was a bad one last night, not too long before you brought in the baby." Her smile faded and her pretty dark eyes grew serious. "Anyway, what can I do for you?"

Jane Winthrop was a refreshing change from Alma Lindquist.

"I'd like to see the baby, see how he's doing."

"No problem. He's in pediatrics, on two. Take the elevator up one floor and turn to your left. Through the double doors and you're there. The admitting nurse, Shannon Pratt, is still with him, I think. She'd just started her shift when they brought the baby in."

Chandra didn't waste any time. She followed Jane's directions and stopped by the nurse's station in the pediatric wing on the second floor. Chandra recognized Nurse Pratt, the slim brunette, but hadn't met the other woman, plump, apple cheeked, with platinum blond hair, a tanning-booth shade to her skin and pale blue eyes rimmed with eyelashes that were thick with mascara.

"You're back," Shannon said, looking up from some paperwork on the desk. "I thought you would be." She touched the eraser end of a pencil to her lips as she smiled and winked. "And I bet you're looking for one spunky little guy, right?" Before Chandra could answer, Shannon waved toward one of the long corridors. She leaned closer to the other nurse. "I'll be back in a minute. This is the woman who brought in the Baby Doe."

The blond nurse, whose nameplate read Leslie Nelson, R.N., smiled and a dimple creased one of her rosy cheeks. "He's already won over the entire staff—including Alma Lindquist!" She caught a warning glance from Shannon, but continued blithely on. "You know, there's something special about that little guy—" The phone jangled and Leslie rolled her huge, mascara-laden eyes as she picked up the receiver. "Pediatrics. Nurse Nelson."

"She's right about that," Shannon agreed as she led Chandra down the hallway. "Your little friend has wormed his way into the coldest hearts around. Even Dr. O'Rourke isn't immune to him."

"Is that right?" Chandra asked, lifting an eyebrow. She was surprised to hear Dr. O'Rourke's name, and even more surprised to glean a little bit about the man. Not that she cared. He was just a doctor, someone she'd have to deal with while visiting the baby.

"One of the nurses caught him holding the baby this morning. And he was actually smiling."

So there was a more human side to the gruff doctor. Chandra glanced down the hallway, half expecting to see him, and she was surprised at her feeling of disappointment when he didn't appear.

Shannon clucked her tongue and shook her head. "You know, I didn't think anyone could touch that man, but apparently I was wrong." She slid Chandra a glance. "Maybe there's hope for him yet. Here you go. This little guy's still isolated until we get the results of his tests. But my guess is, he'll be fine."

They stood behind a glass partition. On the other side of the clear wall, the dark-haired infant slept, his face serene as an ultraviolet light warmed him. There were other newborns as well, three sleeping infants, who, separated by the wall of glass, snoozed in the other room. Nearby, a nurse was weighing an unhappy infant who was showing off his lungs by screaming loudly.

"We're busy down here," Nurse Pratt said.

"Looks that way." Chandra focused her attention back on the isolated baby, and her heart tugged. So perfect. So beautiful. So precious. The fact that he was separated from the rest of the infants only made his plight seem more pitiful. Unwanted and unloved, living in a sterile hospital with only nurses and doctors—faces, hands and smells that changed every eight hours—to care for him.

A lump formed in her throat—a lump way out of proportion to the situation. She'd been a physician, for God's sake, a *pediatrician*. She was supposed to handle any given situation and keep her emotions in check. But this time, with this child, she was hopelessly ensnared in the trap of caring too much. Involuntarily her hand touched the cool glass. If only she could pick him up and hold him close....

Chandra felt Shannon's gaze resting on her, and she wondered just how much of her emotions played upon her face. "It looks as if he'll be okay once we get the jaundice under control," Shannon said softly.

"And his caput—"

"Nothing serious, according to Dr. O'Rourke, and he's the best E.R. physician I've ever met."

"And the pediatrician?"

"Dr. Spangler was on duty and looked him over last night. Agreed with O'Rourke right down the line. Dr. Williams will check the baby later this morning."

Chandra felt a sense of overwhelming relief. She stared at the perfect round cheeks and the dark sweep of lashes that caressed the infant's skin, watched as his tiny lips moved ever so slightly, as if he were sucking in his dream. On whose breast did he subconsciously nurse?

Chandra's heart wrenched again and she felt rooted to the spot. Though she'd seen hundreds of babies, they had all come with mothers firmly attached, and she'd never once experienced a pang of devotion so deep. The feeling seemed to spring from an inner well of love she'd never known existed.

True, she had been married, had hoped to bear her own children, and so, perhaps, all her motherly instincts had been turned inward. But now, years later, divorced and having no steady man in her life, her nurturing urges seemed stronger than ever, especially where this tiny baby was concerned.

"Uh-oh." Nurse Pratt exhaled softly. "Trouble."

"What?" Chandra turned and discovered two men striding toward her. Both were of medium height, one with curly black hair, the other straight brown. They wore slacks and sweaters, no hospital ID or lab coats.

"Make that double trouble," Shannon corrected.

"Miss Hill?" the man with the straight hair and hard eyes asked. "Bob Fillmore with the *Ranger Banner.*"

Chandra's heart sank as the curly-haired man added, "Sid Levine." He held out his hand as if expecting Chandra to clasp it. "Photographer."

She felt Sid's fingers curl over her hand, but she could barely breathe. Reporters. Already. She wasn't yet ready to deal with the press. "But how did you know—"

"Have you got permission to be here?" Nurse Pratt cut in, obviously displeased.

Fillmore ignored her. "I heard you found an infant in the woods near your home. Abandoned, is that right?"

"I don't think this is the place to conduct an interview," Nurse Pratt insisted. Behind the glass, the baby started making noise, soft mewing sounds that erupted into the hard cries Chandra had heard the night before. Chandra whipped her head around and the sight of the infant, *her* baby—no, of course he wasn't hers, but he *was* in distress and she wanted desperately to run to him and pick him up.

"Is that the kid?" Fillmore asked. "Any idea who he belongs to? It is a he, right?" He looked to Chandra for verification as he withdrew a small pad and pen from the inner pocket of his jacket. He'd also unearthed a small tape recorder from his voluminous pockets and switched on the machine.

The baby cried louder, and Chandra felt her back stiffen. "Look, I'm not ready to give you an interview, okay? Yes, I found the baby—in my barn, not the woods—but since this is a case the police are investigating, I think you'd better go to the sheriff's office to get your facts straight."

"But why your property?" Fillmore insisted, his tape recorder in his outstretched hand. Memories, painful as

razors, cut through Chandra's mind as she remembered the
last time she'd had microphones and recorders waved in her
face, how she'd been forced to reveal information to the
press.

"I don't know. Now, if you'll excuse me—"

"Just a few more questions."

Obviously the man wasn't about to give up. Chandra
glanced at Nurse Pratt and, without thinking about pro-
tocol, ordered, "Call security."

Fillmore was outraged. "Hey—wait—you can't start
barking orders—"

"If she doesn't, I will." Dr. O'Rourke, who could have
heard only the last of the exchange, strode down the hall.
Dressed in jeans, a long-sleeved T-shirt and down vest, he
nonetheless oozed authority as he glared at the reporter and
photographer with a stare that would have turned the
fainthearted to stone. He motioned to Shannon. "Do as
Ms. Hill suggests. Call security." Nurse Pratt walked to the
nearest telephone extension and dialed.

"Why all the secrecy?" Fillmore demanded, apparently
not fainthearted and not the least bit concerned about
O'Rourke's stature, anger or command of the situation.
"We could help you on this, y'know. A couple of pictures
of the baby and an article describing how he was found,
and maybe, just maybe, the kid's folks will reconsider and
come back. Who knows what happened to them? Or to
him? For all anyone knows, this kid—" he hooked a thumb
toward the glass "—could've been stolen or kidnapped.
Right now some distraught mother might be anxious to
have him back again, and you guys are impeding us."

He's right, Chandra thought, disliking the reporter intensely as she noticed a flicker of doubt cross Dr.
O'Rourke's strong features.

"In due time," the doctor replied, his gaze landing on
Chandra for a heart-stopping second. A glimmer of un-
derstanding passed between them, as if she and the doctor

were on the same side. Quickly, O'Rourke turned back to the reporters. "My first concern is for the child's health."

"The kid got problems?" Fillmore persisted, his eyes lighting with the idea of a new twist to an already newsworthy story.

"We're running tests." O'Rourke, in a sweeping glance, took in the two men and Chandra, and once again she felt a bond with him, though she told herself she imagined it. She had nothing, save the baby, in common with the man.

O'Rourke wasn't about to be pushed around. "Now, if you'll excuse me, I have a patient I have to see. If you want to continue with this interview, do it somewhere else." He turned just as two security guards, hands on holsters, entered the pediatric wing.

"Okay, what's going on here?" the first one, a man with a thick waist and a face scarred by acne, demanded. His partner stood two feet behind him, as if he expected the reporters to draw weapons.

"Just lookin' for a story," Fillmore said.

"Well, look somewhere else."

Levine threw up his hands, but Fillmore stood his ground and eyed the doctor. "What is it with you, O'Rourke? Why do you always see us as the bad guys?"

"Not bad guys, just guys without much dignity." Dr. O'Rourke stepped closer to Fillmore and scrutinized the reporter with his uncompromising gaze. "You tend to sensationalize things, try to stir up trouble, and that bothers me. Now if you'll excuse me, and even if you won't, I've got a patient to examine."

Summarily dismissing both men, O'Rourke stepped into the nursery to examine the baby. With a nudge from the guards, both reporter and photographer, muttering under their collective breath, headed out of the wing. "You, too," the heavier guard said, motioning toward Chandra.

"She can stay." O'Rourke, though on the other side of the window, pointed toward Chandra before focusing his attention on the crying infant. Chandra had to swallow a smile as she stared at the vest stretched taut across O'Rourke's back.

The guard shrugged and followed his partner through the double doors while Chandra stood dumbstruck. She didn't know what she expected of O'Rourke, but she suspected he wasn't a particularly tolerant man. His demeanor was on the edge of being harsh, and she was certain that just under his facade of civility, he was as explosive as a volcano.

On the other hand, he touched the infant carefully, tenderly, as he gently rolled the screaming baby from front to back, fingers expertly examining the child. It was all Chandra could do to keep from racing into the room and cradling the baby herself, holding the infant close and rocking him.

This has got to stop, Chandra, she told herself. *He's not yours—he's not!* If she had any brains at all, she'd tear herself away from the viewing window, walk out of Riverbend Hospital and never look back. Let the proper authorities take care of the child. If they could locate the parents or next of kin, so be it. If not, the Social Services would see that he was placed with a carefully-screened couple who desperately wanted a child, or in a foster home...

Quit torturing yourself!

But she stayed. Compelled by the child and fascinated by the doctor examining him, Chandra Hill watched from the other side of the glass.

Why she felt a special bond with the child and the doctor, she didn't know. And yet, as if catching a glimmer of the future in a crystal ball, she felt as if they, all three, were inextricably bound to each other.

Chapter Four

Dr. O'Rourke was quick and efficient. His examination took no longer than five minutes, after which he gave Nurse Pratt a few instructions before emerging from the glassed-in room. "I think he'll be out of isolation tomorrow," he said, joining Chandra.

"That's good."

"Know any more about him?"

She shook her head and began walking with him, wondering why she was even conversing with him. She thought she caught an envious look from Shannon as they left the nursery, but she chided herself afterward. Envious? Of what?

"The Sheriff's Department show up at your place?" he asked as they walked. His tone wasn't friendly, just curious. Chandra chalked his questions up to professional interest.

"This morning at the crack of dawn. The same two deputies." She stuffed her hands into her pockets. "They poked around the barn and the grounds. Didn't find much."

O'Rourke pushed the button for the elevator, and the doors opened immediately. "Parking lot?"

"Yes." She eyed him for a second, and as the car descended, said, "I'm surprised to see you here this early. Last night you looked like you could sleep for twenty years."

"Thirty," he corrected, then allowed her just the hint of a grin, and she was shocked by the sensual gleam of white teeth against his dark skin. His jaw was freshly shaven, and the scent of soap and leather clung to him, overpowering the antiseptic odor that had filtered through the hospital corridors and into the elevator. "But I've learned to survive on catnaps. Five hours and it's all over for me." He studied her with that intense gaze that made her throat grow tight, but she held her ground as a bell announced they'd landed at ground level. "What about you?"

"Eight—at least. I'm running on empty now."

He cocked a dubious eyebrow as they walked past the reception area and outside, where the sunlight was bright enough to hurt the eyes. Chandra reached into her purse for her sunglasses and noticed that O'Rourke squinted. The lines near his eyes deepened, adding a rugged edge to his profile. The man was handsome, she'd give him that. Dealing with him would be easier if he were less attractive, she thought.

"That reporter will be back," he predicted. "He smells a story and isn't about to leave it alone. You might be careful what you say."

Though she knew the answer from personal experience, she wanted to hear his side of the story. "Why?"

His lips twisted into a thin line of disapproval and his eyes turned cold. "Words can be misconstrued, taken out of context, turned around."

"Sounds like the voice of experience talking."

"Just a warning. For your own good."

He acted as if he were about to turn away, and Chandra impulsively grabbed the crook of his arm, restraining him. He turned sharply and his gaze landed on her with a force that made her catch her breath. She swallowed against the dryness in her throat and forced the words past her lips. "When can I see the baby? I mean, really see him—hold him."

She didn't remove her fingers and was aware of the tensing of his muscles beneath the sleeves of his shirt and jacket. "You want to hold him?"

"Oh, yes!" she cried, her emotion controlling her tongue.

"You feel something special for the child, some sort of bond?" he guessed.

"I..." She crumbled under the intensity of his gaze. "I guess I feel responsible."

When he waited, for what she knew was further elaboration, she couldn't help but ramble on. "I mean he was found on *my* property, in my barn. I can't help but think that someone wanted me to find him."

"That you were chosen?" He sounded as if he didn't believe her, yet he didn't draw his arm away.

"Yes. No. I mean—I don't know." She'd never been so confused in her life. Always she'd been a take-charge kind of individual, afraid of nothing, ready for any challenge. But one tiny newborn and one very intimidating man seemed to have turned her mind to mush. "Look, Doctor, I just want to hold the baby, if it's okay with you."

He hesitated, and his voice was a little kinder. "I don't know if it's a good idea."

"What?" She couldn't believe he would dissuade her now, after he'd called her to tell her the child had improved and then had let her stick around. But that warming trend had suddenly been reversed.

"Until the Sheriff's Department sets this matter straight, I think it's best for you and the child if you stayed away from the hospital until everything's settled."

Her hopes, which she had naively pinned on this man, collapsed. "But I thought—"

"I know what you thought," O'Rourke said. "You thought that since I rescued you from those vultures, loosely called reporters, that I was on your side, that you could get at the kid through me. Well, unfortunately, it doesn't work that way. Either you're a relative of the child or you're not. And I don't like being used."

"You called me," she reminded him, and watched his lips tighten.

"I've had second thoughts."

"To hell with your second thoughts!" Her temper, quickly rising, captured her tongue. "I'm not going to hurt the baby. I'm just someone who cares, Doctor. Someone who would like to offer that poor, abandoned child a little bit of love."

"Or someone who enjoys all the attention she's getting?"

"If that was the case, I wouldn't have tried to throw the reporters out of the hospital, now, would I?"

That stopped him, and whatever he was about to say was kept inside. He stared at her a few minutes, his gaze fairly raking over her, as if he were examining her for flaws. She almost expected a sneer to curl his lip, but he was a little too civilized for outward disdain. "I'm just being straight with you. There's a lot I don't know about that baby who's up in pediatrics, Ms. Hill. And a lot more I don't know about you. If it were up to me, I'd let you hang around. Based on first impressions, I'm guessing that you do care something for the infant. But I don't know that, the hospital administration doesn't know that and Social Services doesn't know that."

He turned then, and left her standing in the middle of the parking lot, her mouth nearly dropping open.

He didn't understand why he'd come to her rescue in the hospital, only to shoot her down a peg or two.

Instinctively, Dallas knew that she was a different kind of woman than those he'd met. There was something about her that attracted him as well as caused him to be suspicious. She seemed at once strong willed and yet innocent, able to take care of herself and needing something—a man?—to lean upon occasionally.

There had been a desperation in her eyes, a pleading that he hadn't been able to refuse in the hospital, but here, out in the light of day, she'd looked far from innocent—in fact, he suspected that Ms. Hill could handle herself in just about any situation.

Dallas felt himself drawn to her, like a fly buzzing around a spider's web. He didn't know a thing about her, and he was smart enough to realize that she was only interested in him because he was her link to the baby. Yet his stupid male pride fantasized that she might be interested in him—as a man.

"Fool," he muttered to himself, kicking at a fragment of loose gravel on the asphalt. The sharp-sided rock skidded across the lot, hitting the tire of a low-slung Porche, Dr. Prescott's latest toy.

He must be getting soft, Dallas decided. Why else would he let a woman get under his skin? Especially a woman who wasn't being entirely honest with him.

He slid behind the wheel of his truck and flipped on the ignition. What was it about Chandra Hill that had him saying one thing while meaning another? He didn't want to keep her from the child, and yet he had an obligation to protect the baby's interests. Hospital policy was very strict about visitors who weren't relatives.

But the baby needed someone to care about him, and Chandra was willing. If her motives were pure. He couldn't believe that she was lying, not completely, and yet there was a wariness to her, and she sometimes picked her words carefully, especially when the questions became too personal. But that wasn't a sin. She was entitled to her private life.

Yet he felt Chandra Hill was holding back, keeping information that he needed to herself. It was a feeling that kept nagging at him whenever he was around her; not that she said anything dishonest. No, it was her omissions that bothered him.

He crammed his truck into gear and watched Chandra haul herself into the cab of a huge red Chevrolet Suburban, the truck that last night he'd thought was a van. Her jeans stretched across taut buttocks and athletic thighs. Her skin was tanned, her straight blond hair streaked by the sun. She looked healthy and vibrant and forthright, and yet she was hiding something. He could feel it.

"All in your mind, O'Rourke," he told himself as he drove out of the parking lot and toward the center of town. He had hours before his meeting with Brian, so he decided that a stop at the sheriff's office might clear up a few questions he had about Chandra Hill and her abandoned baby.

Chandra drove into Ranger, her thoughts racing a mile a minute. Automatically, she adjusted her foot on the throttle, managing to stay under the speed limit. She stopped for a single red light and turned right on Coyote Avenue. Without thinking, she pulled into a dusty parking lot and slid into one of a dozen available spaces, her mind focused on the infant. Baby John Doe. Already she'd started thinking of him as J.D. Kind of a bad joke, but the child deserved a name.

Lord, who did he belong to?

And that damned Dr. O'Rourke, telling her she shouldn't "hang around" the hospital. That man—kind one minute, cruel the next—set her teeth on edge! Well, the less she thought of him, the better.

Flicking off the ignition, she grabbed her jacket and climbed from the cab onto the sun-baked asphalt. A few blades of grass and dandelions sprouted through the cracks in the pockmarked tarmac, but the neglect seemed only to add to the casual allure of this tourist town. Most of the buildings, including the gas stations, coin laundry, banks and restaurants, sported a Western motif, complete with false facades, long wooden porches and, at the veterinary clinic, a hitching post.

Years before, the city fathers had decided to mine whatever gold was left in Ranger—not in the surrounding hills, but in the pockets of the visitors who drove through this quaint village in the foothills of the Rocky Mountains. Those same far-thinking civic leaders had persuaded the town to adopt a Wild West atmosphere, and the mayor had encouraged renovating existing buildings to adopt the appearance of the grange hall, livery stable and old hotel, the only remaining structures built before the turn of the century, and therefore, authentically from the eighteen hundreds.

In the past twenty years, all the businesses facing Main Street and a few more on the side streets reeked of the Old West. Wild West Expeditions had willingly embraced the idea.

Situated near the livery, on the second floor of a building constructed in 1987 and made to look a hundred years older, Wild West Expeditions, owned by once-upon-a-time hippie Rick Benson, was Chandra's place of employment.

She climbed the exterior stairs, noticing a soft wind rush through the boughs of a birch tree, spinning the leaves so that they glittered a silver-green.

The door was propped open. The sign above, painted red and yellow, swung and creaked in the breeze.

"Hey—I heard a rumor about you!" Rick greeted her with a toothy smile. He was a big man, six-two with an extra twenty pounds around his middle. His hair was extremely thin on top and had turned to gray, but he still wore his meager locks in a pony tail that snaked halfway down his back. He had a flushed face, an easy smile and no enemy in the world. Not even the mother of his children, who, in the seventies, he hadn't bothered to marry, and ten years later hadn't needed to divorce when she took the kids and packed them back to "civilization" in St. Louis.

"A rumor, eh?" Chandra hung her jacket on a peg near the door. The interior of the establishment was as rustic as the rest of the town. Rough-hewn cedar walls, camping equipment, including ancient snowshoes and leather pouches, hanging from wooden pegs, a potbellied stove and a long counter that served as the reception desk. "Only good things, I hope."

"Something about an abandoned kid. Found by your mutt down near the creek. I heard the kid would've drowned if Sam hadn't led you to him."

"Well, that's not quite the truth, but close," Chandra said, thinking how quickly a story could be exaggerated in the gossip-riddled coffee shops and streets of Ranger. She gave Rick a quick rundown of what really happened, and he listened, all the while adding receipts on a very modern-looking adding machine, swilling coffee and answering the phone.

"Why'd'ya s'pose the kid was left in your barn?" he asked once she'd finished with her tale.

She poured herself a cup of coffee. "Beats me. That seems to be the million-dollar question."

"Must be a reason."

"Maybe, maybe not."

"The army jacket a clue?"

Chandra sighed and blew across her cup. "I don't know. The deputies took it and the blanket, but it seemed to me they think nothing will come back from the lab."

Rick pushed up the sleeves of his plaid shirt, which he wore as a jacket over a river boatman's collarless shirt, usually cream colored and decorated by a string of beads that surrounded his neck. "Well, whatever happens with the kid, the press will be all over you." He scowled, his beefy face creased. "Bob Fillmore has already called."

"We've met," Chandra said dryly.

"Watch him. He's a shark," Rick warned, his light brown gaze meeting hers. He never probed into her private life. Not even when, two years before, she'd shown up on this doorstep and applied for a job as a white-water and camping guide. He hadn't lifted an eyebrow at the holes in her résumé, nor had he mentioned the fact that she was a woman, and a small one at that. He'd just taken her down to a series of rapids known as Devil's Falls in the Rattlesnake River and said, "Do your stuff." When she'd expertly guided the rubber raft through the treacherous waters, he'd hired her on the spot, only insisting she learn basic first aid and the lay of the land so that she would become one of his "expert" guides. She'd passed with flying colors. As far as she knew, Rick had no knowledge of her past life and didn't seem interested. She doubted that he knew that she'd been married or had been a pediatrician. He didn't care about the past—only the here and now.

Rick rubbed his chin. "Fillmore wants you to call him back and set up an interview."

"And you don't think I should."

Lifting a big shoulder, Rick shook his head. "Up to you. Just don't let that piece of slime inside here, okay?"

"You don't like him."

"No." He didn't say why, but Chandra remembered hearing that Fillmore had once written a piece about Wild West Tours. The crux of the article had been a cynical evaluation of Rick's alternative life-style, his "sixties values" in the late eighties.

"What've we got going today?" she asked. "There's a group coming in—when?"

"Soon, but I've changed things around a little," Rick replied, glancing at his schedule. "That group of six from the Hastings Ranch want a medium-thrill ride. I thought the south fork of the river would work for them. But I've got one lone ranger who wants to play daredevil . . . let's see . . . the name's McGee. Brian McGee. Young guy. Twenty, maybe twenty-two. He wants, and I quote, 'the ltimate thrill—the biggest rush' we can give him before he eads back to college. You think you want to deal with im?''

With pleasure, Chandra thought, recalling the so-called e-men she went to college with. The boys who didn't think he'd cut it in medical school. "Grizzly Loop?" she asked.

"If you think *he* can handle it. I know you can, but who nows what kind of a nut this bozo is. If he wants to play macho man and doesn't know beans about rafting, you ould be in a pile of trouble."

"I'll check it out."

"Good. He'll be in at eleven."

"And the other group?"

"Randy and Jake'll handle them. Unless you'd ather—"

"Oh, no," Chandra replied crisply, noticing the teasing ft of Rick's brow. "Bring on Mr. Macho." Maybe she just eeded to throw herself into her work to forget about the aby and, most especially, Dr. O'Rourke.

The Sheriff's Department had ignored the Western mo- f of the other buildings in town. A single-story brick uilding, there wasn't the hint of pretension about the lace. Inside, the walls were paneled in yellowed birch, and e floor was a mottled green-and-white tile that was worn ear the front desk and door.

The receptionist recognized Dallas as he walked through e door. He'd helped deliver her second child two years arlier. With a grin, she slid one of the glass panels to the de. "Dr. O'Rourke!"

"Hi, Angie." He leaned one arm on the counter. How're the boys?"

"Hell on wheels," she said with a heartfelt sigh. Behind er desk, officers in uniform or dressed in civilian clothes at at desks and pushed paper, drank coffee, smoked and radled phones to their ears as they filled out reports. "But you didn't come here to discuss the kids," Angie said "What's up?"

"I'd like to talk to the dispatcher on duty early this morning, around one-thirty or two o'clock. A call came in about an abandoned baby."

"Let me check the log." Angie's fingers moved quickly over a computer keyboard, and she squinted into the blue light of a terminal. "Let's see... Here it is—1:57. Marla was on duty, but she won't be in until ten tonight."

"But the call was recorded?"

"They all are. You want to listen to the tape?"

"If it's all right."

Angie winked. "I've got connections around this place," she said. "Come on in." As Dallas walked through a door to the offices, he heard Angie ask another woman officer to cover for her, but his mind wasn't on the conversation. He was, as he had been ever since meeting her last night contemplating Chandra Hill.

"So, you've got an abandoned kid on your hands," Angie said, snapping him out of his thoughts. She opened door to an interrogation room. "Who would leave a baby alone like that?"

"I wish I knew."

"So do I. I'd personally wring her neck," Angie said fiercely. "Here, just pull up a chair. I'll get a copy of the tape. It'll be just a minute."

The room was windowless, with a long table, four folding chairs and little else. Just the basics. The faint scent of stale cigarette smoke hung in the air, and the two ashtrays on the table had been emptied, but not wiped clean.

He waited less than ten minutes for Angie to return, as promised, with a tape, a player and a cup of coffee, "compliments of the department."

"Thanks." He accepted the cup as she slipped the tape into the player.

"All the comforts of home," she teased, her dark eyes sparkling as she glanced at the bare walls and uncomfortable chairs. "Let me know if you need anything else."

"Will do."

She closed the door behind her as she left, and Dallas played the tape. Chandra's voice, at first frantic, calmed as she described the condition of the child. Cool and professional. And the medical terminology was used precisely—hardly typical of a first-aid class graduate. No, Chandra sounded very much like a physician.

Dallas sipped some of the coffee—stronger and more bitter than coffee served at the hospital—and rocked back in the chair. Chandra Hill. Beautiful and slightly mysterious. Sure, she came on strong and she seemed forthright, but there was more to her than what she said.

So what if she's a physician? Big deal. Maybe she just wants a little privacy. And, really, O'Rourke, it's none of your damned business. She brought you a patient, and you've got an obligation to care for him—and not for her.

Yet, as he heard her take-charge voice on the tape, he smiled. What, he wondered, would it be like to kiss a woman like that? Would she bite his lips and kick him in the groin, or would she melt against him, growing supple and compliant? The thought of pressing his mouth to hers caused an unwanted stirring between his legs.

"Damn," he muttered, angry at the turn of his thoughts. What the hell was he thinking?

Scowling darkly, he rewound the tape and listened to it again, his eyes narrowing through the steam rising from his cup. The tape gave him no more clues to the baby's parentage or to Chandra Hill. In fact, he thought sourly, he had more questions about her than ever.

"You're the guide?" Brian McGee couldn't swallow his surprised grin. He was handsome in a boyish way, with oversize features, large green eyes and a smile that was dazzlingly white. And he was shocked to his socks as he stared down at Chandra.

"I'm the guide," she quipped.

Brian glanced from Chandra to the counter, where Rick was busily working on the wording of a new brochure.

"I, uh, expected someone more—"

"Male?" she asked, tilting her chin upward and meeting his quizzical, amused gaze with her own steady eyes.

"Well, yeah, I was. I mean, not that you're not capable—"

"She's the best riverwoman I've got," Rick put in, never looking up from his work.

"But—"

"Come on, Mr. McGee. It'll be fun," Chandra assured him, though she was beginning to doubt her own words. This young buck definitely had ideas about male-female relationships on all levels. She grabbed a couple of life vests and a first-aid kit. "Believe it or not, you don't need extra testosterone to paddle a canoe."

He gulped. "Is anyone else going on this trip?"

"Nope. Just you and me."

McGee glanced back at Rick. "And this is a serious ride?"

Rick slid him a glance. "I guarantee you'll get the biggest rush of your life," he mocked, chuckling softly.

"That's what I want," McGee replied with a grin.

"Good." Chandra was already at the door. "The raft's tied to my rig. You follow me in yours, and we'll drop your car off at the south fork. Then you climb in my Suburban with me and we'll continue up the river. It'll only take about an hour to get there." She eyed him over her shoulder. "You have rafted before, haven't you?"

"Absolutely."

"Then let's get going."

While McGee paid for the excursion and signed the release forms, Chandra packed the truck. Within ten minutes, she was on the road, McGee following her in a beat-up

Pontiac. They dropped his car off at Junction Park, and he climbed into the Suburban. Mentally crossing her fingers, Chandra hoped that Brian McGee wouldn't be too much trouble on the trip. She glanced at his profile as she put the truck into gear. For a second, she thought she was looking at Dallas O'Rourke. The profile, though much more boyish, was similar, the clear green eyes intense...but that was crazy. Calling herself every kind of fool, she snapped her sunglasses onto the bridge of her nose and vowed she wouldn't think of Dallas O'Rourke for the rest of the day!

She must really be losing it. To think that this...college boy resembled O'Rourke was ludicrous. And why Dr. O'Rourke wouldn't leave her mind alone was too obnoxious to contemplate.

"Somethin' wrong?" McGee asked, and she shook her head, as if to clear out a nest of cobwebs.

"Nope. You just..." She laughed. "You reminded me of someone I know."

His grin was enchanting. Boyish, but enchanting. "Someone you like?" he asked, his voice smooth as silk.

"I'm not sure," she said, and decided to end the conversation by turning on the radio. She wasn't interested in a college boy, or any man, for that matter.

McGee seemed to take the hint. He reached into his pocket for a pack of cigarettes and, rolling down the window, lit up. Tapping his foot to the sultry beat of an old Roy Orbison song, he seemed lost in his own world, which was fine with Chandra. She coveted her own thoughts, and they had nothing to do with the boy next to her.

Instead, her mind was crowded with images of a tiny baby and the doctor who cared for him. The baby, she understood. She'd wanted a child for a long, long time. But why Dr. O'Rourke? He was the baby's physician. And a man who was much too complicated for her—not that she wanted a simple man. She didn't want a man at all, thank you very much. And especially not a man like Dallas O'Rourke.

She gripped the wheel more tightly and realized that her palms were sweating as they drove upward, on a gravel road that twisted and turned along the forested banks of the Rattlesnake River.

Late, again. Dallas glanced at his watch and scowled. Brian had suggested they meet here, at the Rocky Horror Pub, at six. It was now 6:40, and Dallas had nursed one beer in the smoky interior. The after-work crowd had gathered. Pool balls clicked in the corner, a lively game of darts had begun, and the tables, as well as the bar itself, were packed with the regulars who always enjoyed a couple beers before heading home.

Five more minutes. That's all he'd give his irresponsible brother, then Brian could go borrow money at a bank, like a normal person.

Dallas finished his beer just as the saloon-type doors swung open and Brian, all one-hundred-eighty-five pounds of cockiness, strode in. Dressed in dusty jeans, a cowboy shirt and Stetson, Brian glanced around, spotted Dallas and waved.

"Sorry I'm late," he announced, plopping down on a chair at Dallas's table. He waved to the waitress and pointed at Dallas's empty. "Two more of those...wait a minute. Is that a *light?* Forget it. I want the real thing. Whatever you got on tap."

"And you?" the waitress asked, her eyebrows lifting at Dallas. "Do you want the 'real thing,' too?"

"Nothing," Dallas replied, glancing at his brother. "Better watch out, Brian. You could end up with a Coke."

"Bring this guy the same thing I'm having," Brian insisted, and the waitress, rolling her eyes, left them.

Settling back in his chair, Brian took off his hat and hung it on a hook near the table. His thick hair was unruly, springy and slightly damp. "I've just had the experience of a lifetime, let me tell you."

The waitress deposited the two glasses on the table and, surprisingly, Brian paid for them both. Reaching for a handful of peanuts and shaking his head, Brian asked, "Ever shot the rapids at Grizzly Loop?"

"No," Dallas replied.

"Hell, man, you should. It was incredible."

"Sounds dangerous." Dallas waited as Brian tossed peanuts into his mouth. Sooner or later, he would get to the point, which was, of course, how much.

"It was. But the woman who was in charge, man, could she shoot those rapids. Scared the living hell out of me!"

"Woman?"

"Yeah." Brian hooked his thumb toward the windows. "She works over at Wild West Expeditions. Chandra something-or-other. Just a little thing, but, boy, does she know how to ride a river."

"Does she?" Dallas asked dryly. He took a swallow of the beer he didn't want. What were the chances of there being more than one woman named Chandra in a town this size?

"Believe me, I was skeptical. This little thing, couldn't be more than five-three or four, drives a huge red rig, carries a backpack that's half her size and shoots rapids like some damned Indian guide!"

"She blond?" Dallas couldn't resist asking.

"And gorgeous." Brian smiled slyly and winked at his older brother. "Built a little on the slim side for my tastes, but good-lookin'." Dallas felt his back stiffen. "With women like that," Brian continued as he lifted his glass to his lips, "maybe I'll just hang around for a while. I could go back to school after Christmas."

"Like hell!" Dallas replied in a loud whisper. A few heads turned in his direction, and he immediately put a clamp on his runaway emotions. What the hell was wrong with him? Brian was only kidding around, anyone could see that. Yet Dallas's temper had flared white-hot, probably because he was guilty of the same thoughts himself.

"Hey, man, I was only—"

"I know." Dallas waved off his explanation. "Maybe we should get down to business."

Brian's smile left his face, and for the first time that Dallas could remember, the younger man seemed genuinely sincere. "Look, I hate to ask you again, but I do need a few bucks to get through the next couple of terms."

"How much?" Dallas asked, taking a swallow from his "real thing."

Brian turned his glass uneasily. "I don't know. Four—" he glanced up to see how far he was getting "—maybe five grand could get me through to spring."

He wasn't asking a lot, Dallas knew. Though part of Brian's tuition and books were paid by his scholarship, his room and board were not. Brian's dad helped him a little, but the monthly checks didn't stretch far enough. And living expenses alone would mount up to more than he was asking for. However, Dallas couldn't get over the fact that Brian hadn't bothered to earn one red cent all summer. It wasn't loaning Brian the money that bothered Dallas so much as wondering if the kid would ever get enough gumption to actually get a job and become self-reliant.

"I looked for a roommate," Brian added, and Dallas's head snapped up.

"I thought you had two roommates."

"They dropped out."

"So you're living alone?"

"It's only temporary. I'll hook up with someone once school starts. There's always guys looking for a place to stay, and I'm not too far from campus...."

Without roommates to share the expense of a Southern California apartment, Brian would go through five thousand dollars quickly.

Dallas frowned and rubbed the back of his head. "I'll send you the money once you get back to L.A.," he said, eyeing his half brother and wondering why, with the same mother, they were so unlike each other. Dallas had never shied from work; in fact, he'd been accused of having no emotions, no room for anything in his life but his profession. He'd put himself through school with a little help from a small inheritance from his grandmother. When that had run out, he'd borrowed money from the government. School had been a grind—long hours, no money, no room for anything but classes, studying and sleeping. And it had taken him years to pay off the debt. However, he didn't wish what he'd gone through on anyone, especially his younger brother.

Brian looked straight at Dallas. "I was kinda hoping you'd, uh, give me the check now." He licked his lips nervously, and Dallas noticed a tightening around the corners of his half brother's mouth.

"Are you in some kind of trouble?"

"Nah! Nothing serious," Brian said quickly, his mouth twisting into a boyish grin again. "It's just that I've got a temporary cash-flow problem and I thought . . . well, I was hoping . . ."

Dallas reached into his jacket pocket and pulled out his check book. "How much?"

"Just a couple of hundred . . ."

Wondering if he was doing more damage than good, Dallas wrote a check for three hundred dollars and handed it to his brother.

With obvious relief, Brian stuffed the check into his wallet. "I don't know how to thank you."

"Finish school."

"No worry about that. Oh, by the way, I bought you something."

"You *bought* me something?"

"Yeah, well, I couldn't resist."

"But I thought you were broke."

"I am. But I've got a bank card and . . . I guess I was in a generous mood."

Dallas was about to protest. No wonder the kid couldn't stretch a buck, but Brian withdrew some sort of coupon from his wallet and slid it across the table. It was a pass for a white-water camping trip from Wild West Expeditions.

"You need to lighten up," Brian said. "I thought you should do something besides hang around the hospital all the time."

"This must've cost you—"

"Relax, will ya. Think of it as your money. Have Chandra take you up to Grizzly Loop—I told the old man who runs the place you're to specifically ask for her. You'll never be the same, I guarantee it." He reached into his shirt pocket, grabbed a pen and, clicking it, scratched Chandra's name on the coupon. "There ya go! The experience of a lifetime!"

"If you say so," Dallas said, his lips twisting at the thought of spending a day alone with Ms. Hill. It could be interesting.

And dangerous. He didn't know anything about her, and her story about the baby didn't ring quite true. No, he was still convinced she was hiding something—something she didn't want him to find out about her. What it had to do with the abandoned infant, he didn't understand. But he would. In time, he'd figure it out and, he thought bitterly, he probably wouldn't like what he found.

Except that she was interesting, far more interesting than any woman he'd met in a long, long while. He considered her tanned skin and gray-green eyes. A day or two alone with Chandra Hill could spell more than trouble. His emotions were already on edge whenever he thought of the woman—which was too damned often. But the idea of being close to her, seeing her without all her attention centered on that baby, was far too appealing to turn down. And, even if she were trouble, he decided he was willing to take that chance. He slipped the pass into his wallet.

Chapter Five

A couple of days later, Dallas had his first weekend off in two months. Seated in his pickup, he stared through the glass at the rustic building where Chandra worked.

Baby Doe was doing well. Just yesterday, Dr. Williams had allowed the infant to be put in the general nursery with the others. Had the child a parent, he would be released soon. However, no one as yet had claimed the baby, despite the front-page story in this morning's *Banner*. Dallas glanced to the passenger seat, where the paper still lay open. "Mystery Baby Abandoned in Barn." Fortunately there were no photographs of the child. Chandra had only been quoted once, and it seemed that Bob Fillmore, a man Dallas didn't trust an inch, had gotten most of his information from the Sheriff's Department.

However, the first story in the *Banner* was unlikely the last. The press would keep sniffing around, Dallas thought, his gaze returning to the rough-finished building where Chandra worked. Fillmore, like the proverbial dog after the bone, wouldn't stop until he'd dug through every corner of Chandra's life. Things could get ugly.

Retrieving the coupon from his wallet, Dallas reached for the door handle and wondered, not for the first time, what the devil he was doing here. He was afraid his reasons had more to do with Chandra than with relaxing in the mountains. Yes, he was curious about her, but logic told him he was making a big mistake by taking up his brother's offer. Long ago, Dallas had decided he didn't need any complications in his life. Hadn't he had enough of complex relationships in L.A.? Weren't difficulties in his life in southern California the express reason he had retreated to this sleepy little mountain town? To his way of thinking, women always spelled trouble—with a capital *T*.

Chandra Hill would be no different—perhaps she was the most complex of all the women he'd ever met. Certainly she was fascinating. And she was crazy for that little boy. He'd checked with the nurses in pediatrics. It seemed Chandra was more often in the pediatrics wing of Riverbend Hospital than not. In two days, she'd visited the child five times—drawn inexplicably to the baby, as if she were the infant's mother or, at least, were nurturing some maternal bond.

He started up the steps leading to Wild West Expeditions. It wouldn't hurt to find out a little bit about the mysterious Ms. Hill, he decided. After all, he did have some stake in Baby Doe's future, in so far as he was the admitting physician. And the child had no one to fight his battles for him. Unless Dr. Dallas O'Rourke stepped in. His mouth twisted at the irony of it all—he'd never considered himself a hero of any kind. And here he was, deluding himself, making excuses just so he could spend a little time with Chandra Hill. Just like a schoolboy in the throes of lust. He hadn't felt this way in years.

"You're a case, O'Rourke," he muttered under his breath as he leaned on the door at the top of the stairs. It opened easily, and a brass bell jangled as he crossed the threshold.

Chandra was inside. Alone. She was seated at a makeshift desk, and glanced in his direction. Her fingers froze above the keyboard of a calculator, and surprise and anxiety registered in her even features. "Dr. O'Rourke," she said quietly. Standing, she yanked her glasses from her face and folded them into a case. As she approached the counter separating them, she asked. "Is...is anything wrong? The baby—is he—"

"He's fine," Dallas said, cutting in, and noticed relief ease the tension from her shoulders.

"Thank God. When I saw you here...well, I assumed the worst."

She blew her bangs from her eyes in a sigh of relief, and Dallas couldn't take his eyes from her face as he crossed the room and slapped his coupon onto the desk. "Actually, I'm here to cash this in."

Chandra picked up the voucher and eyed it carefully. "You want a white-water trip?"

"Overnight camp-out, I think it says."

"When?" She seemed ill at ease, drumming her fingers as she read the damned coupon again.

"As soon as possible. I've got three days off and thought we could get started whenever your schedule allows." He watched her and wondered if she'd try to beg out, try to palm him off on someone else—a man probably. He didn't blame her and, considering his fantasies of late, she would probably be right. Nonetheless, more than anything, Dallas wanted to spend the next couple of days alone with her.

"This coupon has my name on it," she said, glancing up at him with assessing hazel eyes. "Did you request me?"

"It was a gift. From my brother."

"Your brother?" She pulled her eyebrows together, and a deep line formed on her forehead.

"Half brother really. Brian McGee."

"McGee? Oh!" A smile of recognition lighted her eyes. "Mr. Macho."

"Was he?" Dallas wasn't certain he liked this twist in the conversation. Obviously Chandra had noticed Brian's dubious charms, and Dallas had hoped that she would be a little more selective. He saw her as a cut above the women Brian usually dated.

"He wasn't too thrilled to have a woman guide," she explained with a soft chuckle that struck a chord deep within Dallas. "But he changed his mind."

"Whatever you did, he sang your praises for two hours."

She laughed, and the sound was deep and throaty. "I scared him."

"You what?" Dallas couldn't help the grin that tugged at his lips. The thought of this little woman besting his brother was music to his ears.

"I scared the living tar right out of him." She glanced to the coupon and back to Dallas, and the laughter died in her eyes. "Am I supposed to do the same for you?"

"Do you think you can?"

"Without a doubt," she said, arching one fine eyebrow.

Was she teasing him? Women rarely had the nerve to joke with him; he'd heard his nickname, Dr. Ice, muttered angrily behind his back more than once. The name and the reputation suited him just fine. Kept things simple.

"Well, Ms. Hill, you're on."

"In that case, call me Chandra—I'll try to forget that you're a doctor." She flashed him a cool smile of even, white teeth that made him want to return her grin.

"Will that be possible?"

"Absolutely. But I think we should get some things clear before we set out—in case you want to back out." She leaned over the counter that separated them. "When we're in the boat, *Dallas*, I'm in charge. And that goes for the rest of the trip, as well. It was hard enough to convince your brother of that fact, so I hope I don't get any guff from you. Understood?"

For a little thing, he thought, she certainly could lay down the law. He couldn't help feeling slightly amused. "What time?"

"Let's see what we've got available." She turned, picked up a clipboard with several charts attached to it and ran her fingers along the top page. Scowling, as if she was disappointed to find she wasn't booked up, she said, "Be back here at ten-thirty today. I'll have everything ready by then."

"What do I need to bring?"

"Besides your nerve?" she asked, and slid a list of supplies across the desk. One column listed the equipment and food that would be provided, the other suggested items he might bring along. "Just remember we travel light."

"Aye, aye, captain," he said mockingly, and started for the door.

"One more thing," she called. He stopped short, turning to catch a glimpse of what—worry?—on her small features. "Will you be coming alone—the coupon is only for one. Or is anyone from your family... your wife, anyone, coming along?"

At that he snorted. "My wife?" he asked, and thought of Jennifer. Though they'd been divorced for years, she was the only woman who had become missus to his mister. "Nope. Just me." With that, he strode through the door.

Chandra let out her breath. If Rick was here right now, she'd personally strangle him. What did he mean to do, hooking her up with O'Rourke? And what about the cryptic comment from O'Rourke about his wife? Was he married or not? Already, Chandra was getting mixed signals from the man, and not knowing his marital status made things difficult. Not that his marital status mattered, of course. Dallas O'Rourke was nothing more than the doctor who had admitted the baby.

Nonetheless, Rick Benson had a lot of explaining to do! Putting her name down on the form!

Within ten minutes, her boss waltzed through the door. "What's gotten into you?" she demanded.

"Hey—what's wrong?"

"Everything." She threw up her hands in disgust. "You signed me up for an overnight with Dr. O'Rourke. Remember him? The guy who's about as friendly as a starving lion and as calm as a raftload of TNT going over the falls!"

"Hey, slow down. What's all this about?" Rick asked before spying the coupon on the desk. "Oh."

"'Oh' is right."

"Don't blame me. That college kid insisted that you give his brother the ride of his life."

Chandra's eyes narrowed suspiciously.

"The kid even paid for an overnight, but if you don't want to do it, I'm sure that Randy would—"

"No!" Chandra cut in, feeling cornered. "I already said I'd meet him today. I can't back down now."

"Sure you could. Get a headache or claim you have P.M.S. or—"

"Just like a man!" she said, throwing up her hands and glaring at him. "I swear, Rick, sometimes I think you're on *their* side."

"On whose side? Men's? No way, Chan, I'm just walking a thin line between the sexes." He looked up, trying to swallow a smile. "I hired you, didn't I? You should have heard all the flack I took about that."

"I know, I know," Chandra said, though she still felt betrayed. It wasn't that she didn't want to be with Dr. O'Rourke, she told herself; the man was interesting, even if his temper was a little on the rough side. But the thought of spending a day *and* a night with him...

"Hey—isn't he the guy who took care of the baby at the hospital?" Rick asked as he walked into the back room. He returned with a gross of pocket knives, which he put on display in the glass case near the door.

"Just the admitting doctor."

"Well, he works at the hospital, doesn't he? Maybe you could get a little more information on the kid. I know that you've been eatin' yourself up over it."

"Is it that obvious?"

"And then some." Rick opened one pocket knife to display the blades, then locked the case. He moved back to the desk, where Chandra had tried to resume tallying yesterday's receipts. "If you ask me, you're getting yourself too caught up with that little tyke."

"I don't remember asking." She took her glasses out of their case, then slid them onto her nose.

Rick pushed the sale button on the cash register and withdrew a five-dollar bill. A small smile played upon his lips. "This trip with the doc might be the best thing that happened to you in a long time."

O'Rourke was prompt, she'd give him that. At ten-thirty, his truck rounded the corner and pulled into the lot. He guided his pickup into the empty slot next to Chandra's Suburban. "Ready?" he asked as he hopped down from his truck.

"As I'll ever be," Chandra muttered under her breath, forcing a smile. "You bet." Dr. O'Rourke—no, Dallas— was as intimidating outside the hospital as he was in. Though he was dressed down in faded jeans, beat-up running shoes, a T-shirt and worn leather jacket, he still stood erect, his shoulders wide, his head cocked at an angle of authority. *What am I doing?* Chandra wondered as she, balancing on the running board of the Suburban, tightened a strap holding the inflated raft onto the top of her rig.

"Need help?"

"Not yet." She yanked hard, tied off the strap quickly and hopped to the ground. Dusting her hands, she said, "Just give me a hand with your gear and we'll get going. You follow me in your truck. You can park at the camp. We'll take my rig up the river."

"Sounds fair enough," he said, though he couldn't hide the skepticism in his voice.

Within minutes, they were ready—or as ready as Chandra would ever be—and the Suburban was breezing along the country road, which wound upward through the surrounding hills. Behind her, Dallas drove his truck, and she couldn't help glancing in the rearview to watch him. There was something about the man that was damned unsettling, and though she told herself differently, she knew her attraction to him—for that's what it was, whether she wanted to admit to it or not—had nothing to do with Baby J.D.

The drive took nearly two hours, and in that time the smooth asphalt of the country road deteriorated as they turned onto a gravel lane that twisted and turned up the mountains.

Tall pines and aspen grew in abundance along the roadside, their branches dancing in the wind and casting galloping shadows across the twin ruts of the sharp rock. Through the forest, flashes of silver water, the Rattlesnake River, glinted and sparkled in the trees.

Chandra pulled off at a widening in the road, just to the south of Grizzly Loop. Dust was still billowing from beneath her tires as Dallas's rig ground to a stop. Through the surrounding stands of trees, the river rushed in a deafening roar and the dank smell of water permeated the air.

Dallas cut the engine and shoved open the door of his truck. "I must be out of my mind," he said as he hopped to the ground. "Why I ever let Brian talk me into this . . ." He shook his head, and sunlight danced in his jet-black hair.

"So it wasn't your idea?"

"No way."

Chandra opened the back door of the Suburban and started pulling out crates of supplies. "Let me guess. You didn't really want to come today but your male pride got in your way, right? Since your brother—"

"Half brother," Dallas clarified gruffly.

"Whatever. Since he made the trip, your ego was on the line. You had to prove you were man enough to challenge the river." She smiled as she said the words, but Dallas got the distinct impression that she wasn't just teasing him. No, she was testing his mettle.

"Maybe I couldn't resist spending time with you," he said smoothly, then cringed at the sound of his own words. Good Lord, that corny line could've come straight out of an old black-and-white movie.

"I figured as much," she tossed back, but a dimple in her cheeks creased, and her hazel eyes seemed to catch the rays of the sun. Her eyes sparkled the same gray-green as the river that he glimpsed through the trees. "Well, are you going to give me a hand or what?"

"I thought you were the guide."

"On my trips, everyone pitches in." She reached into the truck again, withdrew some tent poles and tossed them to him. "I think we should set up camp at the edge of the forest."

"Whatever you say. You're the boss," he mocked, carrying tent poles, tarp and a heavy crate down a dusty path through the trees. Branches from the surrounding brush slapped at his thighs, and a bird, squawking at his intrusion, soared upward past the leafy branches to the blue sky.

For the first time, Dallas didn't doubt the wisdom of this little adventure. Though he hated to admit it, he decided that Brian might have been right about one thing—he did need a break from his sterile routine. For the past three years, he'd had no social life, contenting himself with work and sleep. He swam daily in the pool of a local athletic club, taking out his frustrations by swimming lap after tiring lap, and he skied in the winter.... Well, he hadn't last winter or the winter before that. He'd been too busy....

"This should do."

He hadn't even been aware that Chandra had joined him or that the path had ended at a solitary stretch of sand and rock. Chandra strapped on a tool belt and took the tent stakes from his hands. "Put the rest of the equipment right there and unload the back of the Suburban. But don't bring down the first-aid kit, life preservers or anything else you think we might need on the trip—including the small cooler." When he didn't move, she smiled sweetly and added, "Please."

Dallas wasn't used to taking orders. Especially not from some tiny woman puffed up on her own authority. And yet, she'd been straight with him from the beginning, so despite his natural tendency to rebel, he dropped the things he was carrying and, turning, started back up the path.

When he returned, Chandra was bent over her work. The stakes were driven into the earth, and the ropes were strung tight. She leaned her back into her efforts as she stretched the nylon tarp over the poles.

She'd tied a handkerchief around her forehead and had begun to sweat; shiny drops beaded over her eyebrows and along the gentle ridge of her spine where her blouse separated from her shorts. He wondered about the texture of her skin, so firm and supple, then closed his mind to that particular topic. What was coming over him? Since he'd moved to Ranger, more than his share of women had shown interest in him. Patients, nurses, even fellow doctors had been bold enough to try to get to know him, but he'd held firm. No woman, no matter how beautiful, no matter how interesting, was allowed past a certain point. He had made the mistake of putting his faith in a gorgeous woman once before, and he wasn't about to suffer that fate again.

Even if, as he was beginning to suspect, Chandra Hill was the most exciting female he'd met since stepping foot on Colorado soil.

Ignoring the obvious curve of her behind, he dropped the rest of their supplies. "Here, let me give you a hand with that."

"You know how?" she asked skeptically.

"Mmm."

"Don't tell me, you're an Eagle Scout in disguise," she joked sarcastically, but took the sting off her words by offering him that sexy smile again.

"Nope. The military."

"You were in the service?" she asked, turning all her attention his way. Her face, touched by the sunlight, seemed younger and more innocent than he'd first thought, and yet there was a trace of sadness in her eyes, a flickering shadow that darkened her gaze momentarily.

"My father was," he clarified, wondering why he was giving her any information about himself. "Career military doctor."

She rocked back on her heels and wiped her palms on her shorts. "And you decided to follow in his footsteps?"

"Something like that," he admitted, though the subject, as far as he was concerned, was closed. He'd come on this trip with the firm intention of gaining some insight on Ms. Hill, not the other way around.

They finished setting up camp, and Chandra, swinging a rope over a tall tree branch, hoisted a nylon bag of food twenty feet into the air. "Bears," she explained when she caught his questioning gaze. "They're as hungry as Yogi and twice as clever. So let's not leave any 'pic-i-nic baskets' around. Even this—" she hooked a thumb toward the tree "—might not be effective."

"No one mentioned bears on this trip."

"Don't worry, I'll protect you," she said, and laughed. That husky sound continually surprised him. Checking her watch, she said, "Come on, let's go. We want to get back here before dark."

He had no choice but to follow her back up the path, and though he tried to train his eyes on the steep curving trail, his gaze wandered continually to the movement of her tanned legs and the sway of her hips beneath khaki-colored shorts.

Her clothing, an aqua T-shirt and shorts, wasn't innately sexy, but there was something about her, some emotions simmering just beneath the surface of her calm smile, that hinted at a slumbering sexuality ready to awaken. His thoughts leapt ahead to a vivid picture of her lying naked on that sandy beach, hair wild and free, water from the river still clinging to her skin. Her arms were outstretched, her legs, beneath an apex of blond curls, demurely crossed, but her dark-tipped breasts pointing upward, beckoning—

"Ready?"

His heart slammed against his chest as he started from his fantasy and found her staring up at him. They had emerged from the forest, and the sunlight seemed harsh after the filtered shadows of the woods.

"Anytime you are," Dallas replied, his voice lower than usual as he shook the inviting image of her bare body from his mind with difficulty.

"Good." Crawling into the cab of her truck, Chandra added, "Hop in." She fired the engine and threw the big rig into gear. Dallas had barely settled into his seat and closed the door when she tromped on the accelerator and they were off to God-only-knew-where.

Dr. O'Rourke wasn't exactly as Chandra had expected him to be. He was quiet—too damned quiet. She never knew what he was thinking, and now, bumping over the lane to the start of Grizzly Loop, she wished she'd never agreed to be his guide. His brooding silence made her nervous, and the directness of his gaze made it impossible for her to relax. And that didn't even begin to touch his sexuality, which, now that she was alone with him in the wilderness, seemed more potent than ever.

She switched on the radio, hoping that music would dull the edge of tension that seemed to emanate from the man beside her. A Kris Kristofferson ballad drifted from the speakers.

"Where, exactly, are we going?" the doctor finally asked.

"To a point known as Fool's Bluff."

"Appropriate," he muttered, and slipped a pair of mirrored sunglasses onto the bridge of his hawkish nose.

She let that one slide. But as the gravel of the lane gave way to rocky ruts, she hazarded a glance at this man who was to be her companion for the next thirty-six hours. He was handsome, no doubt of that, and his profile, made more mysterious by the dark glasses, was potently virile and male. His features were hard, his hair wavy and willful, for the black strands appeared to lie as they wanted, refusing to be tamed by any civilized comb or brush.

He seemed to fill up the interior of her truck, the smell of him pure male and soap scents. His long legs were cramped, even in the roomy interior.

She knew that he was watching her from the corner of his eye, and she felt self-conscious. Never before had she needed to rack her brain for conversation; her clients had always, through anxiety or their outgoing personalities, managed to keep up a steady stream of small talk.

But not Dr. O'Rourke. No way.

The noon sun was intense, and the sky offered no traces of clouds. Chandra drove along the winding road that followed the twisted course of the river. Through the passing trees, flashes of gray-green water sped by. "Okay, let's go over a few safety rules," she said as she fished a pair of sunglasses from the glove box and slid them onto her nose. "First, as I told you before—I'm in charge. I'll let you guide the raft, but if we're getting into trouble, you've got to trust me to take over."

O'Rourke snorted, but inclined his head slightly.

"Secondly, you wear your life vest and helmet at all times."

"I read all the rules," he said, rolling down his window and propping his elbow on the ledge. Cool mountain air, smelling of fresh water and dust, rushed through the rig's interior, catching in Chandra's hair and caressing the back of her neck.

She rattled off a few more pieces of information about raft safety, but Dallas was way ahead of her, so she fell silent, watching the road as the Suburban jarred and bumped up the hillside. Shafts of sunlight pierced through the pines and aspen that clustered between the road and the river. Nearby, the mountains rose like stony sentinels, sharp-peaked and silent.

The road began to lose its definition, becoming nothing more than a pair of tire tracks between which grass, weeds and wildflowers grew.

"This part of the river is known as Grizzly Loop," Chandra said, glancing over at Dallas.

"So, there are really bears up here. I thought you hauled our provisions into the trees just to scare me."

"Did I . . . scare you?"

His smile was arrogant and mocking. "I was terrified."

"Right," she said sarcastically. "As for grizzlies, you'll see about as many as you see rattlesnakes. The river and parts of it were named a long time ago. I suppose there were a lot of bears here once, and there could be rattlesnakes, but I've never seen either, nor has anyone I know. Disappointed?"

"Relieved."

The radio, playing a mixture of soft pop and country, finally faded in a crackle of static, and the grass strip between the tire ruts grew wider. Long, sun-dried blades brushed the underbelly of the truck. Chandra fiddled with the dial, found no discernible signal and flipped off the radio. "I guess we'll have to settle for brilliant conversation."

"Suits me." He leaned against the passenger window and studied her more closely. "What do you want to talk about?"

"Baby Doe," she said automatically. No reason to beat around the bush, and that way she could avoid discussing her life.

"What about him?"

"Has anyone tried to claim him?"

Dallas shook his head, and Chandra felt a release of anxiety, like the rush of water from a burgeoning dam. Ever since she'd found the small child, crying and red faced in her barn, a tiny idea had sprouted in her mind, an idea that had grown and formed until she could recognize it for what it was. She wanted the baby, and though she'd argued with herself a million times, she knew that she was on a path to requesting guardianship. It was time she became a parent. She needed the baby, and, oh, Lord, the baby needed the kind of loving mother she could well become.

They drove a few more miles until they reached Fool's Bluff, which was situated some forty feet above the river. The rocky ledge provided a view of the curving Rattlesnake as it sliced through a canyon in the mountains. "That's where we'll be going," Chandra said, parking the truck and climbing out to point south, toward the wayward path of wild, white water.

"It looks pretty tame from up here," Dallas observed.

Chandra laughed. "Don't you know that looks can be deceiving?"

"I'm beginning to," he said, and he sent her an assessing glance that caused her heart to trip-hammer for a second as their gazes touched then moved away. Quickly, she turned back to the truck, and balancing on the running board, began to unleash the raft.

Dallas worked on the other side of the Suburban, and soon they were packing the raft and a few supplies along the narrow trail leading through the undergrowth and pines surrounding the river. "You're sure this is safe?" he asked, a smile nudging the corner of his mouth.

"You're insured, aren't you?"

He snorted. "To the max. I'm a doctor, remember? Insurance is a way of life."

"Then relax. You've got nothing to worry about," Chandra mocked, her eyes seeming to dance.

But Dallas wasn't convinced. With the single-minded perception he'd built a reputation upon, he realized that the next hours, while he was alone with Chandra in the forested hills, might prove to be his fateful undoing.

Chapter Six

Like an awakening serpent, the river bucked and reared, rolling in a vast torrent of icy water that slashed furiously through the terrain. Chandra propelled the raft through the rapids, concentrating on the current, guiding the craft away from rocks and fallen trees.

The raft hit a snag and spun.

Adrenaline surged through Chandra's blood as the raft tilted, taking on water. *Hold on,* she told herself. Freezing spray splashed in her face, and water drenched her shirt and shorts as she tried to concentrate on the idiosyncrasies of the river. The raft pitched and rolled as the Rattlesnake twisted back upon itself. "Hang on," she yelled, putting her shoulders into the task of balancing the inflatable boat.

Blinking against the spray of water, she was aware of Dallas shifting the position of his oars, of his body moving with the flow of the current as easily as if he, too, were a river guide.

The raft hit a submerged rock and bounced upward, landing back on the water with a slap and a curl, spinning out of control for a heart-stopping second before Chandra found the channel again.

Dallas, his black hair wet and shining, his face red where the water had slapped him, paddled with the current, helping Chandra keep on course.

"You lied. You *were* a Boy Scout," she screamed over the roar of wild water.

His laugh filtered back to her. "No. But I was taught to be prepared for anything."

"By your father?"

He didn't answer, but threw his back into his oar, and the craft whipped past a slick boulder that protruded from the frigid depths.

They shot past the final series of ripples, and finally, as the Rattlesnake's strength gave out, their craft slowed in the shallows to drift lazily in the ebbing current.

Chandra let out her breath in relief. Though she was always eager to challenge the river, she was also relieved when the most difficult part of the journey was over.

"You do this every day?" Dallas asked, settling back against the stern of the raft to look at her.

"No, thank God! Sometimes I guide trail rides or supervise camp-outs or rock climbs. In the winter, I work on the ski patrol and give lessons."

"The outdoorswoman who does it all."

"Not everything," she countered, shoving her wet hair from her face. "I don't hunt."

"No?"

She narrowed her eyes against the lowering sun and paddled slowly, anticipating the next series of rapids. Though smaller than the last, they were still treacherous. "I'm afraid that if meat didn't come wrapped in plastic on little trays in the store, I'd become a vegetarian."

He smiled at that, and his grin, honest in the outdoors, touched her.

"Show time," she said as the river picked up speed again, and together they slid through the rapids, following the Rattlesnake's thrashing course until, half an hour later, they glided around a final bend to the beach beneath Fool's Bluff, where their camp was waiting.

"Home sweet home," Chandra quipped, and Dallas couldn't help thinking she was right. The faded tents and supplies stacked nearby, the bag of food swinging twenty feet in the air, the tall pines and rocky shore all did seem as much home to him as anyplace he'd ever lived.

Skimming her paddles through the water, Chandra guided the boat to the bank. Near the beach, she hopped into the icy water. Dallas, sucking in his breath, followed suit, and soon they'd pulled the raft onto the beach, leaving it upside down to drain.

"Now what?" Dallas asked.

"Well, you can change into some dry clothes, or you can leave those on, they'll dry soon enough. We'll get started on dinner. Then, once it's dark, we'll tell ghost stories around the campfire and scare ourselves out of our minds," she deadpanned.

Dallas laughed, and Chandra couldn't help but grin. Beneath his hard facade, Dallas O'Rourke was a man with a sense of humor, and here in the mountains, he seemed less formidable, more carefree. What else was he hiding beneath his surgical mask and professional demeanor? she wondered before closing her mind to a subject that was strictly off-limits. He was the client, and she was the guide. Nothing more. And yet, as the time she shared with him passed, she found her thoughts drifting to him as she wondered what kind of a lover he would be. What kind of husband? What kind of father?

Before twilight descended, they drove upriver in his truck to retrieve the Suburban. By the time they returned, the sun was behind the mountains and long shadows stretched across the beach. Dinner consisted of sandwiches, fruit and cookies that Rick always purchased from a bakery on the first floor of the building housing Wild West Expeditions.

"Not exactly Maxim's," he remarked, leaning his back against a large boulder and stretching his legs in front of him.

"You complaining?"

"Me? Never."

"You could have bought the deluxe trail ride and rafting trip," she said. "The one with caviar, champagne, Thoroughbreds and a yacht."

His mouth lifted at the corner and he said lazily, "My brother's too cheap."

"Are you two close?" she asked, and was rewarded with silence. Only the swish of water and drone of insects disturbed the silence. The sky, as if painted by an invisible brush, was layered in bands of pink and lavender. Above the darkening peaks, the boldest stars glimmered seductively.

Chandra, leaning against a log, drew her legs to her chin and wrapped her arms around her shins. "It's gorgeous up here, don't you think? The first time I saw this place, I *knew* this was where I had to stay."

"Where're you from?" he asked. She turned to find him watching her so closely that her breath stopped for a second. For the first time since the river run, she realized that she'd be spending the night with this man—all alone in the wilderness. Though it wasn't a new experience—she'd led more than her share of trail rides and camping excursions—she could feel in the air that this night would be different. Because of Dallas. There was something that set him apart from the other men she'd guided along the river—or was there? She edged her toe in the sand, unwilling to admit any attraction for a man she'd met so recently, a man who could, for all she knew, be married.

The scent of water filled her nostrils and the night seemed clearer than usual. The evening air was warm, its breath laden with the scents of spruce and pine.

"I take it you're not a native," he pressed, those inscrutable eyes still staring at her.

"No, I'm originally from Idaho," she admitted. "Grew up there. My dad was a real outdoorsman, and since he had no sons and I was the oldest daughter, he spent a lot of time showing me the ropes of canoeing, horseback riding, swimming, rafting and mountain climbing."

"And you made it a profession?"

Picking up a stick, she nudged over a rock, exposing a beetle that quickly scurried for cover. "With some stops along the way," she admitted. "Why are you so interested?"

He looked at her long and hard. "Because I've never met a woman who, with a few first-aid courses, could so quickly and accurately diagnose a patient as you did. You were right on target, Ms. Hill."

"Chandra. Remember?" she said, and considered telling him the truth. He deserved that much, she supposed. "And you're right," she admitted, though she couldn't confide in him, not completely. There was too much emotional scarring that she wouldn't reveal, at least not yet. So she hedged. "I've had more training than basic first aid. I was in medical school for a while, but I dropped out."

"Why?" he asked. The word seemed to hang between them in the night air. The moon had risen, and dusk, like a familiar warm cloak, closed them off from the rest of the world. The river rippled by, shimmering with the silvery light of the moon. The mountains, craggy and black, loomed toward the twilight sky.

"I didn't think it was right for me," she lied, cringing inwardly. Why not tell him the truth and get it over with? But, though she tried, the words wouldn't pass her tongue. Standing, she dusted her palms on her shorts. She felt a chill, though the air still held warmth from the afternoon, and she didn't know how much she should tell Dallas.

He was leaning forward, hands clasped, watching her every move, but when she didn't explain any further, he stood and walked toward her, his gaze still fastened on her face. He stopped just short of her, and she was all too aware that he was standing inches from her, his sleeve, still damp, brushing the crook of her arm. She tried not to notice how close he was, how intimate the night had become. Dry leaves fluttered in the wind, rustling and whispering as the breeze moved along the course of the river.

Lifting her head, she focused on the straight line of his chin, his square jaw, the way his hair ruffled in the wind. As if he understood her pain, he didn't ask another question, just took her in his arms and held her. Her throat burned with his sudden gentleness, and tears threatened her eyes. She didn't try to break away, just let his arms and the sounds of the river envelop her. How long had it been since someone had held her?

His breath whispered across her crown, and his body was warm, a soothing balm for all the old wounds. Her arms wrapped around his as if of their own accord, and he groaned. "Chandra," he whispered, and his voice had grown husky.

Good Lord, what was she doing, embracing this . . . this stranger, for crying out loud? And why did she feel the need to tell him her life story? This was all wrong. Even if his arms felt right, he was a client, a doctor, for God's sake, not a man she could get involved with. He could be married, for all she knew! She tried to break away, but his arms, strong as hemp, wouldn't budge. "I think...this isn't right.... I don't know anything about you." She gazed up at him steadily. "Look, Dallas, I don't fool around. Especially with married men."

"Then you're safe."

"You're not married?"

The muscles surrounding her tensed. "Not anymore."

"Oh." She didn't know what to say.

She tried to slip out of his arms, but his grip tightened. "I still don't think this is very smart."

"I know it isn't."

"I don't get involved with *any* men," she clarified, her voice unusually low, her pulse beginning to race wildly. They were talking about a very serious subject, and yet she felt that there was an undercurrent in their conversation, and she couldn't concentrate on much more than the feel of his hard body pressed so close to hers.

Embracing him was crazy! Downright insane. She didn't even know the man—not really. All she had were impressions of an honest, overworked physician, who at times could be cuttingly harsh and other times as textured and smooth as velvet.

"I know you were right on the money with the baby," he said, his breath fanning across the top of her head. "I've seen you handle Alma Lindquist and Bob Fillmore. I know for a fact that I couldn't put you off when you demanded to know about the infant's condition. And I've seen you navigate one helluva river. My guess is that you do whatever you set your mind to, Ms. Hill."

"Chandra," she reminded him again, but the words strangled in her throat as his night-darkened gaze locked with hers for a heart-stopping instant. She knew in that flash of brilliance that he was going to kiss her and that she was unable to stop him. He dropped his head then, and his mouth molded intimately over hers.

It's been so long... she thought as a river of emotions carried her away. The smell of him was everywhere—earthy, sensual, divine. And the feel of his hands, so supple against her skin, caused tiny goose bumps to rise on her flesh. He locked one of his hands around the back of her neck and gently pulled her hair as his tongue traced the rim of her mouth.

Her breath was stilled, her heart beginning to pound a cadence as wild as the river rushing through this dusky canyon.

This is a mistake! she told herself, but didn't listen. She heard only the drumming of her heart and the answering cadence of his. Warm, hard, primal, he provoked a passion so long dormant, it awoke with a fury, creating desire that knew no bounds. He shifted his weight, drawing her down, and her knees gave way as he pressed her slowly, intimately, to the beach.

Cool sand touched her back, and he half lay across her, the weight of his chest welcome, the feel of his body divine. She didn't protest when his mouth moved from her lips to the slope of her chin and lower, against her neck. She was conscious only of the feel of the coming night, the cool sand against her back, the whisper of his lips against her skin, the firm placement of his hand across her abdomen, as if through her clothes he could feel the gentle pulsing at her very core.

He moved slightly, and his hand shifted, climbing upward to feel the weight of her breast. Chandra moaned as her nipple, in anticipation, grew taut and desire caused her breast to ache.

Dear Lord, this is madness! she thought, but couldn't stop. She gripped his shoulders and sighed when she felt him push aside the soft cotton of the T-shirt until his flesh was nearly touching hers and only the simple barrier of white lace kept skin from skin.

"Chandra," he groaned, as if in agony, against her ear. "Oh, God..." He tugged off her T-shirt then, as the first pale glow from the moon filtered through the forest. He stared at her, swallowing hard as his gaze centered on the dark nipple protruding against filmy lace.

Chandra shivered, but not from the coolness of the night so much as from that critical gaze that seemed to caress the border of tan and white flesh across her breast, below which the white skin, opalescent and veined with blue lines, rounded to a pert, dark crest.

Dallas closed his eyes, as if to steady himself, but when he looked at her again, none of his passion was gone. "This is crazy," he whispered, and she couldn't reply; her mouth was dry, her words unformed. But she felt him reach forward again, slowly push down the strap of her bra, peel away the gossamer fabric and allow her breast to spill free.

"You're beautiful," he said, and then, as if he knew the words were too often spoken in haste, looked her straight in the eyes. "It's probably as much a curse as a blessing."

Beautiful? She wasn't blind and knew she was pretty, but beautiful? Never. She felt herself blush and hoped the night hid the telltale scarlet stain creeping up her neck. "You don't have to say anything," she replied in a voice that sounded as if it had been filtered by dry leaves.

His arms surrounded her, and he drew her close, his mouth finding hers in a kiss that drew the very breath from her lungs. No longer tenuous, he pressed his tongue into her mouth and explored the wet lining, one hand surrounding her back, the other softly kneading her breast.

Chandra melted inside. Heat as intense as a fire burning out of control swirled inside her, through her blood and into her brain. She wrapped a leg around him and arched upward. He slid lower, then snapped the fastening of her bra, letting both breasts swing free. He captured one nipple in his teeth and sucked as if from hunger, his tongue flicking and massaging the soft underside of her skin.

Her passion igniting, Chandra cupped his head and pulled him closer, crying out in bittersweet agony when, as he breathed, his hot breath fanned her wet nipple.

"Please," she whispered, caught in this hot whirlpool of desire and unable to swim free. "Please."

He found the fastening on her shorts, and his fingers brushed against her abdomen and lower still.

Somewhere in the trees high above, an owl hooted softly, breaking the stillness of the night. Dallas's lips stopped their tender exploration, but the breath from his nostrils still seared her sensitive skin. He jerked his head away. "This is a mistake," he muttered, swiping a hand impatiently through his hair, as if in so doing, he could release the tension that was coiling his muscles. He rolled away from her. "Damn it all to hell, Chandra, I don't know what got into me."

Embarrassment crept up Chandra's spine at his rejection. Silently calling herself a fool, she scrambled for her clothes.

"Look, I'm sorry—"

"Don't apologize," she interrupted. "There's nothing to apologize for. Things just got out of hand, that's all." She wished she felt as calm as she sounded, but inside, her heart was pounding, and she wanted to die of mortification. She'd never played loose and fast. Never!

She'd been the butt of cruel jokes while in medical school. Doug's friends had wondered aloud and within her earshot if it were possible to light a fire in her or if she, so conscientious with her studies, were frigid. Doug had stood up for her, if feebly, and they had married, but she'd never forgotten how wretched those remarks had made her feel.

Nonetheless, she didn't see herself in the role of femme fatale, and this little escapade with Dallas was certainly out of character.

"This doesn't happen to me," he said.

"And you think it does to me?"

His lips compressed into a hard line, and Chandra nearly laughed. What did he think of her? She should be incensed, but she found his confusion amusing. She smothered a smile as she pulled her T-shirt over her head. "Well, what just happened between us is usually not part of the expedition, not even the most expensive trips," she teased, hoping to lighten the tension. Dallas wasn't in the mood for jokes. "Don't worry about it," she said, though she could think of nothing but the touch of his hands on her skin, the smell of him so close, the taste of his lips on hers. She turned back to the campsite. "Come on. We should start dinner, and if you think just because I'm a woman that I'm going to do it all myself you've got— Oh!"

He caught hold of her wrist and spun her around. She nearly tripped on a rock, and he caught her before she fell.

Strong arms surrounded her, and his face, not smiling, but as intense as the night closing in on them, was pressed to hers. "I just want you to know," he said so quietly she could barely hear him above the wind soughing through the pines, "I don't play games."

She gulped. "I wouldn't think so."

"So when something like this…happens, I can't just take it lightly and shrug it off like you do."

"It's easier that way," she said, lying.

In the darkness, his eyes narrowed. "Just what kind of woman are you?"

She sucked in her breath, ragged though it was. "What kind of woman am I?" she repeated, incredulous. "I'm a woman who doesn't stand around waiting for a man to trip all over himself to open her car door, a woman who doesn't believe in love at first sight, a woman who would someday like a child but doesn't necessarily need a man, and a woman who expects any man she meets to pull his own weight," she managed to spit out, though she was all too aware of the feel of his hands against her skin and the tantalizing passion flaring in his eyes.

His grin slashed white in the darkness, and his hand was tight over her wrist. A chuckle deep and rumbling erupted from him. "Are you really so tough?"

"Tough enough," she replied, tilting her chin defiantly, though inside, she quivered. Not that she'd let him know. She didn't want Dallas to suspect any weakness. She twisted in his arms, afraid that if he saw into her eyes, he'd read her hesitation. Together, while the river flowed on in bright glimmers of silver moonlight, they stared at the water, and Chandra couldn't help feeling as if they were the only man and woman on earth.

"Come on," she finally said, afraid this intimacy would only make spending the night together more difficult. She drew her hand from his and, reluctantly, he let her go. "I'm starved."

They barbecued steaks and warmed bread, boiled pota-
toes and stir-fried fresh vegetables. Conversation was min-
imal. After dinner, they sat near the tents, the lanterns
glowing in the wilderness and attracting insects. The smell
and sound of the river filled the night, and Chandra felt
more at peace than she had in a long, long while. There was
something comforting about being with Dallas, something
warm and homelike. And yet, there was another side to
him, as well, the volatile, passionate side that kept her on
edge. They drank coffee slowly, sitting apart, not daring to
touch.

She wrapped her arms around her knees and stared at the
man, whom she'd met as a doctor for J.D., but now knew
as . . . well, not a friend . . . but more than an acquaintance.
And possibly a lover? her mind teased, but she steadfastly
shoved that absurd thought into a corner of her mind.
Though she wanted to think of him as a man, she forced
herself back to the issue at hand. She had more important
things to think about.

"How long will Social Services wait until they place the
baby?" she asked, sipping from her cup.

"As soon as we release him from the hospital. Probably
in a day or two."

"That soon?" Chandra's heart took a nosedive. She'd
have to work fast.

"He can't stay in the hospital forever." Dallas reached
for the coffeepot, still warm on the camp stove, and, holding the enamel pot aloft, silently asked if she'd like more.

Shaking her head, Chandra bit her lower lip, her mind
racing in circles. If no one claimed the baby, she'd try to
adopt him. Why not? Tomorrow, when she returned home,
she'd call her lawyer, have all the necessary applications
filled out, do whatever she had to do, but, damn it, she intended to make a bid for the baby. . . .

As if he saw the wheels turning in her mind, Dallas said,
"What's on your mind, Chandra? You've been bringing up
the baby all day." He stretched out on a sleeping bag and

levered up on one elbow while his eyes, cast silver by the soft shafts of light from the moon, centered on her.

Could she trust him? She needed a friend, an ally, but Dr. O'Rourke was an unlikely choice. Licking her lip nervously, she decided to gamble. "I hope to adopt him," she admitted, holding his gaze.

"If no one claims him."

"If J.D.'s—" she saw the doctor's bushy eyebrows elevate a notch "—that's what I call him. You know, for John Doe." When he nodded, she continued. "If J.D.'s mother shows up, she'll have to prove to me that she's fit. What kind of woman would leave a baby in a barn?"

"A desperate one?"

"But why not stick around? Or knock on my door? I would've helped her, taken her and the child to the hospital," Chandra said, shaking her head and turning her attention back to the few swallows of coffee left in her cup. "Oh, no, there's no reason, no good reason, to leave a baby to die."

Dallas finished his coffee. "The baby didn't die," he pointed out. "Maybe the mother was in an abusive situation. Maybe she was trying to protect the child. The reason she didn't show her face is that she doesn't want her husband or boyfriend or whoever to show up, claim the baby, then perhaps hurt him or her. She could be on the run for a good reason."

"There are agencies—"

"Not enough."

Chandra glanced up at Dallas and noticed the serious lines deepening along his eyes and mouth. So there was a humanitarian side to Dr. O'Rourke. The man had many layers, Chandra decided, and she would all too willingly unravel each and every one to get a glimpse of the real man hidden beneath his cold, professional facade.

"I work in E.R. We see a lot of 'accidents' to children and women," he added, his voice deep and grim. "You don't know that the boy's mother wasn't a woman who, given her fear and limited knowledge, did the best she could.''

"Leaving a baby alone and defenseless is never the best. That woman—whoever she is—had other options. She didn't have to take the coward's way out. She could have taken that baby with her wherever she was running."

"And what if she had a couple of other kids?" He sighed and threw the dregs of his coffee into the woods. "There's no reason to argue this. We don't know the woman's motives, but I think there's a chance the mother will surface, and when she does, she'll want her baby back."

Chandra knew he was right, and when her gaze met his eyes, she noticed a trace of sadness in their steely depths. Her heart grew suddenly cold.

"Just don't get too attached to...J.D.... Don't be giving him names and thinking about swaddling him in blankets and knitting little blue booties. You could get hurt."

"It's a chance I'll have to take."

Dallas drew one knee up and leaned over it. His face, illuminated by the fire, was serious as he studied the crackling flames. "There are other ways to become a mother—easier ways. Ways that will ensure that no one takes the child away from you."

She snorted. "Most of those ways involve a man." She stared boldly across the short space separating them, and asked, "Are you applying for the job?"

He returned her gaze for a long, tense moment, and Chandra wished she could call back the words, said too quickly. He probably thought she was seriously propositioning him.

"I just thought you could use some friendly advice," he finally said.

Chandra felt a rush of warmth for the man. "Thanks."

"You're still going to go through with it, aren't you?" When she didn't reply, he continued, "You know, you might still need a man. The system still likes to place children in homes where there is a role model for each parent.

And, no, since you asked a little earlier, I don't go around fathering children." An emotion akin to anger pinched the corners of his mouth. "Call me old-fashioned, but I think it's a father's duty, responsibility and privilege to help raise his child."

"Well—" she stood and dusted her hands "—now we know where we stand."

"Almost." He tossed down his cup and stood, closing the distance between them. He grabbed both her shoulders in big, hard hands. "Be careful, Chandra. If you don't watch out, you and the baby and God-only-knows who else might be hurt by this."

"It's my business," she said simply, unmoving.

"It's my business, too, like it or not. We're both involved." He dropped his hands, and Chandra took the opportunity to step back a pace, to keep some distance from him. Her crazy heart was thundering. What was wrong with her? She'd been with dozens of men on trips like this. A few had even made the mistake of making a pass at her. But until tonight, resisting a man's advances had come easy.

To make herself look busy, she rinsed her cup in the warm water simmering on the stove. "I'd better get this food back in the bag and hang it from the tree, then we can turn in." She wished she'd never gotten close to O'Rourke. He'd only reinforced her fears that adopting the baby would be difficult, even painful, and might not work. But then he didn't know her, did he? He couldn't understand that once she'd set her mind on something, it would take the very devil himself to dissuade her.

Later, tucked snugly in her sleeping bag, she thought about the night stretching ahead of her, of the starlit sky, the mist rising off the river, the man who slept only a few feet away. Kissing him had seemed natural and safe. She touched her lips and quietly called herself a fool. Dallas O'Rourke was a doctor, for crying out loud, a man married to his job, a man who might stand in her way in her efforts to adopt J.D., a man of whom she knew very little.

She'd had a physical response to him, that was all. It was no big deal. She hadn't been with a man since her divorce, and in those few years, she hadn't so much as let another man kiss her, though more than a few had tried.

It wasn't that she was a prude; her response to Dallas was evidence to the contrary. She just didn't want an involvement with any man, including Dr. O'Rourke.

Chapter Seven

Chandra was up at the crack of dawn and insisted they break camp early.

"That's it? We're finished?" Dallas asked, his chin dark with the shadow of a beard, his eyes a midnight blue as he stretched and yawned. A few clouds hovered in the sky, but the temperature was cool, the mountain air crisp with the promise of autumn.

"Not quite. We still have one run before you can return to civilization. We'll eat, take down the tents, check the supplies and make sure we haven't sprung any leaks in the raft. Then we'll shoot the lower flats."

"Lower flats? Calmer than Grizzly Loop, I hope."

"Different," she replied as she retrieved the supply sack. Fortunately, no bears had disturbed the food, though once before, on a camping trip in the mountains, she'd awakened to see her fat supply sack flapping in the breeze. It had been slashed at the bottom, the contents long gone, with only scraps of carton and paper and the wide tracks of a bear visible the next morning. That trip, they'd relied on the fish they'd caught and a few berries for the day. Fortunately, this time she wasn't embarrassed by a persistent and clever bear making a mockery of her precautions.

After a quick breakfast of muffins, fruit and coffee, they made preparations to break camp. Before she folded up her tent, Chandra changed into a swimsuit, shorts and blouse. She tied her hair away from her face, ignored any thoughts of makeup and yanked on a nylon parka.

Dallas, who hadn't bothered shaving, wore a khaki-colored pair of shorts and blue pullover. "You know, we could call it quits here," he said as he loosened a rope and his tent gave way.

"Your brother paid for a specific excursion," Chandra replied. "I wouldn't want to disappoint him."

"He'll never know."

Bending over her own flattened tent, she smiled at him over her shoulder. "Cold feet, Dr. O'Rourke?"

"I just thought I'd save you some trouble, that's all." His blue eyes gleamed with a devilish spark.

"No trouble at all."

Dallas didn't argue any further. Chandra could sure change a man's mind, he thought as he watched her move expertly through the campsite, packing gear, bending over without even realizing she was offering him a view of her rounded buttocks and tapered legs.

"Well?" she asked, turning to cast him an inquiring look. Her rope of tawny hair fell over one shoulder.

"You're the boss." He slapped his knees, and as he stood, he looked younger, more boyish, as if he were really enjoying himself.

She chuckled. "Now we're making progress." They packed the remaining gear and carried it up the shaded path to the strip of road where their trucks were parked.

Dallas pumped the throttle and flicked the ignition switch of his truck. The engine revved loudly, and despite his reservations, he felt a surge of excitement at the coming raft trip. Being alone with Chandra in the wilderness was more than a little appealing, and he remembered their embrace vividly, more vividly than he remembered caressing or kissing any other woman in a long, long while.

He forced his thoughts away from the impending rafting trip and the possibilities of kissing her again, of the silken feel of her skin against his, of the proud lift of her breasts, pale in the moonlight.

"Stop it," he muttered to himself, grinding the gears as he shifted down and wrenched on the wheel in an effort to follow her Suburban onto the flat rise of dry grass. She parked in the shade of some aspens that bordered the field. He stopped and willed his suddenly overactive sex drive into low gear.

The river curled close to the shore, cutting through the dry land in a shimmering swath that reminded him of a silvery snake.

Chandra cut the engine, hopped to the ground, locked the door, then climbed into the passenger side of Dallas's truck. She shoved her sunglasses onto the bridge of her nose and pretended she didn't notice the handsome thrust of his chin or the way his eyes crinkled near the corners as he squinted against the sun. She didn't let the masculine scent of him get to her, either.

He was just a man, she told herself firmly, forcing her gaze through the windshield to the rutted lane that wound through pools of sunlight and shadow. But he was her link to the baby—that was why she was attracted to him, she thought.

Deep in her heart, though, she knew she was kidding herself. Dallas was different, a man who touched a special chord deep within her, a chord that she didn't dare let him play.

She drummed her fingers on the armrest, and the hairs on the back of her neck lifted slightly when she felt him glance in her direction.

"Nervous?" he asked.

She shook her head. "Anxious to get back," she said evasively. Just being around Dallas was difficult; she felt she was always walking an emotional tightrope.

"Already she wants to get rid of me," he mocked.

Chandra laughed a little. "It's the baby. I wonder how he's doing," she replied, though the infant was only part of the reason. She needed to find her equilibrium again, something that proved impossible when she was with Dallas.

"I'll bet he's screaming for breakfast, or—" he made a big show of checking his watch "—or lunch. Demanding food seems to be what he does best."

Chandra glanced at the doctor, caught the sparkle in his eyes and was forced to smile. She relaxed a little, her spirits lifting with the morning sun as it rose higher in the sky.

Once they'd parked near the river, they checked the equipment one last time, shoved the raft into the frigid water and hopped in. The current was lazy near the shore, but as the craft drifted to the middle of the river, the stream picked up speed, narrowing as the current turned upon itself and the surge of white water filled the canyon.

The raft plunged into the first set of rapids, and the river became a torrent that curled around rocks and the shore. Chandra, jaw set, narrowed her eyes on the familiar stretch of water, shifting her weight and using her paddles against the primal force of the river.

Over the deafening roar of the water, Chandra shouted orders to Dallas, who responded quickly, expertly, his shoulders bunched, his eyes glued to the frothy water and rocks stretching before them.

He moved as they approached a rock, and they skidded past the slick, dark surface. Chandra bit her lower lip. Downstream, Ridgeback Ripples foamed in furious waves, and Chandra braced herself for the pitch and roll that would occur as they rounded the dead tree that had fallen into the river.

She managed to steer clear of the fallen pine, avoiding the part of the stream that swirled near the blackened, dead branches. The water was clear, the rocks below shimmering gold and black. She shoved in her paddle, intending to move into deeper water.

"Watch out!" Dallas yelled.

Too late! The raft hit a snag in the water and responded by spinning, faster and faster, out of control. Water thrashed over the side. Chandra paddled more firmly.

The raft plunged deep, then bobbed up again, bucking wildly, out of control.

Hang in there, she told herself, refusing to lose her calm. They rammed a large rock and pitched forward. Chandra fell against the inflated side. Before she could get up on her knees again, the raft, still spinning, hit a shoal and buckled, flipping over.

"Hold on!" Chandra screamed as she was pitched overboard. Roaring ice-cold water poured over her in a deluge, forcing its way down her throat. Sputtering, she couldn't see, but reached out instinctively, grabbing hold of the capsized raft.

Dallas! Where was he? Oh, God! She surfaced, pulled by the drag of the current as it whisked the overturned raft downriver. Water rushed everywhere. "Dallas!" she yelled, coughing and looking around her as she tried vainly to tread water. Trees along the bank flashed by, and the sun, still bright, spangled the water, the light harsh against her eyes.

She didn't see him.

Come on, Dallas, come on. Show yourself. She looked upriver and down, searching for some sign of him as she was carried along with the current. "Dallas!" she screamed. Oh, Lord, was he trapped beneath the raft? Trying to grab on to a rock with her free hand, she scraped her arm. If she could only stop and look for him! Her heart pumped. She gasped in lungfuls of air and water. Adrenaline surged through her blood, bringing with it fear for the man she'd only recently met. *Where was he?*

If she'd inadvertently hurt him...

"Dallas!" she screamed again, just as the rapids rounded a bend and dumped into a relatively calm pool. She flipped the raft over, half expecting him to be caught beneath the yellow rubber.

Nothing.

Oh, God. Please don't let him drown! She couldn't lose someone in her care again...someone who had trusted her with his life...someone she'd begun to care about. "Dallas!" she screamed, her voice growing hoarse as she shouted over the roar of the river. "Oh, God, Dallas!" Her heart dived, and she struggled until she found a toehold where she could stand and scan the river as it roared by in fierce torrents. Coughing, her teeth chattering, she prayed she'd see him, his lifejacket keeping him afloat, his helmet preventing a head injury. "Come on, Dallas...please!" The river flowed past in swift retribution. "Dallas!" she yelled again, her voice catching in fear. *Think, Chandra, think! You know what to do!* She wouldn't just stand here. She'd had survival training, and she'd find him. He had to be alive—he had to! But fear kept her rooted to the spot, drew her eyes to the dark and suddenly evil-looking river.

She forced her legs to move with the current, knowing that he would have been swept downstream—

"Hey! Chandra!"

His voice boomed, and she turned to find him waving his arms on the shore at a bend in the river. He was the most beautiful sight she'd ever seen. Wet, bedraggled but grinning, he shouted her name again. Relief brought tears to her eyes, and she nearly fell on her knees and wept openly. Instead, she sent up a silent prayer of thanks. To think that he might have drowned...oh, God.

Still dragging the raft, she sloshed through the shallow water near the shore, wading toward him, and he, grinning sheepishly, slogged upstream. They met in waist-deep water, their lips blue, water running from the helmets and down their necks. Without thinking, Chandra flung her arms around him, wanting to feel his heartbeat, the strength of his body.

His arms, as sturdy as steel, surrounded her, drawing her close, and for a second in the frigid water, they forgot all propriety. She wanted to laugh and cry, scream in frustration and kiss him, all at the same time. Relief poured through her. Her senses, already charged by the fear that had stolen into her heart, filled with him. He smelled of the river, but his touch was warm and electric. He smoothed a strand of hair from her cheek, as if he, too, were savoring this moment when they were both alive. Her heart wrenched and her throat clogged. She pounded a fist against his chest. "You scared me half to death," she said, drawing her head back to stare up at him.

"It was my fault."

"Yours?" Shaking her head, she wouldn't let him take the blame. "No way. I was in charge. I shouldn't have let her capsize."

"But I steered the raft into the snag—"

"The current did that. It was my job to avoid the situation." Suddenly weak, she sighed and, ripping off her helmet, tossed the hair from her eyes, spraying his chest with icy pellets of water. "I'm just glad you're in one piece." His arms tightened a little, and when she glanced up at him again, her breath caught in her throat. His gaze, blue and intense, drilled deeply into hers. He, too, removed his helmet and cast it beside hers on the rocks of the shore.

"I'm glad you're in one piece, too," he said, his breath warm against her chilled skin. He lowered his head and kissed her, his cold lips molding to hers, his hands drawing her so close, she could scarcely breathe.

His tongue pressed lightly against her teeth and she responded, her heart soaring that they'd both survived the accident. Her mind, usually calm and rational, was now fuzzy with emotions she didn't want to dissect. She lost herself in his touch and the smell of his clean, wet skin. Clinging to him, her breasts flattened against the hard wall of his chest, she thought of nothing save his touch and the tingling of her skin whenever their bodies pressed close against each other.

He slid his hands across her back, and through her wet shirt she felt the warmth of him. He scaled her ribs with gentle fingers and slowly eased a palm over her breast.

She gasped, and he kissed her harder, his tongue plunging deep as his fingers moved insistently beneath the top of her swim suit, to her nipple, stroking the already hard peak until her entire breast ached.

The cold seeped away. The water rushing past their knees and slapping their thighs didn't exist. Chandra was only aware of Dallas, his kiss and the expert touch of his hands on her flesh.

She shivered deep inside as desire crept through her blood. Moaning, she wound her arms around his neck, her own tongue searching and tasting, delving and flicking.

He groaned in response and slid downward, moving his hands slowly to her buttocks, kissing the column of her throat.

Chandra sucked in her breath and he pressed his warm face against her abdomen before he pulled down her vest and suit and then rimmed her nipple with his tongue.

"Oooh," she whispered over the rush of wild water. Her fingers twisted in his hair as he suckled. Between the cold air and the warmth of his body, Chandra was suspended in tingling emotions that wouldn't lie still. She knew she should stop this madness, but couldn't. His body, hard and anxious, demanded exactly what hers wanted so desperately.

When he drew his mouth from hers, he gazed up at her and shook his head. "What're we going to do about this?" he wondered aloud, obviously as perplexed with the situation as she was.

"I don't know."

He slowly covered her breasts and stood, his arms still surrounding her. "Overused phrases like 'take it slow' or 'one step at a time' seem the appropriate thing to say, but I'm not sure slow is possible with you. And I'm sure it isn't with me." He sighed loudly in frustration. "You turn me inside out, Ms. Hill," he admitted, "and I don't think this is the time in my life for that kind of imbalance."

"Imbalance?" she repeated, shivering. "I'm causing you an imbalance?" Shaking her head, she turned back to the raft. "Well, we certainly wouldn't want to mess around with your well-ordered life, Dr. O'Rourke," she said, her anger rising. "It's not like I planned this, either, you know. It just happened!"

She was suddenly angry, and wondered if her fury was aimed mostly at herself. "Let's just forget this happened and get on with the trip."

"I don't know if I can."

She'd been reaching for the rope when his voice arrested her. Turning, she found him still standing in the river, his features thoughtful, almost disbelieving, as if something were happening to him that he couldn't control.

She cleared her throat. "We only have about a mile of river left, then we can pack up. You can go your way and I can go mine. And trust me, I won't try to imbalance your life again. Just make sure your brother doesn't buy you another expedition, okay?"

She grabbed his helmet off the beach and tossed it to him, then strapped hers on. "Let's get this over with."

"You're the boss."

"Right. So get in and we'll shove off!"

They both climbed into the raft, and Chandra, determined to be professional, guided them downstream. They didn't say another word, though a few blistering phrases leapt to Chandra's mind. She'd love to tell Dr. O'Rourke what she really thought of his attitude.

She didn't like being played with, and yet, every time he kissed her, she hadn't stopped him—hadn't been able to.

Her traitorous body seemed to tingle with anticipation at his touch, and that thought alone disgusted her.

He was just a man! How many times did she have to remind herself of that one simple fact? She hazarded a glance in his direction and took comfort in the fact that he seemed as irritated and out of sorts as she was. And she consoled herself that he wasn't immune to her.

The raft glided around the final bend in the river. Chandra, feeling a mixture of relief and sadness, spied her truck parked beneath the tree. Soon, this wretched, lovely trip would be over.

Dallas saw the play of emotions on Chandra's face. She barked orders at him as he helped her drag the raft out of the water and lash it across the top of her rig. Silently, still wondering what the hell he was going to do with her, he admired how quickly and efficiently she worked, her arms tanned and strong, her fingers sure as she tied square knots and half hitches, and stored the gear in the back of her Suburban.

She moved with the natural grace and assuredness of an athlete, and yet her femininity was impossible to ignore. Her legs were supple and tanned, her buttocks round and firm, and her breasts, hidden beneath several layers, were soft, fleshy mounds that fit so perfectly in his palms.

But more intriguingly feminine than her obvious physical attributes was the sparkle of green in her gray eyes, the lift of her lips when she smiled, the arrogant toss of her hair over her shoulders. Chandra Hill was used to dealing out authority, probably from her year or two in medical school. He wondered how she could have ever given up medicine. Maybe she hadn't been able to afford the schooling. She claimed that she'd found out once she'd enrolled that she wasn't cut out to be a doctor, but he doubted that story. Chandra Hill seemed to be a woman who set goals for herself and then went about attaining them, no matter what the odds.

Somehow, guiding the idle rich down a dangerous stretch of water paled when compared with the ecstasy of saving a life. There were downsides to being a doctor, and tragedies that were impossible to ignore, but he'd learned to live with those, and he couldn't imagine giving up his livelihood as a physician. He'd rather cut off his right arm.

"That's it," she said, opening the driver's side of her truck. Dallas slid into the sunbaked interior and rolled down his window. He propped his elbow on the window frame as she started the truck and headed up the mountain road in a plume of dust. Reaching into the compartment between the two bucket seats, Chandra found a pair of sunglasses—ostensibly to replace those she lost during the rafting excursion—and set the shaded lenses across her nose. "Well, what d'ya think? Ready to go out again?"

"Maybe," he said, and she cast him a quick glance.

"Even after that spill?"

"Does it happen often?"

"This is only the second time," she said, a frown puckering her brow as she braked and the Suburban hugged a sharp turn in the road and slid to a stop. "Shh—look." She pointed to the undergrowth where a doe stared at them with huge, liquid eyes. A fawn pranced behind its mother until it saw the truck and froze, unmoving, blending into the background of dry grass, brush and trees.

"You love your job, don't you?" he asked.

Lifting a shoulder, Chandra shoved the rig into first and appeared to concentrate once again on the road that wound through the forest.

"And you're never going back to finish studying medicine," he predicted.

She flashed him a dark look. "I don't think so," she said, unhinged by his sudden display of compassion. "I-um—the trip's over. I really have to get back," she said, though a part of her wanted this trip to last forever.

"Someone waiting for you?"

She smiled slightly. "Oh, yes," she admitted, thinking of Sam. The old dog would be looking for his dinner. She'd fed him early yesterday morning, leaving enough food for two days along with several gallons of water, but by this time, he'd be starved. And lonely.

"There is?"

"Mmm. And he's very jealous."

Dallas cocked a thick eyebrow, his expression neutral, though his eyes had darkened a shade.

"His name is Sam and he lives with me," she clarified, smiling inwardly when she caught a gleam of jealousy in Dallas's eyes. Did he really think she would let him kiss her when she was seeing someone else? "He wanted to come along, but I told him that he'd just be in the way."

"Is that so? And how'd he like that?"

"Not at all. In fact he growled at me all night long."

The doctor's eyes narrowed, and all of his friendliness, so visible earlier, disappeared from his features. "You're *involved* with someone? And he lives with you?"

"Has since I moved in," she teased, waiting as Dallas opened the door. "He's become very possessive. In fact, he's been known to bite intruders."

A slow smile spread across Dallas's chin and Chandra couldn't help but chuckle. "Tell your 'friend' that I'm not afraid of him," he said with a laugh as he slammed the door shut.

"He'll be disappointed."

"I'll bring him a steak bone. Will that solve the problem?"

"He'll be forever in your debt," she said, ramming the Suburban into reverse and roaring off, her laughter hanging on the air as Dallas fished his keys from his pockets.

What was wrong with him? He'd almost acted as if he were planning to see her again. And he wasn't. If he'd learned anything from this fiasco of a trip, it was that he had to keep his distance from Chandra Hill. The woman was just too damned attractive for her own good. Or his.

But the thought of not seeing her again bothered him, and he took heart with the realization that, as long as Baby Doe—or J.D., as she insisted upon calling him—was a patient at Riverbend Hospital, Chandra Hill would be underfoot. She could very well pretend interest in Dallas just to get close to the baby. In fact, her interest in the infant explained why a strong-willed woman like Chandra could so easily be seduced.

He believed her when she said she didn't get involved with her clients—so why him? A physical attraction she couldn't deny? He scoffed at the idea, though his passion for her was something he could barely control. But, no, he suspected that Chandra was just using him to get close to the baby. Still, he couldn't just forget her. She was an impossible woman to forget.

He opened the door of his truck and sighed. Damned if you do and damned if you don't, he decided, pushing the key into his ignition. He didn't want to see Chandra again—well, at least he told himself that he didn't—and yet, he couldn't imagine not ever looking into her eyes again or catching the glimpse of her smile.

He hadn't felt this way since Jennifer. That realization was more shocking than a plunge in the icy depths of the Rattlesnake. He'd fallen hard once before, and, after more emotional pain than he'd ever thought existed, he'd proclaimed that he'd never fall again.

Since the divorce, he'd clung to his vow as if to life itself. He'd made sure that he had no time for a woman in his life, no time for anything but his work. And he'd been happy, or so he'd told himself.

Chapter Eight

Chandra, one hand pressed against the glass, stared at the baby. He was awake, his eyes bright, his face relaxed as he lay in the bassinet in the nursery with the other infants. There was a group of six small bodies wrapped in warm blankets, sleeping or blinking or yawning. Nurse Nelson was changing a squalling, tiny red baby without a trace of hair.

"Hi," she said from the other side of the glass that separated the nursery from the hallway where Chandra stood. "Would you like to hold him?" Leslie finished with the diaper, then motioned to J.D.

"Are you serious?" Chandra asked in a voice loud enough to be heard through the glass.

"Why not?" Opening the door a crack, Leslie flashed her dimples and tucked a blanket around the baby she'd been changing. "All these other guys—" she gestured to the bassinets with their squirming bundles "—get more than their share of attention. Of course, they're lucky. They have mothers." She disposed of the dirty diaper, then walked to J.D.'s bassinet and wrapped his blanket tightly around him. "Come on, you," she said as she carried him through the double doors and placed him in Chandra's waiting arms.

Chandra's heart felt as if it might break. The baby cooed and shifted, nuzzling her chest. Emotions tore at her soul. Tears gathered behind her eyes, and her throat closed as she gazed down at this precious child with the perfectly arched eyebrows, pudgy round cheeks and loud voice. Any lingering doubts she had concerning this baby were quickly washed away. She had to adopt him. She had to! She had no other choice. She thought of all her reservations, but she couldn't help herself. Who cared if the baby's natural mother showed up? This child needed her. And she needed him. Desperately. To make her life complete. Or would it be? Even with J.D., her life might still be missing something vital, the third part of a perfect family—the husband and father.

She rocked gently back and forth, ignoring her disturbing thoughts, whispering to the infant, touching his downy hair, unaware that Dallas was watching her as Leslie Nelson returned to the nursery. On rounds, Dallas had worked his way through the second floor and ended up at the nurses' station, where he'd stopped when he'd spied Chandra cradling the infant.

A smile toyed with the corner of her lips, and her eyes were downcast, focused on the bundle in her arms. Dark lashes, looking slightly damp, swept her cheek as she, dressed in denim skirt, white sweater and suede vest, held the baby. She was talking to the infant, maybe singing to him. Dallas could only hear a word or two, but the scene resurrected an old dream of his—the dream of one day being a husband and a father. Now this woman—this woman he barely knew, with her blond hair and mischievous gray-green eyes—awakened feelings in him he'd hoped he'd long since destroyed. An unfamiliar tightness bound his chest, and he couldn't for the life of him drag his eyes away from Chandra and the child.

He folded his arms across his chest and wondered if Chandra's love for this child—for she obviously already did care for the baby as if it were her own—would cause her any heartbreak.

> "Hush, little baby, don't say a word,
> Mama's gonna buy you a mockingbird..."

Dallas felt an unlikely tug on his heart.

> "And if that mockingbird don't sing,
> Mama's gonna buy you a diamond ring..."

He cleared his throat, and she jumped, her head snapping up, her eyes focusing on him. "Looks like I've got some competition," he said, sauntering slowly up to her.

She blanched, as if she felt guilty for being caught with the child. "Com—competition?"

"For your affection."

"I didn't know it was a contest," she replied, turning her gaze back to the swaddled child in her arms. "And neither does he—do you, J.D.?"

"So, you're still calling him J.D.?"

A wonderful, soft shade of pink crawled up the back of her neck and stained her cheeks. "It sounds so much more..." She blinked as if she truly were embarrassed. "So much more personal than Baby John Doe."

"You can call him whatever you like," Dallas said, wondering if she were setting herself up for an emotional fall from which she'd never recover. She was building her dreams on this child, he could see that hope shining in her eyes, and it broke his heart. The child had only been here a few days. The mother—or some other relative—could still turn up. If not, the baby would end up with Social Services, a foster home, then be adopted. "Can I buy you a cup of coffee?"

One eyebrow lifted, and he could see that she was surprised by his offer. Surprised but pleased. "Thanks, I'd like that—but I have an appointment. Maybe some other time."

"Later today?" What was wrong with him? Why couldn't he just leave her alone? She'd been on his mind, in his thoughts, ever since she'd left him at the river just yesterday. Last night had been pure hell. Her vision had followed him into bed and never left him even as he'd dozed in the final hours before dawn. He'd awoken fully aroused, hoping his dream had been real. "I know we didn't part on the best of terms."

"I thought that's the way you wanted it."

He wished it were that simple. "To be honest, when it comes to you, I don't really know what I want," he admitted, baring his soul for the first time in years.

"That's what I like," she said sarcastically, "a man who knows his own mind."

He reached for her arm, wanting to shake some sense into her. Couldn't she see that this was hard for him? But he didn't touch her as she was holding the infant—the only person, it appeared, she truly cared for. "I'm trying to be big about this," he insisted, knowing emotion registered in his eyes. "It's not easy for me. All I'm asking is for a little of your time."

She eyed him speculatively, chewing on the corner of her mouth while she chased away what appeared to be indecision. So she was as wary of him as he was of her. "Sure. Coffee would be good," she finally said, her gaze lingering for a second too long in his. Beyond that, she didn't commit, just checked her watch, frowned and reluctantly handed the baby back to Nurse Nelson. "But not today. I've really got to run," she said as she clipped down the hall to wait for the elevator. Dallas watched her disappear through the parted doors.

He knew where she lived—she'd given her address to the dispatcher when she'd called 911—someplace on Flaming Moss Road, clear out of town.

"Dr. O'Rourke. Dr. Dallas O'Rourke." The page brought him out of his thoughts, but he decided he'd call on Chandra. To hell with the fact that he didn't need any complications. She definitely was a complication, but like it or not, she was already a part of his life. At least until the identity of the baby was discovered. After that... well, he didn't want to project that far into the future. Soon the baby would be released from the hospital and, no doubt, Ms. Hill would lose interest in him.

Dallas plucked a pen from his pocket and clicked it several times before writing instructions on a patient's chart. But as he started down the corridor toward the maternity wing, he passed the elevators and smelled the clean scent of Chandra, the whisper of her perfume still clinging to the air.

What was he doing thinking about her? he wondered angrily. He couldn't start fantasizing about her while he was working. He had a job to do, a job that required complete concentration. A job that was his whole life!

He stopped by a phone to pick up his page, and while the operator connected him to Dr. Spangler, Dallas rubbed his chin. He couldn't afford to get involved with a woman; he knew the price he'd have to pay. Closing his eyes briefly, he muttered irritably, "Come on, come on," hoping the operator would put him through to Spangler and get his mind off Chandra.

But her image wouldn't leave him alone. As he waited, his damned thoughts drifted to her again. He decided he was handling the situation all wrong. As long as she was distant, she would always be the forbidden fruit and her allure would never diminish. Before he got caught up in something he couldn't control, he needed to know more about her. He'd trusted a woman at face value once, and she'd proved far from the woman he'd thought he'd married. As for Chandra, what would it hurt to check out her story before he or the hospital was duped? She seemed sincere, and yet her tale about finding a baby and not knowing the mother was hard to believe.

He had a friend in Denver, a guy he'd gone to school with, a private detective who made a decent living out of poking into other people's lives. Guilt stiffened the back of his neck; he knew that Chandra was a private person and she'd be furious if she had any idea he was checking her out. But if he were going to see her again, it only made sense—

"Dallas?" Spangler's voice broke him out of his thoughts. "Would you mind looking in on a patient in 107? Eleanor Mills. Fractured tibia..." Dallas's mind jerked back to the present, but he knew he wasn't finished with Chandra Hill.

Roy Arnette stared at Chandra as if she were certifiably insane. "You want to adopt the kid you found in the barn?" he repeated, eyeing her over the tops of his wire-rimmed glasses. Roy had been her attorney ever since she'd landed in Ranger, and he was as straitlaced as a Victorian corset and just as inflexible. At sixty-three, he sported a thick shock of white hair, dark eyebrows and a quick smile. He was tall, six-two or three, and dressed the part of a Texan, with his gleaming lizard-skin cowboy boots and string tie. Even his office had a Southwestern motif, which fit right into the town's Western look. Cacti sat in clay pots in the corner, pictures of coyotes and adobe Indian villages graced the walls, and a Native American rug in hues of rust, blue and gray was spread over a bleached plank floor.

"That's right," Chandra said. "I want you to draw up the necessary papers and file whatever petitions are necessary. I want that child for my own."

Roy shook his head. "Whoa, darlin', aren't you gettin' the cart before the horse? You don't even know that baby won't be claimed. Hell, it's only been a few days."

"And any mother worth her salt would never have left J.D. in the first place."

"J.D.? You've already got a name for him?"

"Yes," she said firmly. She was on her feet, pacing in front of Roy's red-oak desk, a bundle of restless energy.

"As your lawyer, I'd advise you to take this slow," he drawled, licking his lips and staring up at her with worried eyes.

"I don't want to take it slow. In fact, the sooner we can get the child, the better."

"It's not that easy. You're not dealing with a private adoption, you know. The state's gonna have to get involved. Social Services. And there may be other people— the child's kin or just some couples anxious for a child of their own—who might want him."

"Who? If the boy had any family, surely they would've come forward."

"If they knew about him. And even if not..." He reached behind him to a stack of newspapers, unfolded one and searched until he'd found the section he wanted. With a rustle of paper, he snapped the page open, pressed the newsprint onto his desk and pointed a long finger at the personals column. "Take a look-see."

Chandra swept her gaze over the advertisements:

ADOPT—Loving couple awaits your newborn. Expenses paid. Contact our attorney...

ADOPTION—Dear Birthmother: Professional couple willing to give your newborn love and affection. Expenses paid. Secure future for your child with all the opportunities you'd hoped for. Contact the law firm of...

LOVING ARMS WAITING TO ADOPT...

CHICAGO COUPLE WILLING TO ADOPT
YOUR NEWBORN...
WANTED TO LOVE: YOUR NEWBORN...

There were more. Lots more. The requests for babies
filled two columns. Chandra felt her knees go weak. She
sank into one of Roy's overstuffed leather chairs positioned near the desk and let the breath out of her lungs at
the thought of the uphill battle that was before her.

"This is just one paper, from Denver. Ads like this appear in newspapers all over the country. Sterile couples
want babies. I have three clients myself who are interested
in private adoption. But you know this—it isn't new to you.
You worked with kids, and in a hospital."

Of course she knew the facts, but she'd been hiding from
them, unwilling to accept the reality that someone else
might want her baby. And that was how she'd come to
think of J.D.: as hers.

"There's something else you might consider," Roy said,
refolding the paper and speaking to her in a kindly voice
that reminded her of her own father. "When the judge
grants someone custody of the child, he'll probably award
that custody to a married couple."

"But—"

Roy held up a flat hand. "I know, I know, single person's rights and all that baloney. But you can argue till
you're blue in the face, I'm just tellin' you the facts. A
married couple—a *stable* married couple—with a house
and a few dollars in the bank to provide security for the
baby will have the best shot at adopting B.J."

"J.D.," she corrected automatically. "I think I'd do a
damned good job as a mother."

"And a father?"

"Yes, and a father!" she argued. "Look at my job, for
crying out loud!"

"Being a father takes more than a job," Roy said calmly,
reminding her without words that he and his wife had raised

five children. "It's a way of thinking—the male perspective. And there's the most obvious reason for placing a child with a couple."

"Which is?" she asked, knowing and dreading the answer.

"That if one of the parents dies, the kid's got a backup. He won't be orphaned again."

Chandra's shoulders slumped. She couldn't argue against that simple logic, and yet, she told herself, if she gave up now, didn't even fight for custody, she'd always look over her shoulder and wonder if she'd made a mistake. "I don't care what the odds are, Roy," she said, slowly lifting her gaze to meet the questions in his. "I want you to do everything in your power to see that I adopt J.D."

"And you—are you willin' to do the same?"

"Do you even have to ask?"

"Then, if I might make a suggestion," he said, his lips twitching a little, "you might want to find yourself a husband. It'll increase our odds of winnin'."

"Got anyone in mind?" She threw the words back at him, in no mood for jokes.

"That's your department. I'll do my bit—you do yours."

"I won't get married," she said, shoving herself upright.

"No hot prospects?"

Unbidden, a picture of Dallas O'Rourke formed in her mind, a picture she quickly shoved aside. "No," Chandra replied with a wry smile, "no prospects whatsoever."

"Then you'd better start prayin'," Roy advised, "'cause without a little help from the man upstairs, I don't think you've got a ghost of a chance."

"Try, Roy, okay? Just try."

"I'll do my best. You know," he said with an ingratiating grin, "I always aim to please."

Chandra left the attorney's office with her spirits dragging on the concrete sidewalk that flanked the building. She spent the next few hours at the office of Wild West Expeditions planning a day trip for the following weekend. When Rick asked her about her trip with Dr. O'Rourke, she didn't go into much detail, deciding the less said on the subject of Dallas, the better.

For the next few days, Chandra went about her life. She stopped by the hospital on the way to work, then again before she went home. Even the days on which she led a trail ride or guided a rafting excursion, she found time to spend a couple of minutes staring at the baby.

Every day she expected him to be released, but the doctors at the hospital were taking no chances. J.D. had come into the hospital dehydrated and undernourished, as well as jaundiced, and the swelling in his little head was still apparent, though only slightly.

Soon, however, he'd have to leave.

Dallas wanted no part of the baby. Or so he told himself. Getting involved with the infant was as dangerous as falling for Chandra Hill. Yet, even he was intrigued by the infant with the dark eyes, lusty voice and shock of black hair.

No wonder Chandra wanted to adopt him. Had circumstances been different, Dallas would have been interested in the boy himself. But, of course, he had no room for a child in his life—a child or a woman. And this baby, whoever he was, had parents out there somewhere. Sooner or later, they'd show up, either together or alone, but someday a woman would claim to be J.D.'s mother.

"And then what are we going to do?" he asked the baby as he rubbed a large hand over his tiny ribs. The infant stared up at him with those eyes that reached right into Dallas's soul. The doctor knew what it was like to be unwanted and unloved, and he pitied this poor child.

It would be a blessing if Chandra were allowed to adopt him, Dallas thought; at least, then J.D. would know a mother's love. He wrapped the baby back in his blanket, and rather than kiss the downy head, Dallas patted the little bottom. "You're gonna be okay," Dallas assured him, though he wished he could predict the baby's future. As well as his own. He hadn't seen Chandra all day, and he'd made excuses to show up in pediatrics hoping for a glimpse of her.

Deciding he was hopeless, he headed back to the emergency room.

Chandra did everything possible to assure herself the best chances of adopting J.D. She filled out all the appropriate papers and even began interviewing baby-sitters. She wanted all her ducks in line before she talked to Social Services.

In the meantime, Roy Arnette assured her he was doing everything possible to petition the court for guardianship. Aside from having Chandra fill out forms and sign statements, he'd begun collecting personal references from her friends and acquaintances, even checked on her parents in Idaho, since she knew few people in Ranger. In fact, she was beginning to feel that the hospital staff, particularly the nurses on the pediatric floor, were fast becoming the best friends she had in town.

Even Dr. O'Rourke was more than an acquaintance. She'd seen him several times at the hospital, and for the most part he'd been friendly, though professional. Never once had the rafting trip been mentioned between them. And, if O'Rourke remembered the passion that had burned so brightly for a few magical hours, he didn't show it. Once she'd thought he'd been staring at her, but that flicker of interest she'd seen, or hoped to see, in his eyes was quickly replaced by the cool exterior that had earned him the name Dr. Ice.

"No woman has ever gotten through to him," Shannon Pratt had divulged once when she and Chandra were sharing a cup of coffee in the cafeteria. "I remember when he came here, several of the single nurses zeroed in on him." She'd smiled at the memory. "Every one of them struck out. And these gals were big leaguers. He wasn't the least bit interested.''

Chandra had stared at the bottom of her cup, wishing she could confide in Shannon, but unable to bring up the rafting trip. What had occurred between Dallas and her had been special. ''Surely the man must have dated someone.''

''Not that I know of. Rumor has it that he was burned badly by his ex-wife.'' Shannon had finished her coffee. ''Believe me, if there were a way to that man's heart, no one's found it yet. And the best have tried.''

Now, two days after Shannon's revelation about Dallas, Chandra stopped by the hospital again. Gathering all her courage, she dropped by Dallas's office, hoping to see him, but his receptionist told her that he wasn't available.

In the pediatrics wing, Leslie Nelson was off duty, but Shannon was stationed at the second-floor desk. She let Chandra hold J.D., and once again Chandra's heart wrapped possessively around this little boy. ''It's going to be all right,'' she whispered into his cap of dark hair. ''We're going to work this out.''

Eventually, she gave the baby back to Shannon, who suggested Chandra drop by at feeding time so that she could give J.D. his bottle. Chandra asked a few questions, but was told that, as far as Shannon or any of the nursing staff of the hospital knew, no one had yet found the mother.

From the hospital, Chandra called the Sheriff's Department and was eventually connected with Deputy White, who informed her that there was nothing new on the case. No one, it seemed, was missing an infant. All the hospitals in a three-hundred-mile radius had been contacted, and no babies had been stolen from the nurseries. It was as if J.D.'s mother didn't exist.

''Nobody just leaves a baby in a barn,'' Chandra told herself as she walked through the breezeway connecting the parking lot to the hospital. Of their own accord, her eyes swept the staff lot, but Dr. O'Rourke's truck wasn't tucked into any of the parking spots reserved for hospital physicians, and she chided herself for looking.

"Oh, for crying out loud!" Chandra felt like cursing when, two hours later, she drove down the lane to her house. A tan station wagon was parked near the back porch, and the driver, sitting and smoking, was Bob Fillmore from the *Banner*. Blast it all, she should've known he wouldn't give up. One little article wasn't enough.

Sam, teeth bared, black lips snarling fiendishly, paced by the vehicle. The hairs on the back of his neck stood on end, and every time Fillmore moved, Sam lunged at the car, barking ferociously.

Just what I need, Chandra thought, bracing herself, though the retriever's antics amused her. Sam yipped excitedly as she parked her rig near the back porch.

Knowing that she couldn't duck the reporters forever, she decided to tell everything she knew to Fillmore, hopefully ending any interest the press could have in her.

"Slow day for news?" she asked, hopping out of the truck and forcing a smile she didn't feel. "Sam, down!" She snapped her fingers and pointed to the ground at her feet. Sam reluctantly trotted over and lay by her side, his steady gaze never leaving the car.

"That animal should be locked up!" Fillmore tossed his cigarette butt onto the gravel as he crawled out of his car, but his eyes never left the retriever. "I thought he was going to tear me limb from limb."

"That's the general idea," Chandra said.

Suddenly, the reporter was all business. "Back to your question—about the news? Seems that most of the news is right in your backyard these days. I didn't get much of an interview at the hospital. And the Sheriff's Department hasn't been overly helpful. I thought you could fill in a few of the holes in my story." As if he read denial forming on her lips, he continued, "Look, you're the only one who knows exactly what happened, and I just want to get this story right. The kid's parents may be looking for him right now. He could've been stolen, right? You might be doing them and the baby a big favor...." He let his sentence trail off, implying that there might be a big reward for finding the child. As if money were the answer.

Her stomach lurched and a bad taste filled her mouth. The dislike she'd felt for Bob Fillmore grew more intense. "I just want to do right by the child," Chandra said in the same confidential tone he'd used with her, "and I don't want to interfere with the investigation by the Sheriff's Department." She said nothing about wanting to become the baby's mother. Right now, a statement to that effect would have the same result as spraying gasoline on a slow-burning fire. Fillmore's interest in the story—and in Chandra herself—would definitely heat up. Time enough for that later.

He smiled easily. "No chance of messing anything up with the police. I just have a few questions. Simple ones. Really. Questions that might help the baby find his mom."

Chandra bit back a hot reply about the woman who had forsaken her son. And as for Fillmore, she didn't trust the reporter for a minute. In Tennessee, her life had been ripped open, the focus of several "in-depth" interviews after Gordy Shore had died and his parents had filed suit against her. All of those reporters had seemed a cut above Fillmore, and they'd made her life a living hell. There was no telling what the reporter from the *Banner* might do.

Yet she couldn't very well hide the truth, could she? She couldn't refuse to talk to the man. She'd only make him think she had something to hide. Frowning, she unlocked the back doors of the Suburban and pulled out two sacks of groceries. Sam followed obediently at her heels and only growled when Fillmore, trying to help, grabbed the handle of a gallon of milk. "I could carry those bags."

"Already got 'em." Balancing the groceries, she unlocked the back door, and Sam streaked inside. The retriever settled on the rug under the table and, with one final growl of disapproval, watched Fillmore enter the cabin.

Chandra stuffed a carton of eggs into the refrigerator. "You know, I thought people usually called ahead for an interview."

"I did. This morning. No answer. I left a message. When you didn't call back, I figured the time and place was okay with you."

"And what if I hadn't shown up?" she asked, waving him into a chair. Casting a glance at her answering machine, she noticed the red light flashing. She had no option but to get this over with.

"I would've waited. Speaking of which—" he checked his watch and scowled "—the photographer should be here by now. He knew about this shoot. Would you mind if I used your phone?" He was already picking up the receiver when Chandra nodded. The man was pushy, no doubt about it. He dialed quickly, then tapped a toe while he waited. "Yeah. It's Fillmore," he said into the mouthpiece. "I'm lookin' for Levine. Should've been here by now. I'm at the Hill place on Flaming Moss Road . . . yeah, eighteen, twenty miles out . . . well, tell him to get his butt in gear, okay? We're waiting."

Chandra, only half listening to the reporter, pulled out a couple of sodas from the refrigerator. Her throat was already parched, and at the thought of an interview, her mouth turned as dry as a desert wind. She held one can up silently and Fillmore, still growling orders into the phone, grinned and waved an affirmative. While he was finishing his call, she cracked ice into a couple of tall glasses, not really in the mood to sit down and sip Pepsi with the man from the *Banner.* Her only consolation was that she figured it wouldn't hurt to have the reporter on her side, pretend to go along with him and then, at the first available instant, make some excuse to end the interview early. He'd have a deadline, so he wouldn't be back, and that, thankfully, would be the end of the press camping out on her doorstep. She hoped. If not and he got wind of the fact that she was planning to adopt J.D., so be it. At least he wouldn't be out to smear her. She felt better about offering him the cola.

"Look," she said, once he'd hung up and settled into a chair at the table. She placed one of the dewy glasses in front of him and resisted the urge to press the other to her forehead to ward off a headache. "I just don't want this to get out of hand. No media circus on this, okay?"

"I'm just here to tell a story." After draining half his glass, Fillmore reached into his jacket pocket and pulled out his tape recorder, pen and notepad. "Okay, let's start at the beginning. How did you find the baby?"

Chandra had gone over the same tale so many times that she said the words without much emotion, explaining about discovering the child, calling 911 and driving to meet the ambulance. No, she didn't know to whom the baby belonged. No, she couldn't imagine who would leave a baby alone. Yes, the baby had needed medical attention, but he had seemed strong enough.

They were both about finished with their drinks when Fillmore brought up the baby's future. "What if the mother shows up?"

"Then I guess the court decides if she's a fit parent," Chandra replied, studying the melting ice in her glass. She hoped her face was impassive.

"And where do you fit into it?"

Yes, where? "I don't know," she answered truthfully, just as Sam's ears pricked forward and the dog scrambled to the door with a bark. Chandra glanced out the window and her heart dropped. Dallas's truck slowed to a stop by Fillmore's car. *Great,* she thought, knowing instinctively that Fillmore wouldn't budge if he recognized the doctor who had admitted J.D. into the hospital.

"Well, well, well, the good Dr. O'Rourke," Fillmore drawled, a satisfied smile slithering across his lips. "What's he doing here?"

"I wouldn't know," Chandra said, rising to answer the door. Dallas had, indeed, arrived—all six feet of him greeted her as she swept the door open and invited him in. "Hi," she said, motioning toward Fillmore. "Join the crowd."

Dallas grew rigid and as he walked into the kitchen, the temperature seemed to drop ten degrees. Both men stared at each other for a few agonizing seconds. "Fillmore," Dallas finally said, not bothering to hide his distaste for the man. "What're you doing here?"

"Just checkin' out a story. What about you?" The reporter clicked his pen loudly, and the tape in his machine continued to whir.

"I took an excursion with Ms. Hill over the weekend. She left something in my truck."

"Excursion? You mean a rafting trip?" Fillmore glanced from Dallas to Chandra and back again.

Dallas shrugged. "My brother thought I could use a little R and R." He reached into the pocket of his jeans and pulled out her bandanna, the one she'd used to tie back her hair, clean and pressed.

"So how was the trip? Exciting?"

Dallas turned chilling eyes on the reporter. "Very. Ms. Hill is an excellent guide. In fact, have you ever been on one of those trips down the Rattlesnake at—what was it called?" He looked to Chandra for help, but she had the feeling he knew exactly what he was saying. "Grizzly Loop? I think it's just your speed, Fillmore."

Bob Fillmore smirked, as if he refused to be goaded by Dallas.

"And if Chandra can't help you, maybe the owner can. What's his name—Rick Benson—you remember, the guy you did the piece on a few years back."

The muscles in Chandra's neck tensed. This was no time to intimidate the reporter, for God's sake! What was Dallas doing?

"I'll keep it in mind," Fillmore replied as he scraped his chair back and stood. Chandra hoped fervently that he was finished. "Tell me, Doctor, since I'm writing about the abandoned child, what's his status with the hospital?"

Dallas looked in Chandra's direction. "He's about to be released."

No! So that's why Dallas was here, to break the news and prepare her. Chandra's heart leapt to her throat. "Released to whom?" she asked, trying to keep a calm appearance.

Dallas slanted a glance at the reporter, as if he realized he'd said too much.

"That's right," Fillmore added, "who'll get the kid?"

"I think that's up to Social Services."

Fillmore grinned. "This is getting better by the minute. When, exactly, will he be released?"

"Dr. Williams and Dr. Spangler will decide."

"They the kid's pediatricians?"

"That's right," Dallas said as Sam barked loudly.

A compact Ford, silver-blue in color, roared down the drive, leaving a plume of dust in its wake.

What was this? Chandra wondered. More bad news?

"About time," Fillmore muttered, scooping up his notepad and tape recorder as he scraped his chair back. "It's Sid. He'll want a few pictures of the barn, you know, where the kid was found. And he might have a few questions. Then we'll be outta your hair."

Chandra could hardly wait. They walked outside, and Sid Levine, gathering camera bag, umbrella, light meter and other equipment, unloaded his car. "Hi, fella," he said to Sam as the retriever bared his teeth and galloped toward the newcomer. Sid reached down and scratched Sam behind the ears. "Hey, slow down, I'm not gonna hurt anything."

Growling, Sam sniffed at the proffered hand then, traitor that he was, began wagging his tail so hard that it thumped against the fender of the Ford.

"We were on our way to the barn to get some pictures of the inside," Fillmore said, waving the photographer along as he crossed the yard.

"I'll be there in a minute. Just let me take a few shots out here," Levine said, apparently used to Fillmore's brusque manner.

Inside the barn, Chandra, as she had with the sheriff's deputies, pointed out the stall where she'd found the baby. One of her favorite geldings, Max, a curious buckskin, strolled inside and stood waiting for some oats to be tossed his way. The other horses poked their noses into the barn door and their shadows drifted inside, but they didn't follow the buckskin's lead. Even Cayenne, usually friendly, eyed the intruders, snorted disdainfully and refused to amble inside.

Max draped his head over the top of the stall and eyed Fillmore, who was busy in the end box where the baby was found, then nuzzled Chandra's jacket, looking for a piece of carrot or apple. "Sorry, buddy," she whispered to the horse, who snorted and stamped a foot impatiently.

Dallas had followed her into the barn. He leaned against the ladder to the hayloft while Fillmore asked still more questions and the photographer scurried inside, sending up dust motes and disturbing the cobwebs that draped from the windows. Chandra could feel Dallas's gaze on her back as she petted Max's velvety nose and answered the questions as best she could. Fillmore tried to ignore the doctor, but Chandra couldn't. His presence seemed to charge the air in the musty old barn, and she sensed that some of the reporter's questions were worded more carefully just because Dallas was within earshot.

"This it?" Sid Levine asked, looking around the barn, searching, it appeared, for sources of light. A grimy circular window over the hayloft and a few rectangles of glass at eye level over the stalls gave little natural illumination to the interior.

"In here," Fillmore replied from the stall.

Once again, Chandra pointed out the position of the child. Then, while the reporter asked a few more questions, the photographer took aim and began clicking off shots. Dallas said nothing, just watched the men going through the motions of creating news.

It's almost over, Chandra thought, *it has to be.*

"So...you been a resident of Ranger long?" Fillmore asked.

"A few years," she replied.

"And before that?"

Chandra felt the sweat break out between her shoulder blades. She didn't want her past splayed all over the front page of the *Ranger Banner.* She'd buried her life in Tennessee and hoped that it would stay that way.

"I'm originally from Idaho, up near McCall," she said easily.

"Ahh," Levine said, nodding to himself. "So that's where you get the interest in rafting and trail riding."

"Grew up doing it," she replied. "My father was a real outdoorsman." From the corner of her eye she saw Dallas straighten a little, but Fillmore, evidently satisfied, snapped off his tape recorder and checked his watch. "Thanks for your time. I've gotta shove off if I'm gonna put this story to bed tonight."

The muscles in Chandra's back relaxed a little. If they would just leave, she could find out about J.D. It seemed forever before Fillmore's car was moving down the drive and the afternoon sun was warming her back as she and Dallas watched the reporter take his leave.

Levine was still finishing up in the barn, but Chandra couldn't wait. "What's going to happen to the baby?" she asked, laying a hand on Dallas's arm. She attempted to keep the desperation from her voice, but found it impossible. "What will Social Services do?"

"Probably place the child in a temporary home until a judge decides where he'll be placed permanently."

"Oh, God," she whispered, her throat dry. J.D needed someone who loved him, someone who would care for him. While he was in the hospital, he was being cared for, even loved a bit, by the nurses, and Chandra could see him every day. But now...

To her surprise, Dallas placed a comforting arm around her shoulders. "Don't worry. He'll be fine." Her throat clogged at his tenderness.

"How do you know that?" she demanded, her eyes beginning to burn with unshed tears. She hadn't realized until just then how much she'd thought of the baby as hers. Everyone had been warning her that he could be taken away, but she hadn't listened.

"He'll be placed with someone who'll care for him." Dallas smiled down at her and squeezed her a little. "And I'll make sure that whoever gets him will allow you to see him."

She couldn't believe it. "You can do that?" she asked skeptically.

"I can try." A sliver of uneasiness clouded his features. "But don't get too involved. You don't know what will happen."

"I know, I know," she said, her throat clogging as Dallas offered her the comfort of his arms. She laid her head against his shoulder, drinking in the smell of him, glad for the strong arms that surrounded her. How right it felt to be sheltered by him. For years she'd stood on her own, relied on no one, and now all she could think about was leaning on Dallas. "The mother might show up. Damn that woman, anyway!"

She heard a camera click behind her and jumped. Dallas whirled, his eyes blazing, as Sid Levine lowered his .35 millimeter and snapped the camera back into his case. "All finished," he said, and his eyes held a spark of nastiness that Chandra hadn't seen before.

"I hope I don't see my picture on the front page," Dallas said, and the treachery on the photographer's face was replaced by a glimmer of fear as he slid into his Ford and took off.

"Bastards. Every last one of them," Dallas growled, his eyes narrowing on the silver car as it roared down the lane.

"Just tell me about the baby." Chandra couldn't worry about the reporter or his sidekick. All that mattered was J.D.—her J.D.

Dallas shoved his hands into his pockets of his jeans. "That's why I stopped by," he said, and Chandra felt a jab of disappointment. There was a little part of her that wanted him to have come to visit her on his own. "I talked to Williams, and it's just a matter of days—possibly tomorrow or the day after—whenever Social Services decides to get their act together."

"Oh, God," she whispered, knowing that soon it would all be over. But she hadn't lost. Not yet.

"Maybe it won't be so bad," Dallas said. "As I said, I'll try to arrange it so you can still visit with the baby—"

"Oh, thank you," she said, and, without thinking, she flung her arms around his neck. "Thank you." She felt his arms wrap around her, hold her snug against him for a heartbeat, and for a second she felt as breathless as she had that night by the river. Her heart thundered as his hands moved slowly up her rib cage. But he stopped, pushed her slowly away from him, and when she lifted her eyes to his, she saw his features harden.

He held her at arm's length and dug his fingers into her shoulders. "Look, Chandra, you don't have to thank me, okay? You don't have to do anything to show your appreciation."

"Meaning?"

"Meaning that just because I'm helping you with the baby doesn't mean that there's anything else between us. You're not obligated to show your appreciation."

"Well, that's a relief," she shot back. Did he really think that she would stoop so low as to manipulate him and play with his emotions? "And here I thought I'd have to do something like go to bed with you just to get you on my side.''

He sucked in a quick breath at her sarcasm. His eyes flashed, and he looked as if he'd been slapped.

"That is what you were insinuating, wasn't it? Well, let me tell you something, *Doctor,* I *don't* sleep with men to get what I want. Ever.''

He lifted a skeptical eyebrow and she couldn't help ramming her point home. "You know, I thought you were different, that you weren't the typical egomaniac M.D. who thinks he's God's gift to women. But it turns out that you're just like all the rest—misconstruing motives, thinking women are coming on to you. All I wanted to do was say thanks.''

"Then just say it."

"I did.'' She shoved her hair from her eyes and planted her hands firmly on her hips. "Now, if you'll excuse me—and even if you won't—I've got work to do.'' In a cloud of dust and anger, she stormed to the barn, furious with herself and outraged with him.

Once inside, she climbed the loft ladder, kicked down a couple of bales of hay, then hopped to the floor. Finding her pocket knife, she slit the twine, snapped her knife closed and grabbed a pitchfork. She began tossing loose hay into the manger, throwing her back into her work, filling her nostrils with the scent of sweat, horses, dung and dried grass.

Max, snorting expectantly, wandered back to his stall, tentatively nudging his nose into the fresh hay.

A shadow from the open door fell across the floor. Chandra stiffened and turned, facing O'Rourke again. He looked as he did the first night she'd seen him, unapproachable and deadly serious. "I thought you were leaving,'' she said, throwing another forkful of hay into the manger.

"And I thought we should clear the air.''

"About what?''

"Us."

"Us," she threw back at him. "What 'us'? I'm just *using* you, remember?" She plunged her pitchfork into the loose hay again and threw the bleached strands into the next manger. Brandy, a chestnut mare, ambled inside, her white blaze visible as she sniffed the feeding trough.

Before Chandra knew what was happening, Dallas had closed the distance between them. He grabbed her shoulders with hands made of steel. Spinning her around, he forced her to face the conflicting emotions shading his eyes. "I don't think you're purposely trying to *use* me," he said fiercely.

"What a relief," she shot back, her voice dripping sarcasm.

"But what I do think is that, whether you like it or not, you see me as a link to the baby. You're so desperate to be a part of that child's life that you'll manipulate anyone to get what you want."

"And what I see is a man who runs away from his emotions—a man afraid of being spontaneous because it might upset the careful balance in his life!" Breathing hard, she held the pitchfork with one hand. She didn't want to see the anger in his eyes or feel the warm pads of his fingers digging into her skin. Nor did she want the male smell of him to fill her senses.

She ripped herself free. "Look, don't feel *obligated* to do anything, all right? You don't owe me anything, and I can handle my life by myself. And that includes doing what I have to do to be close to the baby. You can walk away from this . . . just turn—" she pointed to the door "—and leave. That's all there is to it."

"I wish." He lifted his hands as if to touch her face, dropped them again, then swore under his breath. "Damn it all to hell, anyway," he muttered before grabbing her again and pulling her roughly against him. Startled, she dropped the pitchfork and it clattered to the dusty concrete floor.

This time his lips crashed down on hers with a possessive savagery that sent one pulsating shock wave after another down her body. He breathed in her breath, his lips moving insistently, his big hands splayed across the gentle slope of her back.

She tried to drag her mouth away, pushed with all her strength, but was unable to break the manacle of his embrace. Instead she was subjected to an elegant torment as his tongue sought entrance to her mouth and his hands moved insistently, rubbing her clothes against her skin.

She moaned softly, her head falling backward, her throat exposed. One of his hands curled in the thick strands of her hair, and he drew her head back farther still, until he could press hot, wet kisses against the curve of her shoulder.

"No... please... stop..." she whispered, hardly believing the words came from her lips.

His touch was electric, his tongue, teeth and lips nipping and creating pulses of desire that swirled deep inside.

"You don't want me to stop," he whispered against her ear, his breath tantalizing and wet.

"Yes...no... Oh, Dallas, please..." With all her might, she coiled her strength, then pushed away from him and found to her mortification that she was panting, her heartbeat thrumming, her pulse pounding in her temples.

Running a trembling hand through her hair, she stepped backward until she ran into a post supporting the hay loft. The splintered wood pressed hard against her back. "For someone who doesn't want to get involved, you're pretty damned persistent," she said, trying to sound haughty, and failing.

"What I want and what seems to keep happening between us aren't necessarily the same." He, too, had trouble finding his breath. He ran a shaking hand over his lips.

"Then I guess the answer is to stay away from each other."

"You think that's possible?" he asked, sliding her a look with his knowing blue eyes.

"Anything's possible if you want it bad enough."

"Is that so?"

"Absolutely."

"I hope you're right, Ms. Hill," he said as he walked to the door. He stopped and looked over his shoulder. "Because if you're not, we've got one helluva problem on our hands."

Chapter Nine

Dallas dragged himself out of the pool, his body heaving from the exertion, his lungs craving more air. He'd swum over a mile in less than forty-five minutes, and he was breathing hard, his heart pumping crazily.

"What're you tryin' to do, kill yourself?" the man in the next lane asked. The other swimmer ripped off his goggles and cap, letting his wet hair fall nearly to his shoulders.

"I was a little keyed up," Dallas replied. He didn't know the man's name, wasn't really interested. He saw him here at the pool a couple of times a week and usually they swam their laps at about the same pace. Not this morning. Dallas had been wound tighter than a clock spring, his muscles tense, his attitude one notch shy of downright surly.

All because of that damned woman. He didn't know whether to hate her or to love her. She'd upset his well-ordered life, and for that, he was angry with her; but she brought out a part of him he'd kept hidden, a part that felt younger and carefree. He supposed, if he didn't love her, at least he owed her one.

He climbed to his feet, grabbed his towel and rubbed the rough terry cloth over his face, neck and shoulders. Seeing her yesterday with the reporter should have been warning enough, but no, he'd hung around and let down his guard enough to allow that louse of a photographer to snap a picture of them together. Not that it really mattered, he supposed. The picture probably wouldn't be printed, and if it was, so what?

Worse yet, he'd let the man goad him into tracking her down in the barn and acting like some horny barbarian. God, what was happening to him?

In the shower room, he ignored the other men who were in various stages of dressing, shaving or blow-drying their hair. They joked and laughed over the whine of hair dryers and electric razors, but Dallas barely noticed. He'd never been part of that club of men who sought camaraderie in the locker room before facing the day.

He washed the chlorine from his skin and hair and, as they had for the past week, his thoughts swirled around Chandra. Chandra the camping guide. Chandra the seductress. Chandra the would-be mother. God, she was crazy for that kid; that much was obvious.

But Dallas wasn't too sure about how she felt about him. Unless her emotions were as jumbled as his. Dunking his head under the shower one final time, he twisted off the knob and tried not to think about last night, how he, after a short shift at the hospital, had gone home and fallen into bed, only to dream about her—her honey-gold hair, her laughing eyes, her luscious pink lips and her breasts, round and full with dark, sweet tips.

Suddenly embarrassed at the swelling that the thought of her always brought to mind, he turned on the faucet again, gave himself a douse of ice-cold water, then muttering obscenities under his breath, wrapped a towel around his hips and walked briskly to his locker. He changed into clothes quickly, shoved his fingers through his hair and, slinging his bag over his shoulder, strode outside.

The day echoed his mood. Gray clouds clustered over the mountaintops, threatening to explode in a deluge of late-summer rain. Well, great, let it pour. Maybe the drops from the dark sky would cool his blood. He hoped so. Ever since he'd met Chandra Hill, it seemed he'd been battling his body, his mind telling him not to get involved, his damned body wanting nothing more than to plunge into her with a fierce possession.

He'd *never* felt this way before. *Never.* Even with Jennifer, there had been an edge of control in their lovemaking, and not once had he discovered that his passion had ruled him. But now, with Chandra, he couldn't stop thinking about making love to her over and over again.

He unlocked his truck and slipped behind the wheel. Jamming his key into the ignition, he decided that he'd be better off not seeing the lady again.

Maybe another woman . . . He considered the women he knew and, without even realizing the turn of his thoughts, his mind had wandered back to Chandra Hill. Yesterday's kiss . . . a simmering passion . . .

Getting to know her more intimately would either be a blessing or a curse, and he strongly suspected the latter. He shoved a tape into the player and, muttering oaths at the other drivers, he eased his truck into the snarl of traffic and turned toward the hospital.

"I have no choice but to release him," Dr. Williams said with a quiet authority that brooked no argument.

Chandra had caught up with him after his rounds, and they were now in his office at the hospital, he seated on one side of a glossy black desk, she on the other. Behind him, through the window, she noticed the dark clouds that hinted of a late-summer thunderstorm. The thunderheads reminded her of Dallas and the storm she often saw gathering in his eyes, but then, just about anything these days caused her to think about Dr. O'Rourke.

Or the baby. And that was why she was here. She hadn't slept a wink last night, worried about the child. She'd spent the night tossing and turning, her mind spinning with schemes to get custody of the boy, and oftentimes, she hated to admit, those schemes also involved Dallas.

Dr. Williams was staring at her, waiting for her to say something.

"I just think it might be best for the child if he stayed here at the hospital a few more days."

"Why? He's healthy."

"But—"

"Really, Miss Hill, the hospital has done everything it can for the child." Williams gave her a soft smile that was barely visible beneath his neatly trimmed red beard. "He'll stay the night, and tomorrow the caseworker from Social Services will come for him."

"And take him where?" Chandra asked, managing not to sound frantic.

"I don't know." Williams sat back in his chair and shook his balding head. "Her name is Marian Sedgewick, and she's coming for the baby at about eleven. I'm sure you could call her and find out more about his placement."

The phone on the corner of his desk rang shrilly, and Chandra rose. "Thanks, Doctor," she said.

"Anytime." But he was already picking up the receiver.

Chandra walked along the hall of the pediatrics wing, refusing to be discouraged. This was to be expected. The baby couldn't stay here forever. But she'd have to move quickly. Near the nurses' station, she stopped and rummaged in her purse for change, then placed a call to Roy Arnette.

"I'm sorry, but Mr. Arnette isn't in right now. Can I take a message?" Chandra left her name and number. Deflated, she walked to the nurses' station, where Shannon Pratt was busy fielding phone calls.

"Go on back," she mouthed, the phone cradled between her shoulder and ear, as she wrote hastily on a clipboard.

Chandra didn't need any more encouragement. She hurried to the nursery and spied J.D., wrapped in a white blanket, his eyes moving slowly as he tried to focus. Her heart squeezed at the sight of his chubby face. Where would he be tomorrow? Who would change him, feed him, kiss him good-night?

An uncomfortable lump filled her throat as Shannon, all smiles, bustled by. "It's been a madhouse this morning," she apologized. "Leslie told me you were coming in to feed him." She motioned toward J.D.'s crib.

"I'd love to."

"Well, we could use the extra hands." Shannon walked into the nursery, still talking. "This is, and I quote, 'highly irregular,' but I talked long and hard and got the okay from my supervisor who, in turn, worked it out with admin. So we're all set." She handed Chandra gloves and a mask. "You can scrub up in the lavatory, and once you've donned all these glamorous accessories—come back. Believe me, your little guy will be hungry...."

Your little guy. If only. Chandra scrubbed her hands and arms and yanked on her gloves. The smell of antiseptic and newborn babies reminded her of her own practice. She'd been happy back then, treating the patients, getting to know their mothers, fitting into the cozy community of Collier, Tennessee and thinking she would put down roots and start her own family.

But Doug had had other ideas....

"Hey, you look like one of us!" Shannon said as Chandra walked out of the washroom. "And look who's waiting...."

"J.D.," Chandra said, grinning behind the paper mask. "How're ya, pumpkin?" She took the little bundle eagerly, held his tiny, wriggling body close to hers. Nurse Pratt handed her a bottle of formula, and the baby, still blinking up at Chandra, began to suckle hungrily. Tiny little noises, grunts of pleasure, accompanied the slurping sound as he tugged on the nipple.

"You've named him?"

Chandra, startled, jumped and the bottle came out of J.D.'s tiny mouth. He let up a wail that could put a patient in cardiac arrest. Quickly, she nudged the nipple back between the baby's tiny lips. "I'm sorry," she said to Shannon, "I was so into this, I forgot you were there. And, yes, I decided he needed a name."

"Well, I think it's a much better name than Baby John Doe." With a twinkle in her eye, she hurried back to the nursery and, with a black marking pen, wrote "J.D." in large letters on the tag of his bassinet.

Chandra smiled. For the first time since she'd moved to Ranger two years before, she felt a part of the community. Living as she did, miles out of town, meeting only a few townspeople at the market or at work, she hadn't cultivated many friends. Most of the people she dealt with were tourists who wanted a thrill before returning to their cities and nine-to-five jobs. A few returned from one year to the next, but her only real contacts with people in town were the men she worked with.

The nurses and staff of the hospital seemed special. She wondered if it was the hospital surroundings. For the first time since she left Collier, she wondered if leaving her profession had been the right choice.

So she was here. Again. Being set up for a fall. Dallas saw Chandra with the baby, this time taking a bottle from him and swaying gently, brushing the top of his downy head with her lips.

Was she out of her mind? Didn't she know she was playing Russian roulette with her emotions? Yet he, too, could feel the tug on his heartstrings, the unlikely and unwanted pull of tenderness for the child. Seeing them together, she cradling the little dark head so close to her breast, the baby nuzzling closer, caused a tightness in his chest and a deep sadness that he would never be a father, never a husband. He'd tried once and failed.

The familiar metallic taste of loathing filled his throat when he remembered his wife and her betrayal. Though he hadn't loved her as he should have, he'd been faithful to her and fair, and he'd cared about her. And she'd driven a knife into his heart, cutting him so deeply, the scar would never heal. He'd never feel free to love someone like Chandra, to father her children....

He coughed loudly. What the hell was he doing even thinking such ludicrous thoughts? It was one thing to fantasize about making love to her, to consider bedding her and having a quick affair that would end as surely as had his own brief marriage. But to consider a lifetime together, marriage and children? What in God's name was wrong with him?

Clearing his throat, he approached her. She turned, and the sight of her hair fanning her face nearly undid all his hard-fought resolutions to keep away from her. Her lips moved slightly, smiling at the sight of him.

"Thank God you're here," she said, and he realized that she'd somehow become dependent upon him.

This very headstrong, independent woman was beginning to trust him, and he thought guiltily of his detective friend digging into her past. He could call off the investigation, but decided it wouldn't hurt to know more about her. She seemed to have brushed their episode in the barn from her mind.

She said breathlessly, "I just talked to Dr. Williams. They're releasing J.D. tomorrow."

"So it's been decided."

"'Morning, Doctor." Shannon emerged from the nursery and turned her attention to Chandra. "Here, let me change him."

"He hasn't burped yet," Chandra protested, drawing her fine eyebrows together.

"That's all right." Nurse Pratt wriggled her nose at the tiny baby. "We'll take care of it, won't we? And I'll take your lovely accessories..." Shannon accepted the baby, bottle, gloves and mask from Chandra, and after a few quick words with Dallas about a peculiarly obstinate patient in CICU, carried J.D. back to the nursery.

Dallas took the crook of Chandra's arm in his broad hand and pulled her gently toward the nurses' station. "I wouldn't worry too much about the baby. He'll be in good hands."

"How do you know?" She stopped short, looking up at him. "*What* do you know?"

"Rumor is that the child will be placed in temporary custody of the Newells."

"The sheriff?"

"He and his wife, Lenore. She's a part-time nurse here and they've done this sort of thing before. Lenore's known for taking in stray dogs, cats and opening their home to runaways or children who are waiting to be placed in more permanent quarters."

Anxiously, Chandra bit her lower lip and Dallas experienced a sudden urge to kiss her and tug on that very lip. "Come here," he said, all thoughts of denying himself long gone. He pulled her around a corner and down a short hallway to a quieter part of the floor. At the end of the hall, in the landing of the emergency stairs, he tugged on her hand, yanking her hard against him. She gasped, and he captured her lips with his. Seeing the startled look on her face, the surprise in her wide, gray-green eyes, he expected her to frantically push away, but she didn't resist.

His mouth moved over hers, and she leaned against him, circling his waist with her arms, her breasts crushed against the hard expanse of his chest. This time she seemed to melt against his body. He twisted his hands in her hair and played with her lower lip, touching it with his tongue before drawing it into his mouth.

Chandra's heart thumped crazily. What was he thinking, kissing her here, in broad daylight, where at any minute— Her senses reeled, her body reacted and a tingling blush suffused her skin. She closed her eyes and let herself get lost in the smell and touch and taste of him. There was the faint odor of chlorine that clung to his skin, the smell of soap. And his hair was still damp. Somewhere, faraway, a metal cart rattled.

"What the hell am I going to do with you?" he muttered into her hair, breathing deeply, his heart drumming so loudly, she could hear the wild beat.

Before she could answer, he kissed her again, long and hard, creating a whirlpool of emotions inside her. She sighed into his open mouth, and his tongue touched hers before he closed his mouth and every muscle in his body tensed. He dropped his hands to his sides then, and she nearly fell over.

"What?" she asked, before seeing that his eyes, now open, were focused on something or someone standing just beyond Chandra's shoulder.

Chandra turned and found herself gazing into the flushed face of Nurse Alma Lindquist. "Excuse me," the big nurse said, obviously embarrassed. "I, uh, well, I'm looking for you, Doctor, and Shannon said she saw you goin' down this hall." She turned her gaze to Chandra. "She didn't mention—"

"What is it?" Dallas was all business, and Chandra felt like crawling into a hole. Caught like a couple of lusty teenagers—by Alma Lindquist, of all people. Alma's eyebrows were arched over her glasses, and a tiny I-got-you grin was barely visible on her face. Chandra was absolutely mortified.

"Dr. Warren isn't in yet, and I need to get into the medications for E.R. However, if you're busy—"

"I'll be right there," Dallas said, his eyes glittering as Alma tried and failed to smother her knowing smile. She sauntered off down the hall, and Chandra's face felt red-hot.

"This was a mistake," Dallas said, jamming his hands through his hair and shaking his head. "Look, I can't get involved with anyone. It just wouldn't work."

"I don't remember asking you," Chandra replied, though his words stung.

"But you haven't exactly been backing off, have you?"

"I've done nothing to encourage you," she reminded him, wounded. "You came on the rafting trip. I didn't invite you."

"My brother—"

"Whatever. It doesn't matter. And you showed up at my house the other night—and barged into my barn. Again without an engraved invitation."

"And you camp out here at the hospital."

"Because of the baby!" she shot back, knowing in her heart what she would never admit to him. "Don't you understand?" she said instead. "J.D. means everything to me!"

"Oh, Chandra..." he said, and a dark emotion flickered in his eyes.

"And don't give me all the reasons I shouldn't try to adopt him, because I'm going to," she replied, embarrassed and angry and frustrated. She tossed her hair over her shoulders.

"You're serious about adopting him?" Dallas asked, obviously skeptical.

She wished she could call back the words, but the damage was done. There was no reason to play coy. "I hope to. I've already told my attorney to draw up the necessary papers. I'll petition the court—"

"And what did your attorney say?"

"Well, after he tried to talk me out of it," she replied, sliding the doctor a glance, "he told me I'd better go about increasing my chances."

"How?"

"By getting married."

Dallas blanched. Rock solid, all-business Dr. Dallas O'Rourke actually lost his color. Good! Chandra had the feeling O'Rourke needed to be shaken up once in a while.

"That's right, Doctor, I guess I'm in the market for a husband." She straightened her blouse. "Seems that the courts will look more kindly on a couple rather than a single woman."

"You're joking!" He was absolutely stricken, and Chandra's heart nosedived.

"Only about being in the marriage market," she said. "But I'm not going to let any prejudice against single women stop me. If I have to fight this through the Supreme Court, I will."

"Or get married?"

"That was a joke, Doctor," she said, and then decided to drop the bomb. "I was married once. It wasn't all it was cracked up to be."

He didn't move, but his eyes didn't leave hers and she silently counted her heartbeats. "Maybe you married the wrong man," he finally said.

"I did," she admitted, quivering at the thought of discussing her short-lived marriage with him. Once the divorce had been finalized, she'd never spoken of Doug or her marriage to anyone. Not even to her family. "But even if I did marry the wrong guy, I'm not sure I would recognize the right one if he landed on my doorstep."

"Oh, Ms. Hill, I think you would."

She lifted a shoulder dismissively. "I'm not going to lose any sleep over it. See you later," she said breezily, as if his passionate kiss and harsh words hadn't bothered her in the least. With a forced smile, she turned and left him there, trying not to notice that the taste of his lips still lingered on hers.

Dallas tried to ignore the fact that he was jealous—of a man whose name he didn't know. Whoever Chandra's ex-husband was, he was a damned fool.

Now, as Dallas folded his arms over his chest, he tried to keep his thoughts on the business at hand, which was his patient. "The nurses say you've been giving them trouble, Mr. Hastings."

"Call me Ned. And don't give me no guff about not takin' those pills. I've lived eighty-five years without takin' pills, and I'm not about to start now."

"Even though you're in intensive care and have had one heart attack already? All the medication does is help regulate your heartbeat."

Ned scratched his head, his mottled scalp showing through thin gray hair. "I know you're just doin' your job, Doc, and I 'preciate it, but I don't need any goldurn pills to keep my ticker from conkin' out."

"I'm not so sure about that."

"And about those nurses of yours. Always fussin' over me. Pokin' and proddin' and cluckin' their tongues. You're lucky I'm still in this hospital."

Dallas swallowed a smile. The old coot was lovable in his own way. But stubborn. "I don't think you're being realistic about your health."

"Hell, I didn't get to my age by lyin' in a hospital, with tubes run through my body and pills bein' stuck in my mouth every hour of the day. I live alone, I'm proud of it, and I don't need no mamby-pamby women stewin' over me."

"I see he's his usual jovial self," Lenore Newell said. She placed the thermometer into a disposable cover, and with a smile, stuck the thermometer under Mr. Hasting's tongue. "This should keep you quiet a while," she said.

He sputtered, but didn't spit the thermometer out as Dallas had expected.

Nurse Newell took the old man's pulse and, while eyeing her watch, added, "Some people would think spending a few days being pampered by women would be heaven."

"Humph," Ned growled around the thermometer. "They're just plain stupid or they haven't been in this damned place," he mumbled.

"Shh," she ordered, winking at the doctor as she waited for the beep and digital readout of her patient's temperature.

"Keep giving him the medication," Dallas said, seeing the glint of fondness in the old man's glare. "And don't take any abuse from this guy."

Hastings's thick eyebrows shot up.

"I'll be back," Dallas promised him. As he left the room, he heard Ned Hastings still growling around the thermometer.

Lenore caught up with Dallas in the staff lounge. "Cantankerous old son of a gun," she said with a ready smile. Behind big glasses, her eyes gleamed with affection.

"He keeps life interesting," Dallas remarked.

"Don't they all?"

Dallas poured himself a cup of coffee while Lenore rummaged through a basket of tea bags. The lounge was nearly empty. Three nurses surrounded a round table by the window, and a couple of residents, who looked as if they'd each pulled thirty-six-hour shifts, were stretched out on the couches, one in scrubs, the other wearing a rumpled lab coat and slacks. Each supported more than a day's growth of beard and bloodshot eyes.

"Been here long?" Dallas ventured.

One of them, the lanky one with long blond hair, shoved a hand through his unruly locks. "Days, weeks, years...I can't remember."

"We came on duty in 1985," his companion joked. He was shorter and thin, with a moustache and eyes that appeared owlish behind thick glasses.

"Time for a break," Dallas suggested.

"Man, I'm gonna sleep for a week," the tall one said.

"Not me. I'm going out for a five-mile jog and set of tennis."

"Yeah, right!" They struggled to their feet and headed out the door.

Dallas stirred his coffee before glancing at Lenore. "I heard you might have another mouth to feed."

She smiled. "Yep. The abandoned baby. Judge Reinecke seems to think that the baby would be best at our house, at least for a while. We've cared for more than our share of orphans."

Dallas stared into his coffee, not knowing whether he should bring up Chandra or not. Maybe she was better off away from the baby. But he remembered her look of desperation at the thought that the child would be taken away from her. Knowing he might be playing with emotional fire, he nonetheless had to do anything in his power to help her. "Look, there's a woman, the woman who brought the baby in, Chandra Hill. I know she'd like to visit the baby fairly often."

Lenore dunked a tea bag into a steaming cup of water. "I've heard about her. Seems she's pretty attached to the boy."

"Well, it wouldn't hurt for her to drop by."

"Of course not. Tell her to stop in anytime."

"Lenore! Hey, what's this I hear about you and the Baby John Doe?" one of the other nurses called over. "You got any room left over there?"

Dallas took his coffee and left as the two other nurses joined into the conversation. He'd done what he could. Now it was up to Chandra.

He spent the rest of the day in the hospital and finally, at five, stopped in at pediatrics for one last look at J.D. Holding the child, he sighed. "What're we gonna do with you?" he wondered aloud. "You're giving the woman who found you fits, y'know."

The baby yawned, as if he were bored to death.

"Okay, okay," Dallas said, smiling down at the child. "We'll see what we can do."

He left the infant with a nurse and walked outside. The storm that had threatened earlier had cleared up and the day was dry and warm, no lingering clouds in the sky. Whistling under his breath, he walked to his truck and stopped when he spied his half brother chewing on a toothpick, one lean hip resting against the fender, his knee bent and the sole of one boot pressed against the front tire. A grimy duffle bag had been dropped on the asphalt near the truck.

"I thought I might have to spend the whole weekend here waiting for you," Brian said as Dallas approached. As usual, Brian's cocky grin was in place, his eyes squinting slightly against a lowering sun. His jeans were so faded, they'd ripped through the knees, and the denim across his butt was frayed, on the point of giving way completely. His shirt was bright orange, faded neon, and said simply, SURF'S UP!! diagonally in purple letters that stretched from his right shoulder to his left hip.

"What's doing?"

Brian grinned, as if he read the caution in Dallas's eyes. He straightened and held out his hands, surrendering to his half brother's suspicion. "Don't worry, I haven't gone through the money yet. I just came by to say I'm shipping out. On my way back to school."

About time. "That's good."

"Right, and I probably won't see you until Christmas. You'll come to Mom's?"

"I'll see. Christmas is a long way off."

"She'd be disappointed if you didn't come."

Well, maybe. From Brian's point of view, their mother loved Dallas as much as she did her other children. But Dallas remembered a time when, after the divorce from his father and her remarriage, Eugena O'Rourke McGee had been so involved with raising a daughter and the twins that she hadn't so much as smiled at him. She'd been tired most of the time from chasing the younger kids.

Dallas, a reminder of her marriage to a military doctor who had never been able to show any emotion, was, for the most part, left on his own. He'd been enrolled in boarding school while his parents were married, and his status didn't change when his mother remarried, even though none of her other children had ever stepped foot in a school away from home until college. Joanna, Brian and Brenda had been raised at home.

Yes, there was the possibility that his mother might miss Dallas at Christmas, but not for the reasons Brian expected. In her later years, she'd developed a fondness for her firstborn, probably born of guilt, but never had Eugena given him the love she'd lavished on her younger children.

Dallas was no longer bitter about that particular lack of love; he just didn't dwell on it.

"Ahh, come one, it'll be fun. And Joanna and Brenda will kill ya if ya don't show up."

That much was true. For all the love he hadn't received from his mother, his sisters had adored him. "I'll think about it."

"See that you do. Well, I'm outta here." Bending down, Brian slung the strap of his duffle over his shoulder and offered his brother one of his killer smiles. "Thanks a lot. For everything. And, oh—did you manage to go on the raft ride?"

Dallas grinned. "An experience of a lifetime."

"What did you think of the lady?"

"She's something else."

"I'll say." Brian's grin turned into a leer. "Strong little bugger. And great legs! Boy, I bet she's a tiger..." His voice faded away when he caught the set of his brother's jaw. "So you noticed?"

"Just that I already knew her."

"A nice piece." When Dallas's lips thinned, Brian laughed. "Of work. Hey! What did you think I meant?" He glanced down at his brother's hands and grinned even more broadly. Dallas realized that he'd instinctively clenched his fists. "Hey, bro', is there something you're not tellin' me?"

Dallas forced himself to relax. This was just Brian going into his macho-man routine. "Nothing. Just that I already know her."

"And you've got the hots for her."

Dallas didn't reply, but just glared at his half brother, wondering if they had anything in common at all.

"Well, go for it, man! I don't blame you. The lady's nice . . . real nice."

"What do you mean, 'go for it'?"

"Ask her out, spend some time with her, get to know her. For crying out loud, here you are and—pardon me for pointing it out—in the middle of no-friggin'-where, and a woman like that falls into your lap. Take a chance, man. I know you got burned by Jennifer the Jezebel, but not all women are Wicked Witches of the West."

"I should take advice on my love life from you?" Dallas asked, slightly amused.

"Well, you'd better take it from somebody, 'cause the way I see it, your 'love life,' as you so optimistically call it, doesn't exist."

Dallas wanted to smack the smug smile off the younger man's face, but, for once in his life, Brian was right. Instead, Dallas stuck out his arm and shook his brother's hand. "Thanks for the advice."

"Don't thank me. Just do something, man."

"I could give you the same words of wisdom."

Brian's grin was positively wicked. "Not about *my* love life, you couldn't." With a cocksure grin, he strolled over to his car and yanked open the door. Throwing his bag into the back seat, he crawled into the interior, started the engine of the old Pontiac Firebird and took off in a cloud of exhaust that slowly dissipated in the clear mountain air.

Brian's advice hung like a pall over Dallas as he drove to his condominium. This morning he'd wanted to drive

Chandra from his life forever. Then he'd seen her in the hospital and could hardly keep his hands off her. No, he'd better face facts, at least for the present. Brian was right; he should kick up his heels a little. He didn't have to fall in love.

That thought hit him like a bucket of ice water. In love? *I guess I'm in the market for a husband.*

Her words ricocheted through his mind. Had she been joking, or had she been hinting? "Quit this, O'Rourke, before you make yourself crazy."

But forget her he couldn't, and before he knew it, he was making plans to see her again. As soon as he walked into his home, he dropped his mail, unopened, on the table, then picked up the phone book. He punched out the number of Wild West Expeditions. Chandra answered, and he couldn't stop the tug of the muscles near the corners of his mouth.

"I thought we should get together after work," he said, feeling the part of a fool, like some creepy lounge lizard. God, he was just no good at this.

"Why?"

"We left on the wrong note. How about I take you to dinner?"

A pause. A thousand heartbeats seemed to pass. "Dinner?" she finally said. "I don't know...."

"Neither do I, but I've been thinking and..." He let out his breath slowly, then decided honesty was the best policy. "Well, I'd like to see you again."

"Even though I'm only interested in a husband or, more precisely, a father for my yet-unadopted child."

There it was—that biting sarcasm that he found so fascinating. No wimp, Ms. Hill. "Even though," he said, smiling despite himself. "Dress up. I've got a surprise for you. I'll pick you up at your place at six-thirty."

"What if I already have plans?" she asked, obviously flirting with him a little. It occurred to him that she was as nervous about this as was he.

"Cancel them." He hung up, feeling a little like a jerk, but looking forward to the evening ahead. This morning he'd tried to drive her from his mind, but now, damn it all to hell, he was going to fulfill a few of his fantasies with the gorgeous Ms. Hill.

After all, it was just a date, not a lifetime commitment.

Chapter Ten

A date? She couldn't believe it. Yet here she was, pawing through her closet of work shirts, jeans and a few old dresses trying to come up with an outfit for Dallas's surprise.

And her heart was pounding as if she were a schoolgirl. *Take it easy, Chandra,* she told herself, knowing that Dallas's mood could change as rapidly as the weather in these mountains.

She settled for a rose-colored skirt and a scooped-neck blouse, and was just brushing her hair when Sam, ever vigilant, began to growl. "Jealous?" Chandra teased, her heart surprisingly light as she patted the dog on his head, and was rewarded with a sloppy lick of his tongue.

Dallas stood on the doorstep, balancing two grocery sacks. "Wait a minute—I thought we were going out," she said as she opened the door and he stepped inside.

"We are." He placed the brown paper bags on the kitchen counter. "Got a picnic basket?"

"You're kidding, right?" she asked, but caught the glint of devilish mischief in his eyes. *This* was the serious Dr. O'Rourke—this man who seemed hell-bent to confuse her? It seemed that he enjoyed keeping her equilibrium off balance.

"Someone told me I wasn't spontaneous enough, that I needed to get out of my rut," he said with a shrug. "So— the basket?"

"Right. A picnic basket." Wondering what he was up to, she rummaged in the closet under the stairs and came up with a wicker basket covered with dust. She blew across the top and dust motes swirled in a cloud. "Doesn't get much use," she explained, finding a cloth and wiping the woven wicker clean.

"I thought we'd take a ride into the hills."

"Like this?" She eyed his slacks and crisp shirt. "Are you crazy?"

"Just spontaneous."

"Yeah, right," she replied, but wiped out the interior of the basket and lined it with a blanket. Dallas reached into his grocery bag and filled the basket with smaller sacks, a bottle of wine, glasses and a corkscrew. "Did you bring the horses, too, or is that what I'm supposed to provide?"

"The horses and the destination."

"Oh, I get it—you're counting on me to provide you with a free trail ride, is that it?" she teased, feeling her spirits lifting along with the corners of her mouth.

He laughed and the sound filled the cabin, bouncing off the rafters as he snapped the lid of the basket shut. Approaching her slowly, he held her gaze with his. "Are you going to fight me all the way on this?"

"I don't have a side saddle." Oh, Lord, he was so close she could see a small scar near his hairline, obviously old and faded with the passage of time from ruffian boy to man. She had to elevate her chin a fraction to meet his gaze, and her throat caught at the depth of blue in his eyes.

"Improvise," he suggested, his breath tickling her scalp.

"I could change—"

"And leave me overdressed? No way!" His gaze lowered, past her lips and chin, along the column of her throat, to the scooped neck of her blouse and the beginning of the hollow between her breasts, just barely visible. "Besides, you look—" He broke off, his Adam's apple working in his throat. Reaching forward, he touched a strand of her hair and wound its golden length around one finger.

The moment, only seconds, seemed to stretch a lifetime, and as he laid her curl back against her cheek, his finger grazing her skin, her diaphragm pressed so hard against her lungs, she had trouble breathing.

"I think we should go," she said, stepping back from him and feeling clumsy and embarrassed and totally unbalanced. Just being close to him caused her to lose her cool facade. This one enigmatic man had managed, in the span of one week, to create havoc with her emotions. "I—I'll saddle up."

"*I'll* saddle up. You bring the basket." He swung out the door, and Sam, with one look over his shoulder, trotted after him.

"I'm going to change your name to Judas," Chandra warned, swinging the basket from the table and following man and dog to the barn. She was struck by the natural way Dallas strode across the yard, as if he belonged here. Sunlight gleamed in his dark hair and warmed her crown. His dress clothes seemed appropriate somehow, though she could just as easily envision him in faded jeans, a work shirt open and flapping in the breeze as he chopped firewood. And Sam, the turncoat, padded happily behind him, tongue lolling, tail moving slowly with his gait.

Within minutes, Dallas had saddled Max and Brandy, and they were riding along a dusty trail. Chandra had hiked her skirt around her thighs and felt absolutely ridiculous as well as positively euphoric. The sky was a clear cobalt blue, and two hawks circled lazily overhead.

The mountain air was clean, the horses' hooves thudding softly, stirring dust, causing creatures in the brush to scurry through the undergrowth. Once in a while, Sam gave chase, startling the horses as he dashed by, barking wildly at some unseen prey.

After nearly an hour of riding through the forest, the trail forked, and Chandra veered sharply to the right, back-trailing downhill.

"You sure you know where you're going?" Dallas asked.

"Positive." She nudged Brandy in the sides as the pines and blue spruce gave way to a meadow. The game little mare sprinted forward, ears pricked, nostrils flared, her hooves pounding across the field of dry grass and wild-flowers in shades of pink, blue and lavender.

Chandra's skirt billowed behind her, and her bare legs held fast to Brandy's sides. Wind streamed through Chandra's hair, and she laughed as she heard Max close to Brandy's heels, his galloping hooves loud against the dry ground.

"Come on, Brandy," Chandra said, leaning over the little mare's shoulders and watching the horse's ears flatten against her head. She picked up speed, but it was too late. Max, black legs flashing in the sun, raced past. Dallas rode low in the saddle, his shoulders hunched forward, the picnic basket propped between the saddle and his chest.

"We should've beaten them," Chandra told the mare as she pulled up. Both horses were sweating and blowing hard. Chandra, too, was having trouble breathing, but Sam wasn't even winded. He saw a squirrel, streaked off across the meadow and splashed through the creek that zigzagged through the grass. Spring water gurgled and rushed over rocks, and the big gold dog bounded through the stream before disappearing into the woods.

"Should we worry about him?" Dallas asked, swinging off Max at a bend in the creek where the water pooled and reflected the intense blue of the sky.

"He'll be back. He's used to it." Chandra hopped to the ground and felt the tickle of grass against her bare ankles. "That's how I found him, you know. He crawled into the yard, ripped from stem to stern by something—bear, raccoon, possum or something else, I suppose—and I had to sew him up. I've had him ever since."

Dallas's eyes narrowed on the forest into which the dog, joyfully yelping and giving chase, had disappeared. "Hasn't learned much."

"He'll be all right," Chandra replied.

While the horses grazed near the stream, Dallas and Chandra unfolded the blanket in the shade of a pine tree. He uncorked the wine and poured them each a glass of Chablis. "What are we drinking to?" she asked, and his blue eyes deepened to a mysterious hue.

"How about to us?"

She laughed, tucking her legs beneath her as she sat on the edge of the blanket, her skirt folded over her knees. He wasn't serious. This was all a lark, a fantasy. "Us? I thought there wasn't any us—that you couldn't get involved or muck up your life with a woman." She took a long swallow of wine and watched the play of emotions across his face.

His jaw slid to one side, and his hair was rumpled by the breeze that blew from the west. "I didn't want any complications."

"Didn't...?"

"Still don't," he admitted, lying on the blanket and leaning back on one elbow while he sipped from his glass. "But sometimes things change. And what you don't want changes with it." He plucked a dry blade of grass and chewed on it. "From the minute I saw you in the emergency room, I knew you were going to be trouble—big trouble." He squinted as a pheasant, wings beating frantically, rose from the grass as Sam leapt and barked in the frightened bird's wake. "And I thought the only reasonable thing to do, the only sane path to take, was to avoid you.''

She smiled. For the first time since she'd met him, she felt that Dallas was being honest with her. His eyebrows were pinched together, and his lips, moving on the straw, pursed hard, as if he were angry with himself.

''So...'' she prodded.

''So I did. And then my brother gave me that damned coupon.''

''But you still weren't convinced that I wasn't trouble,'' she said.

''Hell, no. Then I knew you were more trouble than I'd even imagined.'' He laughed again and took a long swallow of his wine. ''And that's when things got really out of hand.'' He looked at her directly then, his gaze holding hers. ''I couldn't keep my hands off you, and that's not the way it usually is with me. In fact,'' he admitted, glancing away, as if the admission were embarrassing, ''I was starting to become obsessed.''

''With ... ?'' she asked warily.

''You.'' A muscle in his jaw convulsed, and Chandra realized just how difficult it was for him to bare his soul. They weren't so different, she decided; they both bore wounds that wouldn't heal. ''Anyway, I wasn't sleeping at night, and I couldn't think of anything but you. Making love to you.''

Chandra nearly dropped her glass. Her hands began to sweat, and she took a long swallow of wine to avoid those blue, blue eyes.

''So that's when I decided never to see you again.''

She glanced up sharply. ''But you're here—''

''Believe it or not, I ran into Brian and he told me I was crazy to keep avoiding you. He told me I should loosen up, enjoy life, take a chance or two....'' Dallas lifted a shoulder and beneath the crisp white fabric, his muscles moved fluidly.

A tight knot formed in the pit of Chandra's stomach. He reached over and refilled her glass before adding more wine to his own.

"So, for the first time in my life, I took Brian's advice. Believe me, it wasn't easy." He studied the label for a second before propping the bottle against the inside of the wicker basket.

Chandra felt as if time were suspended between them. Surely she could think of something clever to say, something that would lighten the mood. But all words escaped her, and she could feel his gaze moving slowly over her, caressing her, causing her skin to tingle under his silent appraisal. "So what is this?" she finally asked, her voice as soft as the wind in the pines. "A seduction?"

"If you want it to be."

"No!" she said quickly, breathlessly. She'd thought of making love to him. But it was one thing to fantasize, another to actually do it. She gulped her wine and glanced his way, hoping that she could see some indication that he was joking, but not a glimmer of humor sparked in his eyes.

"Afraid?"

"Look, Dallas. Maybe you can make all sorts of plans—you know, buy the wine, pick out the right cheese and bread, and just . . . just map out some way for us to get together. But it doesn't work that way with me. I can't just drink a little wine and say, 'what the hell,' and start stripping off my clothes. It's just not me. . . ." Slowly, she climbed to her feet and dusted her hands. "This isn't going to work." She whistled to the horses, and while Brandy ignored her and continued to pluck grass, Max responded.

She reached for his reins, but Dallas caught up with her and gently grabbed her wrist. "I've been accused of being blunt," he admitted. "Too blunt."

"Well, at least you don't leave me guessing." She tried to pull away, but his grip tightened, and slowly he tugged, forcing her to face him.

"It's just that I want you," he said. "I want you so much, I can't think of anything else. I ache for you at night, embarrass myself during the day when I start to think of you. I've tried to fight it—hell, I had myself convinced that I didn't want, didn't need, a woman. And I was right. I don't need just any woman, Chandra. I need you."

Her heart turned over, and she felt the pads of his fingers, warm and smooth against the inside of her forearm. Her heart nearly stopped as she dropped the reins and stared into eyes the color of a mountain sky.

"You want me, too." He placed the flat of his free hand over her heart, his fingertips skimming her bare skin, his palm resting over the neckline of her blouse, seeming to press against her breast.

Her heartbeat quickened, and her breath, unsteady to begin with, came in quick bursts through her lips.

"W-wanting isn't enough," she said.

"It was enough on the rafting trip." He kissed the side of her neck then, and her throat constricted. Somewhere she heard a dog barking and the jingle of a bridle, but those sounds were in the distance, and now she heard only the rapid tattoo of her heart and the rasp of air through her lungs.

Dallas pulled her blouse down over one shoulder and placed his lips against her skin. An endless ache started at the apex of her legs and moved slowly upward.

The fingers surrounding her wrist pulled gently, insistently, forcing her to follow him to the ground, and she didn't resist, fell willingly against him, their arms and legs entwining, his body wedged between hers and the bent grass.

He moved his mouth over hers, fiercely, possessively, until it seemed that the fever in his blood had ignited all her senses. She felt the pressure of his tongue, the urgency in his hands, the hot, throbbing desire that blossomed inside her.

He pulled her blouse from the waistband of her skirt and slowly ran his hands over her ribs, moving upward, brushing the lace of her bra. She moaned into his mouth as his thumb skimmed against her already taut nipple.

"Dallas," she whispered as he unbuttoned her blouse and the cool mountain air caressed her skin. He shoved the blouse aside, and then with her above him, craned his neck so that his lips touched her bra and the lace-encased nipple. She writhed, and he pulled her downward, one hand splayed against the bare skin of her back, the other tangled in her hair. He kissed and teased her through the lace, his tongue wet and wonderful in delicious ministrations that caused her to convulse.

"Please, please, please..." she moaned, and he groaned against her flesh, unhooking the bra and letting her breasts fall free, unbound, above him. He took one eagerly into his waiting mouth, suckling hungrily, his tongue and teeth pulling and tugging, creating a whirlpool of warmth deep within her body.

She found the buttons of his shirt and quickly dispensed with them, pushing the white fabric over corded shoulders that flexed, strong and sinewy against her fingers. She arched against him as the shirt was discarded, and her breasts felt the rough hairs of his chest when he lifted his head to stare up at her eyes.

"Chandra," he whispered, his voice rough and pleading, his hands smoothing her back, exploring the cleft of her spine. "You're so gorgeous," he whispered, moving his gaze from her eyes and past her parted lips to her breasts, white and firm, floating above him, enticing him to delirious heights of sexuality.

Never had he felt so free, so anxious, so aroused. His lust was like a living, breathing creature he couldn't control.

With his hand, he sculpted her, teasing the hard nipples and kneading the warm flesh of her breast. Shockwave after delicious shockwave spread through him, and she responded by throwing her head back, her luxurious mane of golden hair falling over her shoulders and back. He didn't stop. Couldn't. He fastened his mouth over her nipple again and slowly slid his hand beneath the waistband of her skirt, skimming her abdomen and reaching lower still.

Sweat broke out on her body, and though he relieved her of her skirt and panties, a dewy sheen covered her body as he continued to touch her, kiss her, caress her.

She found herself helping him with his jeans, and he kicked them off, then lay under her, wanting to delve into her and never stop. When he firmly grasped one buttock, she pressed herself hard against him.

"Make love to me, Chandra," he whispered into her hair. "For now and forever, make love to me."

She closed her eyes and swallowed as he ran one finger down the hollow of her breasts, down past her navel and farther still, until she bucked above him, and he reacted, capturing her lips in his and rolling her over in one quick motion. As he stared down into her eyes, he parted her legs with his knees and hesitated, seeing the trust in her gaze, knowing that she was envisioning a future together.

"Oh, Chandra," he whispered. "I want you...." And in that moment, he knew that life would never be the same. He'd planned all this, to the very seduction. A man of medicine, he never lost his cool, but with this woman, he could very well lose his equilibrium forever. Trying to stay rational, he reached in the grass for his jeans, dug into the pocket for a condom in his wallet. Muttering in frustration, he held up the packet for her to inspect, as if in so doing, they could stop this madness before it went any further.

But it was too late; the bridge had been crossed. A shadow of doubt crossed her eyes for just one second. "Don't stop," she said, as if certain he would deny her. Quickly, he readied himself. She trembled as he brushed the hair from her eyes, and in that moment when their gazes crossed a chasm of doubt, he entered her, in one swift thrust of warmth and need. A hard, primal sound escaped his throat, and he moved, slowly at first, feeling all of her, still aware of her fingertips feather light against his shoulders, her mouth yielding softly to his.

He couldn't stop and wouldn't. His tempo increased, and through fleeting thoughts of satisfying her, he lost control, plunged deep and hard, whispering her name as a litany until he could hold back no longer and he erupted with a roar.

Chandra convulsed beneath him, arching her hips and receiving him with all the ferocity of his own passion. She dug her fingers deep into his shoulders and cried out, and his name echoed through the hills.

"Dallas, oh, Dallas," she said, her throat working, tears filling the corners of her eyes.

Breathing raggedly, afterglow converging upon him, he saw the silent tracks of her tears. Pain shot through him as he realized he'd pushed himself upon her, forced her through seduction and gentle ministrations to have sex with him. Self-loathing swallowed him. "Oh, God, I'm sorry," he said, his throat rough. He pushed her bangs from her forehead, and self-contempt edged his features. What the hell had he been thinking? "I didn't mean to hurt you—"

"No!" She gasped, drawing in deep breaths. "You didn't. Really. It's...it..." She dashed her tears aside with the back of her hand. "It was wonderful. It's just...well, it's been so long."

"For me, too," he admitted, relieved that she wasn't feeling any remorse. He took her into his arms and kissed her crown. "I'm afraid I lost control."

Softly she sighed, and her skin flushed a beautiful pink. "You weren't the only one."

"You're not mad at me for planning this?"

"I could've stopped it." When he was about to protest, she shook her long blond mane. "Really, I could have. If I'd wanted to. But I didn't."

"No regrets?" he asked, kissing a stray tear that slid from her eye.

"None."

Sam loped over to them. Wet from a romp in the creek, he shook himself so hard that his license and collar rattled. Chandra screeched, and Dallas, laughing, picked her up and carried her toward the pool of spring water.

"You wouldn't," she cried, eyeing the frigid water.

"Something's got to cool us off."

"Dallas, no—"

But he waded into the clear depths and sucking in his breath, plunged them both into the icy pond. Shrieking and laughing, Chandra sputtered upward for air, only to find his smiling face next to hers. "You're horrid!" she cried, but laughed when he tickled her.

"Wicked. I'm wicked. Not horrid."

"Worse than that, I think," she said breathlessly as she struggled for the shore. He caught up with her and wrapping arms around her waist, pulled her tight against him. Wet, cold lips pressed anxiously against hers.

"You can't get away from me," he stated.

"Is that a challenge?" She lifted an eyebrow and eyed the shore, judging how far she would have to run should she want to prove him wrong.

"Don't even think about it!"

That was it. With the flat of her hand, she sprayed water in his face, then, laughing, she stumbled up the creek bank, only to be caught midstride and pulled back into the water. "As I said," he repeated, "you'll never get away from me!" He gathered her against him, sliding her intimately against him, pressing kisses against her nape and neck.

"So who's running?" she asked, and kissed him back. She wondered if she loved him and decided it didn't matter. She cared about him, felt a special fondness toward him, and the passion between them was enough to satisfy her. She thought fleetingly of the future, but dismissed it. Today, for the first time in her life, she'd live for the moment.

Eventually the cold water was too much to bear and they returned to the meadow, where, after dressing, they finished the wine and ate sourdough bread, cheese, grapes and strawberries. The sun sank lower on the horizon, and shadows played across the dry grass.

Chandra lay on the blanket, picking a few wildflowers and twirling the stems between her fingers. "You said you didn't want to get involved," she ventured, glancing over her shoulder. Stretched out on the other side of the blanket, Dallas seemed content to stare at her.

"I didn't. Probably still don't. But I am."

"What happened? I mean—that made you so afraid?"

"Afraid?" He rolled onto his back and stared at the sky, still blue as the sun sank lower in the west. "I've never thought of it as being afraid. Cautious, maybe. Smart, for sure, but afraid?"

She arched an eyebrow. "That's the way I see it."

Scowling, he sighed. "I don't believe in reliving the past. No point to it."

"Except when it affects the future."

Dallas stood and dusted off his pants. He walked to the edge of the creek, where he bent down, picked up a smooth, flat stone and sent it skimming over the water to plop near the far bank as rippling circles disturbed the surface.

Chandra followed him to the shore, and, with a twinkle in her eye, picked up a flat river rock and skipped it over the water just as easily as he had. "What is it with you?" he asked, his features pulled into a look of puzzlement. "Studying to become a doctor, guiding white-water trips, backpacking and skipping stones?" He raked his gaze down her body. "For a woman with so many obvious feminine attributes, you sure like to perform like a man."

"Compete," she corrected. "I like to compete with men."

"Why?"

She shrugged. "I guess I'm the son my father never had. He taught me how to throw from my shoulder instead of my wrist, how to rock climb, and he gave me the confidence that I could do anything I wanted to, regardless of my sex."

Dallas eyed her. "You were lucky."

"I think so. My sisters were both glad that I was the chosen one and they didn't have to do any of the tomboy stuff. I think they missed out. But we weren't talking about me," she reminded him.

He feigned a smile. "You remembered."

"What happened to you?"

"It was simple, really," he said in an offhand manner that seemed meant to belie the pain. "My folks split up when I was still in boarding school. My dad was career military, very rigid, a physician, and my mother got tired of moving around. I can't say as I blame her, Harrison O'Rourke would've been hell to live with. He's . . . clinical, I guess you'd say. Didn't believe in showing his emotions, not to me or Mom. It's amazing she stayed with him as long as she did."

Dallas reached down and skipped another stone, and Chandra's chest grew tight. Talking about his past was difficult for him; she could see the reluctance in his eyes, the harsh lines near his mouth. "Anyway, she remarried. Happily, I think. And ended up pregnant right away. Joanna was born a year later, and only sixteen months after that the twins came along. You met Brian." Chandra nodded. "He has a twin sister named Brenda—she's, uh, much more rational than he.

"So, Mom had her hands full, and I was old enough to be on my own, anyway. I finished high school and was accepted at UCLA in premed."

To gain your father's approval, she thought, her heart twisting for a boy who felt unwanted.

"I met the girl of my dreams before I graduated," he said, his voice turning sarcastic. "Jennifer Smythe."

A painful jab cut into her heart, though why it mattered, Chandra couldn't fathom. "Why was she the girl of your dreams?"

He snorted. "She was perfect—or at least, I thought so. Beautiful, smart, clever, witty and a graduate student in law. Even though she was a few years older than I was, I thought the right thing to do was get married, so we did."

Chandra studied his profile—so severe with the on-slaught of memories.

"The marriage was mistake number one. She passed the bar exam and within a few weeks, was hired at a firm where she'd worked during the summers. It was a respectable firm, and the partners were interested in young women to balance the plethora of old men. She supported me while I finished school. Mistake number two. She always felt I *owed* her something."

Dallas frowned darkly and shook his head. "This is really pretty boring stuff—"

"Not at all," Chandra interjected, surprised that he was letting her see so deeply into his private life.

He shot her a look saying more eloquently than words that he didn't believe her, but he continued, though reluctantly. "What I didn't know was that Jennifer didn't want a kid. Period. Now, she never told me this, but she was the only child of rich parents and couldn't see tying herself down to an infant. She thought that between her career and mine, we had it made." Sam galloped up, and Dallas reached down to scratch his ears. The old dog whined appreciatively, and Dallas had to smile.

"Eventually, I graduated and was hired at a hospital in Orange County. Even though we had a few bills, I thought this was the time to start a family, but Jennifer wasn't interested. I should've let it lie, I suppose, but I wanted kids. Badly." He cast Chandra a rueful grin. "In fact, I was obsessed. A bad trait of mine. I figured my folks didn't do the family bit right, so I was going to be the perfect father. As if I knew the first thing about raising kids!"

His eyes darkened, and any trace of humor disappeared from his features. He shook his head, as if in disbelief at his own naïveté.

Chandra felt a whisper of dread as he continued.

"The kicker was that Jennifer did get pregnant, right about the time we were buying our first house. She never told me, of course, and had the pregnancy terminated. I only found out because of a mutual friend who knew the doctor who performed the abortion."

Chandra swallowed hard against the outrage that burned her throat. No wonder he was so bitter. A shadow, dark and pained, crossed his eyes, and the skin around his mouth grew taut.

"That was the last straw. I stormed over to her office, and I didn't care who heard the argument. I was furious that she wouldn't at least have talked to me, have worked things out before she took such drastic measures. But Jennifer wasn't the least bit reticent, and she told me then that she would never have children. It was her body, it had nothing to do with me, and as she saw it, I shouldn't get all worked up over it. Besides, she pointed out, I was doing well at the hospital, and I put in long hours. I didn't need the responsibility of children to make demands on my time—not to mention hers. What did upset her was that I embarrassed her by coming into the law firm in a rage."

Chandra placed a hand on his arm, but he didn't seem to notice. "So that's it. I couldn't deal with her from that point on. I tried to tell myself that losing the baby was for the best, that being married to a doctor was difficult for any woman, that maybe Jennifer would change her mind and there would be other children. But I was kidding myself. I never forgot."

He shoved his hands into his pockets and rotated his neck, stretching his shoulder muscles. For a second Chandra thought he'd finished, but his next words came out in a rush of disgust.

"You'd have to meet Jennifer to understand this, but she assumed everything was A-OK. She was delighted with our new life-style. We had money and social status and interesting careers. She was moving up in the law firm at an incredible pace. Her only real worry was that my position as an emergency-room physician wasn't all that glamorous. She thought I had the brains and skill to become a specialist, a notch up in her estimation. I fought her on that one. I like what I do and couldn't see giving it up."

He rolled his eyes to the sky, now streaked with gold and pink, as if he couldn't believe he'd been so foolish. His shoulders, which had been rigid, began to slump.

"Things got worse, of course. Living in L.A. was a grind. Jennifer and I barely saw each other. When I was offered a position at Riverbend, here in Ranger, I thought maybe we had a chance to start over. But I was wrong. Even though I said I'd set her up in her own practice here, Jennifer wouldn't hear of the move. It was obvious at that point that her job was more important than our marriage and she wasn't about to move to 'some podunk little town in the mountains.' She would be bored stiff in a small town in Colorado, without the nightlife and the glitz.

"Besides," he added bitterly, "she was up for a big promotion. If push came to shove, she'd rather live in L.A. without me than move to Colorado. So we separated. I moved. She stayed. We saw each other a couple of times a month and it was a sham. There was no reason to try to hold the marriage together."

He kicked at the grass. "We agreed on a quick divorce. Three weeks after the divorce was final, Jennifer married her boss, a man twice her age who had grown children and didn't want to start another family. The next time I saw her, she admitted that the baby she'd aborted wasn't even mine."

Chandra thought she might get sick. How could someone use this man—this wonderful man?

"Jennifer had been having an affair with her boss for years—which explained her meteoric rise in the firm of James, Ettinburg, Smith and McHenry," he said, his voice still edged in anger. "And I was the dupe who believed that we still had a chance." He snorted in self-disgust, and

Chandra wished for the right words that would ease hi
pain, but there were none and she had to content hersel
with touching his arm.

"The irony of it all was that it didn't matter. Sure,
would've wanted my own kid, but I would've brought u
Jennifer's baby as if it were my own. But it was too late."

"And that's when you gave up on love and marriage?"
Chandra asked, her heart aching, her fingers still grippin
his forearm.

He slanted a glance down at her. "I think a man who
so involved with his work has no right to ask a woman t
be a part of his life."

"You're wrong," she whispered. "Oh, you're s
wrong." Moved by his agony, she threw her arms aroun
him and kissed his lips. "You would make a wonderf
husband and a terrific father!" Then, realizing what she'
said, she dropped her arms and swallowed hard.

"Why, Ms. Hill," he drawled, his eyes sparkling, "is the
a proposal?"

"I already told you, I'm not interested in getting ma
ried," she said quickly, a flood of embarrassment washin
crimson up her neck. How could she have done anything s
rash? This entire evening had been an exhibition in throw
ing away her self-control. What was happening to her?

"But *I* should be ready to walk down the aisle again?
He laughed without a trace of mirth, and she realized the
the two women in his life who should have loved him, h
mother and his wife, had hurt him so badly, he might nev
trust another woman again.

"You know, Chandra," he was saying, still discussin
marriage, "there's a saying that what's good for the ga
der is good for the goose. Or something like that." H
picked a stick from her hair, and she smoothed a wrinkl
from his shirt, wondering what marriage to him would b
like. Would there be long days of comfortable familiarit
or passionate nights of lovemaking and unexplored emo
tions?

"What about you?" he asked suddenly, and her insides turned to jelly. "I bared my soul. Tell me about your ex-husband."

Chandra wanted to tell him everything, but found the words difficult. "He was a doctor," she finally said, and Dallas froze, his face instantly serious.

"Was he the reason you dropped out of medical school?"

"I, uh, really didn't drop out," she said, then at his look of amazement, shook her head. "I can't talk about it, but Doug was and is a major reason that I decided to give up my practice."

Dallas's hand covered hers. "Whatever happened," he said gently, and Chandra felt tears prick her eyes, "it was a mistake. Whatever he did, it was wrong."

"You don't know—"

"No, but my guess is that you're a helluva doctor."

She blushed, and blinked back tears. "Come on, O'Rourke," she said, eyeing the darkening sky and sensing that they'd said enough for one evening. Someday she'd tell him everything, but not tonight. She didn't want to ruin this night with more bitter memories. "We'd better go while it's still light."

They rode back to her house in relative silence. The forest seemed to close around them, and dusk sent long, purple shadows through the woods. Even Sam seemed to pick up on the mood, and he followed behind Brandy, keeping to the trail, never bounding off into the undergrowth.

By the time they returned to the house, the first stars winked in the sky. The temperature had dropped several degrees with the coming night. Together, Chandra and Dallas took care of the horses, removing the saddles, blankets and bridles, and brushing the animals down. Dallas forked hay into the manger while Chandra filled the water trough and measured out oats.

Max, grinding his ration of grain, nuzzled her chest. "Oh, you think you should get some special favors, do

you?'' she asked, chuckling, then found apples for each
eager set of lips.

Once the horses were cared for, Dallas and Chandra
walked across the yard to the house. The moon had risen
and offered a silvery light to the shadowed hills.

Chandra asked Dallas in for coffee, and it felt natural to
sit with him at the table, cradling cups, watching the steam
rise. He was silent, brooding about something, and yet the
silence was companionable. An unspoken question lingered between them—just how far would this relationship
take them? Was this to be only a one-night stand? An affair? Or a lifetime together?

The coffee was nearly gone when Dallas scraped his chair
back. "So where do we go from here?" he asked, his gaze
roving through the small rooms and up the stairs to the loft
where her bed was visible through the slats of the railing.

"Do we have to make a plan?" She held her empty cup
in a death grip and stared into the stain on the bottom of
the earthenware as if she could read the future from the
dregs of her coffee. But she knew that they couldn't just let
things lie as they were.

Yet, they hardly knew each other. One afternoon of
making love hardly seemed enough of a basis to plan a future together.

"You told me once that you were in the market for a
husband.''

"That was a joke—''

"Kind of a joke,'' he said, his gaze holding hers. "You
were half-serious.''

The air seemed to grow cooler yet. Chandra rubbed her
arms. The conversation was making turns she hadn't expected, turns she wasn't certain she could deal with. But she
had to be honest with him. "Well...actually I'm in the
market for a father for J.D. If I adopt him, and I intend to
I'll need a father figure for him, or so my attorney insists.
So being a husband would probably be secondary,'' she

admitted, hating the awful truth, but knowing it had to be said.

"That could get messy." He glanced out the window to the night beyond the glass before returning his gaze to her. "J.D.'s dad—whomever you choose—might not like me hanging around."

So he wasn't interested. Of course not. What had she expected? she silently chided herself. A proposal? "I suppose not." She tried to hide the disappointment in her voice and refused to back down. She gambled, wondering if she'd lost every last ounce of her sanity. "You told me that you wanted children. And J.D. does need a father—a father he can depend upon, a father to love him." She rotated the cup in her hands and, gathering all her courage, looked Dallas steadily in the eyes. "This could be an opportunity of a lifetime—for both of you."

"Are you propositioning me?" he asked, but there wasn't a glimmer of humor in his eyes.

Why not? she thought, her palms beginning to sweat. "I—I think that getting married for the sake of the baby wouldn't be such a bad idea," she said. "People marry for much worse reasons. And it—it wouldn't have to be forever. You said that if your wife's baby hadn't been yours, you still would have raised it as your own. Well, J.D. doesn't even have a biological father."

Dallas gazed at her face. "What that boy needs is two parents who love each other, two people who will provide a stable life for him."

"No baby is assured of that," she said boldly.

He rubbed his palms on his pants. He appeared more nervous than usual. "I'll be honest with you. I don't know if I can change, Chandra. I was sure that I'd never marry again, never have children. Hell, until today, I was convinced that I should avoid you."

"And now?" she asked breathlessly, her own hands sweaty around her empty cup.

"And now you've nearly convinced me to take the plunge. I'm on the verge of doing something we might regret for the rest of our lives." He held her gaze for what seemed a lifetime, staring at her as if measuring her. "This is absolute madness."

"I don't think so." Good God, was she actually saying this—trying to convince him to walk down the aisle with her? Why? Just for J.D., or did she feel a pang of guilt for making love with Dallas this afternoon? Or were there deeper reasons still, reasons she couldn't yet confront? She studied the handsome lines of his face and knew in an instant that she wasn't speaking from remorse. No, she liked Dr. O'Rourke and thought living with him wouldn't be unpleasant. He evoked emotions within her she didn't want to analyze, so she justified marrying him by telling herself it was all for the baby.

Dallas shoved his hands into his pockets, but he never stopped staring at her. "I don't know if it would work— hell, I'm half-certain it won't, but I'm willing to marry you—for the sake of the child, to help you win custody. Because I don't think that kid could find a better mother."

Time stood still. The clock by the front door was ticking loudly. Here was her chance. He was offering to marry her for J.D.'s sake. And hers. A thousand doubts, like dark moths, flitted through her mind. She ignored them. Touched, she swallowed back the tears that formed in the corners of her eyes. "You—you don't have to be so noble."

He snorted, and the muscles of his shoulders bunched. "Noble? I've never done a noble thing in my life."

"But...this..." She shook her head, and he touched the tip of her chin, raising her face with one long, insistent finger.

"There's a benefit for me, too, you know."

She was afraid to ask, but a warning sensation swept through her, chilling her blood.

"I'll be making love to you every night, and that's worth something. In fact, it's worth a lot." He smiled then, softening the blow.

Nonetheless, all of her romantic fantasies turned to dust. He only wanted to sleep with her. Nothing more. And yet there were times when his gentleness nearly broke her heart.

"I just want you to understand," he said softly, "that I'm not going to accept anything in name only. I won't expect you to cook or clean or pamper me, but I'll want you in my bed. And I'll want to know the truth about your past and the baby."

That seemed more than fair—if a little cold. Gathering her courage, Chandra lifted her chin and met his gaze with hers. If he had the right to bargain, so, she reasoned, did she. "Fair enough," she agreed, her voice shaking. She couldn't believe she was discussing *marriage,* for crying out loud. She'd sworn off men and marriage, and here she was bargaining.

Not exactly the silken thread from which romantic dreams were woven. "But, if you marry me, I'll expect you to be faithful."

His lips moved slightly, and he cocked a dubious eyebrow. "A tough request, Ms. Hill," he mocked, "since I've been celibate for three years. It'll be damned hard to give up all that womanizing. Nonetheless, you've got yourself a deal."

With that, he took her hand and drew her to her feet. Rounding the table, he yanked her toward him, deftly swept her into his arms and carried her up the stairs, sealing their bargain with a kiss.

Chapter Eleven

Marriage. The word rattled around in Chandra's brain until a headache threatened the back of her eyes. And to think how she'd practically gotten down on her knees and begged him to marry her! Good Lord, was she going out of her mind? The idea of marrying him for J.D.'s sake had seemed so right last night. Curled in his arms as she'd tried to sleep, she'd known she'd made the right decision. But this morning, with dawn streaking the hills and the soft call of a morning bird in the distance, she told herself she was crazy. She couldn't marry Dallas. Not even for J.D. Or could she?

She hadn't turned on any lights as she'd crept down stairs to stand at the window, steam from her coffee roll ing across her face as she gazed at the sunrise, blazing magenta in the distance. Dallas was now awake and in the shower. A few minutes earlier, he'd leaned over the rail and playfully suggested that she might join him. She'd de clined, telling him she had to feed the horses, but glancing up at him and catching a glimpse of his naked, well-muscled torso, corded shoulders, beard-darkened chin and blue eyes, she'd almost given in. "Your loss," he'd said with a flash of white teeth, and she'd believed him.

But she had needed time to sort through everything in her mind. Yes, she wanted the baby. Desperately. But to marry a man who wasn't in love with her? What kind of future would a loveless marriage bring? For herself? For J.D.? For Dallas?

Upstairs, the water was still running, but soon she'd have to face him again. And do what? Say last night was a big mistake? Surely he had misgivings—second thoughts?

She gulped her coffee and it burned the back of her throat. "Come on." She whistled quietly to Sam, then, snagging her denim jacket from a peg by the door, set off across the yard. Her boots crunched in the gravel and made footprints on the frost. The air was clear with the sharp bite of autumn. A few dry leaves blew from the trees and danced across the drive.

She shoved open the barn door, and Max nickered eagerly. "Hungry?" she asked, snapping on the lights as the smell of horses, dung, leather and dry hay greeted her. "Stupid question, eh? When are you *not* famished?"

Max snorted. The horses were anxious, pawing or snorting, liquid brown eyes trained on her. "Breakfast's coming," she promised as Brandy shoved her velvet-soft muzzle over the stall. Cayenne eyed Chandra as well, and the other horses nickered softly. "Yeah, you guys all know I got myself into a lot of trouble yesterday, don't you?"

She climbed the loft and kicked down a couple of bales, only to hear the barn door open. "Chandra?" Dallas asked, and the horses swung their attention toward the noise.

"Up here." She hopped down and pulled out her knife, slashing the twine as Dallas grabbed a pitchfork and began scooping hay into the manger.

"I thought maybe you'd run out on me," he said, his eyes dark in the barn. "I figured you might have come down with a case of cold feet."

No reason to lie. "Second thoughts."

Dallas threw another forkful into Max's manger, and his shoulders moved effortlessly beneath his shirt. Chandra's throat went dry at the thought of touching his arms and running her fingers along the ridge of his spine.

"You don't have to go through with it, you know."

"I just don't want to make a mistake." She found the grain barrel, scooped up oats with an old coffee can and began pouring the grain along the trough.

"It's your decision, Chandra," he said slowly.

"Doubts, Doctor?" she accused as she patted Cayenne's head. The sorrel gelding tossed his mane and dug his nose into the grain.

Dallas lifted a shoulder. "It's one thing to be spontaneous, but I'm not sure we really thought this out last night." As Chandra walked past him toward the grain barrel again, he touched her lightly on the shoulder, forcing her to meet his gaze. "Believe it or not, I think we can make this work, but it is a little premature. So let's take things a little slower—one step at a time. Then if either party changes his or her mind, no big deal. We'll call the whole thing off."

Relief surged through her, and it must have been evident in her face, because he laughed.

"You know, Ms. Hill, this was your idea. I'd be satisfied with a hot and heavy affair."

Her cheeks burned hotly. "But that wouldn't help J.D."

A hint of a darker emotion flickered in his eyes, and his mouth tightened slightly. He dropped his hand and started shoving the rest of the hay into the manger. As he hung the pitchfork on the wall, he spotted a mousetrap, tripped, without a victim. "You need a cat," he observed.

"You have one?"

He shook his head. "Animals complicate life."

"So how're you going to deal with a wife and child?"

"And a dog and a small herd of horses," he added, resetting the trap and placing a piece of grain on the trip. "That's the hundred-thousand-dollar question, isn't it? Too bad I don't have any answer. What about you, Ms. Hill, how're you going to deal with a husband and a child?"

"The child will be easy," she predicted, his good mood infectious. She couldn't help teasing him a little. "But that husband—he's gonna be trouble. I can feel it in my bones."

His grin widened slowly. "You'd better believe it." Quick as a cat, he grabbed her and yanked her, squealing and laughing, into his arms. "Somehow, I think you'll find a way," he whispered, just before his lips crashed down on hers in a kiss that melted her knees.

When he finally lifted his head, he stared long into her eyes. "Yes," he said, as if answering some questions in his own mind, "this is going to be interesting. Very interesting." He glanced at his watch and groaned. "We'd better get moving. I've got to be at the hospital by eight. And you've got a wedding to plan."

Chandra didn't know whether to laugh or cry.

"You're getting married?" Roy Arnette's jaw dropped open. "What is this, some kind of joke?" Seated behind his desk, he'd been surprised by her visit, and was even more surprised when she'd told him her intentions.

"No joke, Roy," she assured him, declining comment on the fact that Dallas, only three hours earlier, had given her an out, should she want one.

"Hell, Chandra, you *can't* just up and marry someone for that kid."

"Isn't that what you told me to do?"

"But I was *kidding!*" Sitting on his side of his desk, he yanked on his string tie. "You told me you weren't dating anyone."

"I wasn't."

"And what—the bridegroom fairy came in, waved a magic wand and, poof, instant husband and father?" Frowning, he pushed an intercom button and ordered coffee from his secretary. "Well, tell me, who's the lucky guy?"

"Dallas O'Rourke."

"*Doctor* Dallas O'Rourke? You can't be serious! After what happened to you with Doug—he was a doctor, remember? That was part of the problem—so now you're planning to marry an emergency-room physician? Come on!"

"I'm serious," she insisted. "Look, don't blame yourself. This is my decision."

"What do you know about the guy?" he asked, shaking his head. "What?"

A soft tap at the door announced the secretary's arrival. With a smile to Chandra, she placed a tray laden with coffee cups, a plastic carafe, a small basket of doughnuts and a folded newspaper on his desk. "Thanks, Betty," Roy said as the tall woman poured them each a cup of coffee.

Roy offered her a doughnut, but Chandra shook her head and the attorney, too, left the pastries untouched. He took a long sip from his cup and said, "All right, let's start over. When are you getting married?"

"We haven't discussed it yet," she admitted. "In fact, we haven't exactly ironed out many details. I'm meeting him tonight at the hospital, and he's taking me over to the Newells'."

"The sheriff? You're going to see the sheriff?"

"J.D. is being released today. The Newells have been granted temporary custody as foster parents." Chandra reached for her cup and caught a glimpse of the folded newspaper. Her heart did a somersault. "Oh, no," she said, snatching up the paper and snapping it open. On the front page in big bold letters the headline read, MYSTERY BABY FOUND IN BARN, and near the article were two pictures, one of the barn, the other of her and Dallas, his arm around her shoulder, his mouth pressed close to her ear.

She quickly read the article, which was more informative than the one single-column report that had appeared the day after the baby was found. She and Dallas were identified, in the caption under the picture, and though nothing was blatantly stated, there was an insinuation that she and he, the woman who had discovered the baby and the physician who had first examined him, were romantically involved. There was a plea, within the text, for the real parents of the child to come forward and claim him.

Her heart wrenched painfully. "No," she whispered to herself. "Not now!"

"What? Not now what?"

She handed the paper to Roy, and he scowled as he skimmed the article. "Well, this isn't too bad. Fillmore isn't known to be overly kind with his pen, so you'd better consider yourself lucky. At least it isn't a hatchet job, and since you and Dallas are planning to tie the knot, I don't see that there's any real harm done."

Perhaps not, but Chandra felt as if someone had just placed a curse on her. That was crazy, of course. She wasn't even the kind of woman who believed in curses or voodoo or omens. And yet, her skin crawled as she stared down at the photo of her and Dallas huddled together, consoling each other . . . and falling in love.

"Bastard!" Dallas slammed the newspaper into the trash basket in the staff lounge, causing more than a few heads to turn and gaze speculatively in his direction. He didn't really give a damn. He didn't blame Fillmore for the article; the baby was news. Big news. But the picture of Chandra and him was hardly necessary.

He'd only been at the hospital half an hour and already he'd noticed a few sidelong glances cast his way, a couple of smirks hidden not quite quickly enough. It had started with Ed Prescott. As Dallas had locked the door of his truck in the parking lot, Prescott had wheeled his red Porche into his reserved spot.

"Well, O'Rourke, you old dog," he'd said as he climbed out of the sporty little car and caught up with Dallas's impatient strides. "You made the front page."

"What?" Dallas hadn't seen the paper yet as the weekly *Banner* was usually delivered by mail.

"Haven't you seen it?" Laughter had danced in Prescott's keen eyes. "Here, take my copy!" He'd slapped the newspaper into Dallas's hands and walked briskly toward the building. Prescott's chortling laughter had trailed back to Dallas as he'd opened the folded pages and found his life unraveled in, of all places, the *Banner.*

"Stupid idiot son-of-a-bitch," he growled now, wondering if he were leveling the oath at Prescott or himself. And just wait until Fillmore got wind of the fact that he and Chandra were getting married and hoping to adopt J.D. He'd never hear the end of it!

At the elevator, he waited impatiently, pushing the button several times and opening and closing his fists to relieve some tension. "Come on, come on," he muttered as the elevator stopped and three young nurses emerged.

They saw him, and nearly as one, tried to smother grins as they mouthed, "Good morning, Doctor."

It was all he could do to be civil. He climbed in the car and pushed the button for the fourth floor. He'd check his patients in CICU and ICU, then retreat to the emergency room, where he was scheduled for the day. If everything was under control, he'd head up to pediatrics before J.D. was to be released. Then he'd go to his office, return some calls and check his mail. His investigator friend from Denver had called and said a package should arrive—the information about Chandra. Good Lord, what had possessed him to order an investigation?

He wasn't looking forward to scanning the P.I.'s report, and yet, he may as well. After all, he planned to marry the woman; it wouldn't hurt to know what he was in for.

Crossing his arms over his chest, he watched the numbers of the floors light up. Chandra was so enraptured with little J.D., Dallas was concerned for her. Even if he and she were married, there were no guarantees that they would be chosen as the adoptive parents. What then? Dissolve the marriage? Strike two? "Hell, O'Rourke, you've really got yourself in a mess this time!"

The elevator thudded to a halt and the doors opened. Jane Winthrop, a nurse who usually worked in admitting, was waiting for the car. Pushing a medicine cart, she nearly ran into him. "Oh, Doctor," she said with a smile. "Excuse me."

Was there a special gleam in her eye? Of course not. He was just being paranoid. "No problem," he replied, skirting the cart with the tiny cups of pills arranged neatly on the shiny metal surface.

"I saw your picture in the paper today," she said, and he jerked his head up to meet her eyes, but found no malice in her gaze. "I sure hope that Chandra Hill gets to adopt that baby. He belongs with her, you know. That's why he was in that barn. It's God's will."

The doors closed, and Nurse Winthrop, her cart and her wisdom disappeared.

Rubbing the tension building in his neck, Dallas turned toward ICU and knew that it was going to be a long day. He decided to go directly to his office and only stopped by his receptionist's desk to collect his mail.

There it was, along with the letters, advertisements and magazines—a package with a Denver postmark. His heart stopped for just a second, and he felt guilty as hell, but he took the stack of mail and a fresh cup of coffee into his office. He set the coffee on the ink blotter and dropped the correspondence and bills onto the desk, then ripped his letter opener through the package from Denver.

He couldn't believe he was so anxious that his stomach had begun to knot. There was a computer report, a note from Jay and a few copies of newspaper clippings, mainly of a trial in Tennessee, a malpractice suit brought by the parents of Gordy Shore, a boy who had died while in Chandra's care.

Dallas let his coffee grow cold as he continued to read, and he learned more than he wanted to know about his future wife.

"A shoot down the south fork, a trail ride over Phantom Ridge and a day hike along the west bank of the river," Rick said, eyeing his schedule. He tapped his finger on the last expedition. "Chandra, you can handle the day hike. Randy's got the trail ride, and Jake will take our friends from Boston down the river. All right with you?"

"Fine," she agreed as Jake and Randy began packing gear for their expeditions.

"Good, then I'll hold down the fort here."

Chandra eyed the younger men. Jake was tall and strapping with wheat-blond hair, a tan and blue eyes that cut a person right to the quick. Randy was more laid-back, with a moustache, day's growth of beard and red-brown hair a little on the shaggy side. She turned to see Rick staring at her, his expression uncharacteristically serious. These men, who often joked with her, were the only family Chandra had in Ranger.

"Saw your picture in the paper," Randy said as he tucked trail mix and a couple of candy bars into a backpack. The horses were stabled out of town, so he would meet his clients, drive to the stables and start the ride from that point.

"I hope you're not talkin' 'bout that damned *Banner,*" Rick growled, frowning.

"'Fraid so. Chandra's big news around this town," Randy teased. "You and the doctor looked pretty chummy to me."

"We are," she said with a shrug.

"And here I thought you'd always had the hots for me, but were just too shy to make the first move."

"If only I'd known," she quipped. These men could tease her and needle her because she knew they cared. Once she'd proved herself on the river, they'd both taken on the roles of brothers.

"I just hope O'Rourke knows what a prize he's found," Jake said forcefully. Jake was always more serious than Randy.

"Dallas O'Rourke?" Rick asked. Still behind the desk, he absently counted out the cash, the "seed money" as he called it, that he kept in the safe at night before replenishing the till each morning.

"The one and only."

"How'd you land that one?" Rick asked.

"Must have been that little sashay you took down Grizzly Loop," Randy teased.

"Get a life, Randy," Chandra said, refusing to be baited.

"And keep that rag that some people consider a newspaper out of my shop," Rick ordered. "I'd just as soon wring Bob Fillmore's neck as say hi."

Chandra spent the next hour stocking the shelves with supplies, then met her group of hikers and drove them to the foothills. They spent most of the day walking the trails that crisscrossed Rattlesnake Canyon. At noon, dusty and hot, they paused to eat at the river, then headed downstream until they'd circled back to the car. Clouds were beginning to form over the hills, and the temperature descended as she dropped her tired party off at the offices of Wild West.

For the next hour, she cleaned up and helped Rick close the shop before driving through town and along the road that led to the hospital. At five-fifteen, she dashed up the stairs to the pediatrics wing and discovered Leslie Nelson at the desk. "Is he still here?" she asked without preamble, but she knew from Leslie's sorry expression that J.D. had already been released. Fear, cold as a night wind, touched her soul. What if things didn't go as planned? What if she never saw J.D. again?

Leslie sighed unhappily. "The caseworker—what's her name—Miss Sedgewick ... She was here earlier with Sheriff Newell, and the baby was placed under his care. You know Lenore, don't you?" Chandra shook her head, and Leslie waved aside her doubts. "Well, she's just about the best person J.D. could be placed with. She *adores* kids, and since hers left home, she's been taking in strays, so to speak, kids with all sorts of problems—drugs, family breakups, abuse or runaways. She's one in a million."

"I guess I should be relieved," Chandra said. But she wasn't. She was used to finding J.D. here, and now things had changed. His little life was on its own path, out of her control....

"I think so, and I'm sure she'd let you visit J.D. as often as you want." Leslie leaned over the desk and motioned Chandra closer, as if to tell her a secret. "Just between you and me," she said confidentially, "it's a good thing he's been moved."

"Why?"

"The press! Ever since that story came out in the *Banner* this morning, the phone's been ringing off the hook. Newspaper reporters from as far away as Chicago and Seattle trying to get more information. We're routing all the calls to Dr. Trent's office—he's the chief administrator—and we're not to talk to anyone about the baby."

So the media circus had begun. Chandra's stomach turned over. "Is Dr. O'Rourke in?"

"He was in earlier—checked on a couple of patients, but I don't know his schedule."

"Thanks, Leslie." Chandra turned to leave as the phone at the nurses' station began ringing insistently. Walking on numb legs toward the wing that held the clinic and doctors' offices, Chandra hoped to find Dallas. She'd known the press would come sniffing around, of course, but she'd hoped the public wouldn't be interested.

Dallas wasn't in his office. The receptionist told her he'd be back within the half hour and that she could wait in the lounge. Chandra tried, but the chairs were too uncomfortable and her thoughts were whirling. What if the reporters started digging into her past? The headlines haunted her...

Local Doctor Accused Of Malpractice
By Young Patient's Parents

"My Boy Could Have Been Saved,"
Gordy Shore's Mother Testifies

Doctor Chandra Hill Pendleton Sued By Shores

The headlines had kept coming. Doug's practice had been mentioned, as well as hers, causing a deeper rift in their marriage. Then some of Doug's patients had requested that their files be sent to other cosmetic surgeons. "This'll all blow over," Doug had said, trying to console her, but he couldn't understand the pain and guilt she felt over losing a beautiful boy and suffering the hate of his parents.

No wonder she'd taken back her maiden name and left Tennessee with all its painful memories. Perhaps leaving Collier had looked like the coward's way out, but there had been nothing left for her in Tennessee: no medical practice, no friends, no husband and certainly no children. No, it had been better to make a clean break. And she was still a physician, though unlicensed in Colorado.

Face it, she silently advised herself as she flipped through a dog-eared women's magazine that didn't hold her interest. *You're a lousy judge of character. You married Doug and became friends with Willa and Ed Shore. They all turned on you.*

And now you're planning on marrying Dallas O'Rourke. Good Lord, Chandra, will you never learn?

Bored with waiting, she watched as the receptionist answered the phone and juggled appointments. When the woman's back was turned, Chandra slipped down the hall and pushed open a door with brass letters that spelled "Dallas O'Rourke, M.D." Fortunately the door was unlocked, and Chandra, feeling just a tingle of guilt, rationalized her behavior by telling herself that she was about to become Mrs. Dallas O'Rourke. She needed a little information on the man.

The room was cluttered. A suede-and-leather jacket had been tossed carelessly over the back of one chair, and a tie dangled from the handle of the window. His desk was piled high with papers, though there did seem to be a few distinct piles, as if there were some semblance of order to the paperwork. Medical journals and encyclopedias filled a bookcase and laminated certificates were mounted over the desk. The view from his window overlooked a parking lot, and the two chairs angled near the front of his desk appeared seldom used.

A stack of mail was opened and strewed over the papers on the desk. As she quickly skimmed the letters and bills, her own name leapt out at her: "INVESTIGATIVE REPORT ON CHANDRA HILL."

Chandra's insides froze and her heart turned to ice. Her throat worked, though she couldn't speak. Surely, she'd read the heading incorrectly! She skimmed the first page and felt sick. Dallas had been checking up on her? The tightness in her chest constricted a notch as she sifted through the pages, obviously already read by Dr. O'Rourke. "Why?" she whispered. Why would he ask her to marry him and then check up on her? Or maybe it was the other way around? She found the postmark on the envelope. No. He'd only received this damned report today.

Her hands shaking, she dropped into a chair and began reading about herself, starting with her date of birth and her parents, and later, as they came along, her sisters. Her history inched its way through the pages, a listing of her accomplishments in elementary and high school, as well as in college and medical school. Even names of her friends were listed and those of a few of the men she'd dated.

Nausea churned in her stomach. Her life reduced to eighteen pages of a computer printout, including copies of the newspaper articles about her, her credit history, her health and her marriage and divorce from Doug.

Her stay in Ranger was tagged on at the end, listing Rick as her boss. The first story in the *Banner* about J.D., which had been published just last week, was the final entry.

"Oh, God," she whispered, dropping her head into her hands. How could she ever face Dallas again? Mortified and furious, she clamped her jaw and bit down hard in order to get control of herself. She couldn't let him reduce her to the rubble she'd once been. Never again would she feel this way! She forced her pain to shift to anger. It wasn't hard. She was beyond furious. If and when she ever set eyes on Dallas again, she'd tear him limb from limb! Who did he think he was, sneaking around behind her back, digging up her life to file it neatly onto some private investigator's computer disk?

The door opened, and she twisted her head to find Dallas striding into the room. His eyes dropped to the report in her hands and he sucked in his breath. "What're you doing in my office?"

Chandra stood slowly, dropping the report and pushing herself upright. He was standing in the doorway, his shoulders nearly touching the frame, his face unreadable.

She didn't care how big or intimidating he was. Rage scorched her blood. How could he—this man she'd planned to marry—do this to her? Inching up her chin, she picked up the horrid pages and waved the report in the air. "And what are you doing checking up on me?"

"You're supposed to wait in the lounge."

"Stupid me! I thought being your fiancé gave me a few privileges."

"Not snooping in my office."

"But it's okay for you to snoop into my life, is that right?" She slapped the damned report onto his desk. "How *dare* you have me investigated like some criminal!

Who do you think you are that you can open up my life and check me out? I thought—no, I hoped—you were above that sort of thing!''

A muscle in the corner of Dallas's jaw came to life, but there was no anger in his eyes. ''What did you expect, Chandra?''

''Trust!'' she shot back, and he winced.

''And I expected the truth, which you seemed to twist around to suit your advantage.''

''I did not—''

''You came waltzing in here with a baby whom you claim you've never set eyes on before and a load of medical knowledge. And you ended up turning this hospital upside down—''

''I've done no such thing!''

Dallas snorted, his face a steely mask. ''You read the headlines today in the *Banner?*''

''Yes, but—''

''You see the picture?''

''What, exactly, is your point?'' she asked, leveling a glacial stare at him.

''I just wanted to know whom I was dealing with.''

''Because you thought I might have stolen the baby, then, seeing he needed medical attention, brought him in here?''

''At first, yes, but—''

''Well, you're way off base, Doctor!''

''I know that now.'' Unbuttoning his lab coat, Dallas dragged one hand through his thick hair. ''But I didn't— not in the beginning.''

''And you check up on any person you've never met before?''

''Any person I think I might marry.''

She stiffened. Marriage? Now? After this damned report? She didn't think so. ''When you ordered that investigation, you couldn't have had the faintest idea we might discuss the remote idea of wedded bliss!'' She shook her head, disbelieving that their relationship had come to this.

She was trembling inside, her breathing erratic, and she went to the window to open it a crack and let in some fresh air. "You really are a bastard, O'Rourke," she said quietly.

A cold smile crept across his lips. "Coming from you, that's quite an indictment. Your résumé—" he motioned to the damning report "—is chock full of deadbeats. Especially your ex-husband."

She felt as if she'd been slapped. "A failing of mine, I guess. I just can't say no when a real jerk asks me to marry him!"

"*You* asked me, lady. Not the other way around." He flung the white jacket over an already crowded spoke of a brass hall tree before glancing at her again.

Chandra felt the color drain from her face. "You arrogant son of a—"

"Don't," he cut in. "Let's not sink to name-calling. *Bastard* and *jerk* were good enough. I got the message."

That was it. She'd had it! She grabbed her purse and started for the door. He reached for her arm, but she spun away from him.

"Chandra, wait!" Her hand was on the doorknob, and she, ignoring him, yanked hard.

With a curse, he slammed the door closed. "Don't go—"

She turned frigid eyes on him. "Don't you have some patients to see or, at the very least, some new person in your life that you can sic a private detective on?"

"There's only one new person in my life," he admitted.

"Meaning me?" she spat. "Well, scratch me off the list. I'm not into the humiliation game, okay? I don't hang out with people who dredge up my dirt." She sighed loudly, trying to rein in her galloping rage. With difficulty, she stared into his cobalt blue eyes—eyes that seemed to see into the darkest corners of her heart. "It's too bad, you know," she said shakily. "Maybe if you'd grown up with a little love, if someone had cared for you, you'd know how to care back, how to treat people, how to—'' She stopped suddenly when she saw the raw pain in his eyes. She knew then that she'd hit her mark, that she'd wounded him as deeply as he'd hurt her.

Stonily, he stepped away from the door. ''I don't think we have anything more to discuss,'' he said, his voice flat. He moved to the desk, snatched up the damaging report and held it out to her. ''You can have this.''

Why did she suddenly feel like a heel? She was in the right, damn it! She snatched the report from his hands, but felt the overwhelming need to apologize. She knew she had a sharp tongue, but she didn't usually try to cut someone she cared for so deeply. ''Look, I'm sorry. That crack about your family—was . . . uncalled-for . . .''

''Don't worry about it.'' He sat down in his chair and picked up the telephone receiver, staring at her impatiently, waiting for her to leave.

Sighing, she wadded up the damned report and tossed it into a wastebasket near his desk. ''Can't we start this afternoon over?'' she said, her fury spent.

''Why?''

''Because there's more to us than what's contained in some investigator's printout.''

He dropped the receiver. ''Let's not delude ourselves, okay? What we've got is a baby—that's all. He's our one common bond. Unless you want to count sex.''

Swallowing hard, she glanced through the window to the traffic moving steadily in and out of the parking lot. He was right, of course. Though she'd like to think that love was involved, it wasn't. Love, as far as Dallas O'Rourke was concerned, didn't exist. She'd have to settle for this man who didn't love her, so that she could become J.D.'s mother.

''Well, as long as we understand each other,'' she said, managing to keep her voice steady.

''You still want to marry me?'' he asked, squinting at her, as if looking for flaws.

"I still need a father for J.D."

Dallas drummed his fingers on his desk and pulled his forehead into a frown of disgust. Chandra felt as if her life were on a balance, slowly wobbling, and she was unable to right it.

"I guess I shouldn't have checked up on you," he finally said. "But I thought, when you first brought J.D. to the emergency room, that you could have stolen him or that you were covering for the real mother—that you had a sister or cousin who was in trouble. Believe it or not, I just wanted to help, and I had to be sure that the story you were giving me wasn't a line."

"And now?"

He slid a glance to the wastebasket. "I think the report's filed in the appropriate slot. All I need to know now is that you're playing straight with me."

"I've never lied to you."

"Except about your practice."

"Well, now you know."

"Not everything, Chandra."

"I—I'll tell you about it," she said nervously, her hands beginning to sweat. "But not now. Trust me on this?"

His jaw slid to one side, and as he stood, he retrieved his leather jacket from the hall tree.

"For God's sake, Dallas, don't you trust anyone?" she asked, hating the silence that was radiating from him. She knew why he had trouble trusting people. God knew that she hadn't been completely honest with him herself, and yet she hoped that he would give her the benefit of the doubt.

He slid his arms into his leather jacket, adjusted the collar and looked at her. His features had lost some of their severity, but he didn't smile. "I'm trying," he admitted, "but it's not easy." He walked to the door and held it open for her. Then, as if to leave the argument behind them in the office, he asked, "Okay, it's confession time, how did you get past the sergeant?"

"The what?"

"Dena—the receptionist. She takes her job seriously."

"I've worked in hospitals," Chandra explained. "And your door was unlocked."

"My mistake," he said, smiling crookedly. "Well, one of my mistakes. I seem to be making more than my share lately." He reached forward and took her hand in his. "Come on," he said with a slow smile. "I think there's someone waiting to see you."

"J.D.?" Her heart soared.

"Mmm." He tugged on her hand and led her out of the office before locking the door. "High crime element in the neighborhood," he explained with a glimmer in his eyes. "You never know who you'll catch prowling around."

"Very funny."

"I thought so." He guided her through the corridors to an exterior exit. "Oh, by the way, I thought we'd get dinner first, then visit your friend. But we have one stop first."

"A stop?"

"City Hall. I think we'd better stop by and apply for a marriage license. Unless you're chickening out."

"Me? Chicken out?" she asked, her heart racing. This was it. Her out. If she only dared take it. She licked her lips nervously as she stared into his incredible blue eyes. "No way."

Chapter Twelve

Lenore Newell couldn't have been more delighted with company, or so it seemed to Chandra. She insisted Chandra drink a glass of iced tea while she held the baby. Lenore prattled on and on about the children she'd cared for over the years. The living room of the Newell home, a quaint two-storied farmhouse flanked by a wide front porch, was filled with pictures of children, dozens of them, some who had only stayed a few weeks, others who had lived with the Newells for years.

Over the fireplace, a family portrait, showing Lenore and Frank some twenty years younger and surrounded by four beaming-faced boys, gave testament to the Newells' strong family ties and the house itself seemed cozy and warm.

The furniture in the living room was upholstered in well-worn floral prints that matched a circular rug. Crocheted cloths covered the end tables, and a cuckoo clock near the chimney chirped the hours.

"He's just as sweet as he can be," Lenore said, touching J.D.'s cheek with her finger. The baby, sleeping in Chandra's arms, yawned, then snuggled closer. "I just can't imagine anyone in her right mind giving him up." She glanced over at Dallas, who was standing near an upright piano littered with more photographs of children and teenagers. "Frank says no one's come in to claim him yet. Can you believe that?"

"Hard to," Dallas drawled.

Lenore sighed. "Well, the child's better off with a family who loves him!" She sat in a chair next to the rocker in which Chandra was holding the baby. "Are you thinking of trying to adopt him?"

The question didn't surprise Chandra. Surely Lenore had guessed how close she felt to the baby. "I hope to."

"Good! This child needs a mother." She turned her gaze back to Dallas, and added with a crafty wink, "He could use a father, as well, you know."

"We're already a couple of steps ahead of you, Lenore," Dallas confided, slouching against the upright.

"Are you?" She arched her eyebrows in anticipation of a little small-town gossip. Dallas didn't give her any more details, but Chandra, sending him a murderous look, decided Lenore had the right to know everything.

"Dallas and I plan to be married."

Lenore's mouth rounded, and she couldn't hide the surprise and ultimate delight in her eyes. "Married!" She turned to Dallas for confirmation, but received only a noncommittal shrug. "Don't tell me Dr. Ice is melting."

"Very funny, Lenore," Dallas observed with a dry smile as the screen door squeaked on rusted hinges and Frank Newell, tall and whip-lean, strode into the foyer.

"In here—we've got company," his wife sang out. "There's beer and iced tea in the fridge."

Frank paused under the arch that separated the living room from the foyer. "Well, Doctor," he said with a widespread grin at the sight of Dallas. He motioned to the glass of iced tea in Dallas's hand. "Can't I buy you anything stronger?"

"This'll do."

"You'll never guess what!" Lenore said, bustling to her feet and heading past her husband toward the kitchen. Her footsteps retreated, but her voice still carried. "Dallas and Chandra are going to get married and adopt the baby! How is that for perfect?"

"Is that so?" Frank asked, frowning and looking suddenly tired.

"That's the plan."

"For you and about six hundred other couples."

"*What?*" Lenore asked. Carrying a tray laden with two bottles of beer, a pitcher of tea, pretzels and cookies, she bustled back to the living room.

Chandra felt icicles form in her heart. "Others?"

"The phones down at the station have been ringing off the hook. Seems the story in the *Banner* got picked up by the news services and now we've got TV and newspaper reporters calling in every damn minute, along with attorneys and people wanting to adopt as faraway as San Francisco. From what I hear, the same thing's going on at Riverbend."

The bottom dropped out of Chandra's world. She felt Dallas's gaze on her as she involuntarily held J.D. more tightly. She couldn't give him up. Wouldn't. Desperation wrenched her heart, and it was all she could do to sit and rock instead of scooping the baby into her arms and fleeing. A lump filled her throat, and she sent up a silent prayer that she be given the privilege of raising this precious child.

Frank twisted open a bottle of beer. "I'm surprised the press hasn't camped out in the front yard, but I suppose it's only a matter of time." He took a long swallow and sighed, his kind eyes resting on Chandra. "You won't be out of this, you know. Bob Fillmore and the *Banner* were just the tip of the iceberg. For the next few weeks, Miss Hill, I'm afraid you'll be hounded."

"There are laws about trespassing," she said.

"And we'll uphold them. But your phone will be ringing non-stop. They've already named this guy, you know." He nodded toward the baby. "Some reporter in Denver got wind of the fact that several couples are trying to bid for him. Our Baby John Doe is now the Million Dollar Baby."

Chandra's heart turned to stone, and Lenore protested, "He can't be raffled off like some prize quilt at a county fair!"

"I know. It's just a gimmick. But I don't think this is going to blow over." Frank offered Dallas a beer, but the doctor declined. "And I suppose you'll get your share of the press as well, O'Rourke. Yep—" he shook his head slowly before draining half his bottle "—we're all in for a lot of fun."

Frank Newell was right. By the time Chandra arrived home that night, her answering-machine light was blinking, and the tape was filled with the names and telephone numbers of local reporters as well as a call from a couple in Salt Lake City. Chandra suspected this couple was only the first. Soon there would be a lot of couples desperately calling in hopes of adopting J.D.

"Fat chance," she muttered. The only people she telephoned were her parents. They deserved to hear what was going on in her life from her own lips.

Her mother answered and shouted for Chandra's father to pick up the bedroom extension. "I can understand you wanting the baby," her mother rambled on. "God knows you've wanted a child forever, but what about this doctor fellow? How can you be sure that marrying him won't be a mistake? Oh, well, I don't want to discourage you, honey, it's just that I don't want to see you hurt again."

"I won't be, Mom," Chandra said, winding the telephone cord around her wrist and leaning against the kitchen counter.

"Of course she won't, Jill," Chandra's father cut in. "Chandra knows what she's doing. I'm behind you one hundred percent, girl."

"Well...well...well, so am I," her mother stuttered. "I just think you can take this slow, you know, make sure. You've got the rest of your life—"

"Not if she wants to adopt that baby—"

"Do whatever you think is best," Jill said, sounding irritated with her husband. "And know you've got our blessing. If you tell us when the wedding's scheduled, we'll be there!"

"With bells on," Chandra's father added.

"That I don't know," Chandra replied. They talked a little longer, about everything and nothing, her father asking about her job, her mother sneaking in questions about Dallas. Finally, with both parents in agreement at last that their daughter was old enough to make her own decisions, they hung up and Chandra turned on the answering machine. Whistling to Sam, she walked outside to the small garden, where a few tomatoes still ripened on the vine and the golden tassels on the corn stirred in the breeze. On the other side of the garden was the orchard where pears and apples littered the ground, beyond which were the forested hills. This small ranch would be a perfect place to raise a child, she thought, her heart tearing at the prospect of losing J.D.

And what about Dallas? What would be the point of marrying him when they had no child to hold them together? *You could have other children, Dallas's children.* If he were willing. And there weren't any guarantees that they would be able to conceive. All the advertisements seeking adoptable children were proof enough of the infertility rate. The thought of carrying Dallas's child nearly brought tears to her eyes. For years, she'd given up on the dream of having her own children, and now, with Dallas, it was possible, and what a wonderful baby they could make together. Her throat was suddenly clogged with unshed tears. Dallas's baby! Oh, God, how perfect! Absently, she rubbed her abdomen. A brother or sister for J.D....

She pulled a weed from the garden and tossed it over the fence. Would she be willing to marry Dallas without the prospect of a child? Without J.D.? She cared for him, perhaps even loved him, but was it enough? She felt confused and frustrated and wanted to do something, *anything* to ensure that the baby would be hers. Sitting around and waiting was killing her. *Calm down,* she told herself. She felt the breath of night as the sun sank below the horizon. Would Dallas ever want her to be a part of his life without the baby?

"Oh, God, what a mess," she said with a sigh as she climbed onto the split-rail fence separating garden from orchard. She sat quietly, watching the sky darken in shades of rose and purple. An owl, hunting early this evening, landed in the gnarled branches of the apple tree.

Then the tranquillity was shattered by the intrusion of headlights flashing brightly on the side of the barn.

Another reporter?

She squared her shoulders and squinted against the coming darkness before she recognized Dallas's rig. Relief swelled through her. Maybe he had good news. Or bad. Her pulse thundered, and she waited until he climbed from the cab of his truck before balancing on the lower rails, waving her hands and calling to him. Sam was already bounding through the pumpkin vines and through the yard, yipping excitedly. Even the old dog had allowed Dallas into his heart.

Dallas paused to scratch Sam's ears, then glanced up, catching Chandra's gaze. His face was grim, his expression sober, and Chandra's heart dropped to her knees. Something was wrong. Horribly wrong! J.D.! She vaulted over the fence and told her racing pulse to slow. Maybe J.D. was fine, but she couldn't quiet the screams of desperation that tore through her heart.

"What is it?" she asked, forcing her voice to stay calm. She couldn't lose control. "Something's wrong. Is it J.D.?"

"The baby's fine," he assured her, but drew her into the warm circle of his arms and held her close to calm her. His breath fanned her hair and she felt the tension in his muscles.

"But there's trouble," she guessed as they stood in the rows of corn, the thick leaves rustling in the breeze.

"There could be." He took her hand and pulled her gently in the direction of the orchard, where they sat on the fence rails and stared across the valley. "My beeper went off as I was heading back here. Dr. Trent, chief of administration, wanted me to stop back by the hospital."

"And?"

"He showed me the first of what appears to be an onslaught of gifts, cards and letters for Baby Doe. One corner of his office was filled, and that's just the start. The hospital fax machine has been working overtime with pleas from barren couples from Colorado, Utah, Arizona and California who want to adopt the baby. Lawyers are calling or showing up in person, and the switchboard has been jammed, which is causing all sorts of problems for the hospital."

Her stomach somersaulted.

"Trent's not too happy about this, to say the least, and he called me in because of the article about you and me. Seems it's already gotten around the hospital that you and I are an item. And I didn't deny it. I told Trent we were getting married and hope to adopt the baby."

Chandra's heart was beating like a drum. "What did he say?"

"'Good luck,' and I quote," Dallas replied, holding one of her hands in both of his. "Trent showed me some of the requests for adoption. You wouldn't believe it. Frank was right. Some people are so desperate that they're offering gifts to the hospital, and we're not just talking peanuts. One physician and his wife from South Dakota are willing to buy some very expensive equipment for the pediatric wing."

"But that's bribery—"

"Another couple—both lawyers—offered free legal services to the hospital."

"I can't believe it."

He slung an arm over her shoulder, and his expression had become sober, his eyes dark with emotion. "I think it's time we thought about this long and hard. There's a good chance that the baby will be adopted by someone we don't know, someone who lives thousands of miles away from here."

So this was it—he was breaking up with her. And they've lost the baby. Chandra wanted to crumble into a million pieces, but she wouldn't give up without a fight.

"I don't believe all this," she argued heatedly. "I can't believe that the state or the hospital would...would stoop to blackmail!"

"It's not the hospital's decision, anyway. And a good thing. Trent always has his eyes on possible endowments. But his hands are tied. He and the hospital lawyers are just trying to figure out what to do with all the gifts that are coming in—the pediatric wing is already filled with stuffed animals."

"So we still have a chance," Chandra said, unable to calm the fear that rushed through her blood.

"If you're still willing to toss our hat into the ring."

"Absolutely!"

His lips twitched and a glint of admiration twinkled in his eyes. "I had a feeling you wouldn't back down."

"No way. We haven't lost yet."

"Well, then, I don't think we should wait. Forget the marriage license and waiting period. I think we should fly to Las Vegas tonight. The sooner we're married, the sooner we'll be able to fight this as a couple."

"You're serious?" she whispered, touched. She wanted to throw her arms around him and kiss him over and over again.

Dallas reached into his pocket and withdrew two airline tickets. His eyes never left her face. "Well, Ms. Hill, this is it. Do or die. Are we going through with this?"

Her throat closed for a second. Marriage. Just like that. A quick elopement to the tower of glitz in Nevada. So much for moonlight and roses, candlelight and wine. Romance didn't have any part of this transaction...well, at least not much. But she couldn't deny the feelings of love that were sprouting in her breast, nor could she voice them. She managed a smile. "Where would we live? What would we do—"

"We can live here—or you can move into my condo."

"No, here," she said, her mind spinning with plans for the future. "The cabin's big enough, and I need to be near the horses, and J.D. would love to live out here in the country—" She gathered in her breath and stopped. "But what do you want?"

He hesitated for a minute and drew his gaze away. "I just want to make you happy," he said, and Chandra could hardly believe her ears. This man who had told her all they had in common was the baby and sex?

"You don't have to pretend to fall in love with me," she said, and watched his eyes cloud. She rushed on. "We both know that this is only for the baby."

"And what happens if we lose him?" Dallas asked.

She sighed and her heart seemed to break into a thousand pieces. "That can't happen."

"What if it does?"

Then I'll set you free. Oh, Lord, would she be able to? Or was she falling hopelessly in love with a man who couldn't learn to give love in return? "You won't have to be obligated to me, Dallas. I'll sign whatever prenuptial agreement your lawyers come up with."

"I think it's a little late for prenuptials—that is, if you still want to get married. Well?" He stared at her so intensely that her breath was lost somewhere in her throat. "What do you say?"

"I'd say we'd better get a move on if we're going to catch our flight." She hopped lithely off the fence, determined to ignore the omnipresent doubts.

Together, they walked through the garden and into the house, where she threw her one good dress and a few essentials into a small bag. Then, making sure that her horses and Sam were fed, she climbed into Dallas's truck, and they headed to Denver where they planned to take a ten o'clock flight to Las Vegas. The way Dallas explained it, they'd married sometime after midnight, stop long enough to drink a bottle of champagne over an extremely late dinner, then catch an early-morning flight back to Denver.

They'd lose a night's sleep, but not much more as they would go to their respective jobs as Dr. and Mrs. Dallas O'Rourke tomorrow morning. Just like that. Quick and simple. She wondered what she'd tell her parents, who expected to be invited to the wedding, and her sisters, who had both shied away from marriage. Then, of course, how was she going to handle her new role as Dallas's wife? Life was suddenly becoming complicated.

As Dallas drove through the night-shrouded mountains toward Denver, she glanced at him. His profile was strong and handsome, and his eyebrows were pulled low over his eyes as he squinted against the glare of oncoming headlights.

As far as husbands went, she knew, Dallas would be better than most. Good-looking, rugged, definitely male, passionate and, for all intents and purposes, honest. And as far as their lovemaking was concerned, even now she felt goose bumps. Maybe in time he would learn to love her. They could learn together.

But she didn't kid herself. He wouldn't be easy to live with, and he did brood. His temper was as volatile as hers and as many times as she longed to make love to him, she'd just as soon strangle him.

Well, if nothing else, she decided, seeing the lights of Denver glow ethereally against the night black sky, marriage to him would never be dull.

As far as romance went, the ceremony left a lot to be desired. The minister was red eyed and drowsy, and his breath was laced liberally with liquor. He wore a clerical collar, black jacket and slippers.

His little wife, a mere slip of a woman, smiled through her yawns, and his sister, whose floral dress stretched at the seams, played piano.

Chandra, dressed in a simple pink dress, held Dallas's hand as the minister went through the ritual. Dallas seemed amused by the scene. Wearing black slacks and a white shirt, he was dressed more like a patron of the neon-lit casinos than a bridegroom.

No rings were exchanged, but upon the orders of the minister, Dallas swept Chandra into his arms and kissed her long and hard in the little chapel on the outskirts of Las Vegas.

"It doesn't seem real," Chandra observed as they walked back to the rented car, dodging traffic, that rushed by in the early-morning hours.

"We've got a signed certificate. It's legal.'

"But—"

He snorted as he opened the door of the white sedan for her. "The last time I got married, we had a bona fide church, preacher, six attendants, a three-tiered cake and all the trimmings. It didn't make for any guarantees."

Sighing, she scooted into the interior of the Plymouth. Her first wedding had been complete with a long, white, beaded gown, bridesmaids in lavender silk and ushers in matching tuxedos. A huge reception with flowing champagne, an incredible ice sculpture and hors d'oeuvres hadn't created a perfect marriage. Far from it. Dallas was right.

And yet, as she caught a glimpse of her ringless left hand, she wondered if she'd made the biggest mistake of her life.

"My folks will kill me," she said, thinking of the calls she would have to make, the questions that would be hurled at her, the explanations she'd have to repeat over and over again.

"Mine will be relieved." He started the engine and edged the Plymouth into traffic, toward the hotel where they'd registered earlier.

"Will they?"

His grin turned cynical. "Oh, sure. My mother won't have to feel guilty about not paying me enough attention, and my father will probably think now he'll finally get that grandson he thinks he's owed. I'm the last of his line of O'Rourkes."

"He'll get that grandson," she said firmly, eyeing the glitter that was Las Vegas. People spilled out of casinos, music and conversation filled the air, and the night was as bright as day, lit by a trillion watts of neon.

Dallas stopped for a red light, and in the glow, his face turned hard, his lips compressed. "Sorry to shatter your dreams, Chandra, but J.D. won't count. At least not with my father."

"He damned well better," she said, her fists clenching in determination.

"You don't know Harrison O'Rourke. He's from the old school, and J.D. won't be blood kin."

"And therefore worthless?"

"As far as the family tree goes," Dallas said, frowning as the light changed and he stepped on the accelerator. "Nope, Harrison will expect an O'Rourke son—not a daughter, mind you." He slid her a glance and grinned cynically. "So don't go disappointing him."

"Wouldn't dream of it," she said, her temper flaring at Harrison O'Rourke's antiquated ideas. "I'll tell you one thing, if and when I ever get the honor of meeting your ogre of a father, he'd better treat all our children equally—and that includes J.D. and our daughters!''

Dallas shook his head as he turned toward the hotel. ''So now we've got daughters?''

''We might!''

''Even if we don't adopt J.D.?'' he asked, turning his gaze her way for just a second.

''I—I can't think about not having J.D. Not yet,'' she said softly. She clutched the handle of her purse in a death grip and tried to think about anything other than the awful fact that little J.D.'s future was out of her hands.

Dallas drove to the rental-car parking lot of the hotel. Twenty stories high, the concrete-and-steel building glowed like the proverbial Christmas tree. A marquee announced a famous comic as the weekend's entertainment, and liveried bellboys and ushers welcomed them.

The lobby was awash with light, and a fountain spraying pink water two stories high was situated in the central foyer. Veined marble and forest green carpet covered the floor.

Chandra could hardly believe that she was actually here, married and about to spend the wee morning hours of her honeymoon in the bridal suite.

With the help of the bell captain, they were whisked to the nineteenth floor and left in a three-room suite complete with complimentary champagne, heart-shaped tub and a round bed covered with silk sheets.

''Don't you think this is overdoing it a little?'' she asked, eyeing the bed, beyond which the view of the city, lights winking endlessly, stretched into the desert.

''I thought it was the least I could do. This won't be much of a honeymoon.''

She swallowed a smile and arched a coy brow. ''You think not?'' She glanced meaningfully at the bed. ''Somehow, I think you'll find a way to make up for lost opportunities.''

"You might be right," he agreed, striding so close to her they were almost touching. Only a breath of air separated their bodies, and Chandra's pulse quickened. Slowly he surrounded her with his arms and lowered his mouth to hers. "Maybe we should open the champagne and toast the bride and groom...."

Her breath was already lost in her lungs. "Later," she whispered.

"You're sure?"

Oh, God, was that her heart thumping so loudly when he hadn't yet touched her? "Yes, Doctor," she whispered breathlessly, "I'm positive."

With a wicked grin, Dallas lifted her off her feet and carried her quickly to the bed. "You know, Mrs. O'Rourke, I like the way you think." He dropped her on the silken coverlet, and his lips found hers, molding intimately over her mouth as his body formed to hers. She welcomed his weight and the gentle probing of his tongue.

His fingers worked on the small buttons of her dress, and the pink fabric parted. Dallas groaned as he shoved the dress off her shoulders and stripped it from her body. He moved his hands easily over the silk of her slip and touched the lace that covered her breasts. "You're so beautiful," he murmured against her hair.

She opened his shirt and touched the fine mat of hair on his chest. He caught his breath, and she watched in wonder as his abdomen sucked in and became rigid. "So are you," she whispered, fascinated by this man.

His lips found hers again, and he made short work of their clothes, kicking them into a pile and never once releasing her. Chandra's skin seared where his fingers touched her body, and her breasts ached for more of his sweet, sweet touch. She arched against him, feeling the magic of his hands, lost in the wonder of his mouth.

He kissed her face, her neck, her hair. She writhed against him, trying to get closer, and when his tongue rimmed the delicate circle of bones at the base of her throat, she cried out. He moved lower still, kissing her breasts and suckling on her nipples while he explored her back and hips with sure hands.

"Dallas," she whispered, her voice rough and low, "Dallas." She traced a path along the curve of his spine, and he held back no longer. Suddenly he was atop her, his knee between hers, his chest heaving.

Their lips locked, and he entered her for the first time as her husband. "I can't wait," he whispered, and began his magical rhythm. Chandra clung to him, moving with him, feeling the sweat collect on her skin. She thought he whispered words of love, but in her fevered state she might have heard her own voice as they exploded together and she cried out.

"Dallas!"

"Oh, love, oh, love," he sighed, collapsing against her, spent.

They held each other for endless minutes as the fog of afterglow surrounded them. Chandra closed her eyes, for she knew she might cry, not from sadness, but from deeper emotions that tore at her heart.

When her heartbeat was finally normal, she opened her eyes and found him staring at her. "You okay?" he asked, and she smiled, shyly and self-consciously, as if she'd been a virgin.

"I'm fine. You?"

He swept back the hair from her face and kissed her forehead. "Well, I'm a helluva lot better than fine. In fact, I think I'm great."

She giggled, and to her mortification he picked her up and carried her, stark naked, into the bathroom. "What're you doing?" she asked as he dropped her into the tub and twisted on the faucets.

"If this is going to be a honeymoon, we've got to make the most of it," he replied, his eyes glinting devilishly as warm water rushed into the tub.

"By bathing?"

"Or whatever." He lit two candles, brought in the champagne and turned out the lights. She couldn't take her eyes off his lean muscles, how they moved so easily under his skin. She was intrigued by all of him—the way his dark hair matted across his chest, the corded strength of his shoulders, the white slash of a smile that flashed crookedly in the light of flickering candles.

He stepped into the tub and gathered her into his arms, and their slick bodies melded together. "This is crazy," she said with a laugh as he positioned her legs around him.

"This is wonderful," he corrected. The water rose to their chests, and he turned off the faucets. In the shadowy light, he gazed at her with eyes that seemed to shine with love.

"Now, Mrs. O'Rourke," he said, tracing a drip from her neck to the hollow of her breast, "let's find a way to stretch out these few hours as long as we can."

Hours later, after sipping champagne in the tub and making love on the round bed until they were both exhausted, they awoke and headed downstairs. Dawn was just sending shafts of light across the desert floor and through the streets of the now-quiet city. The neon lights, so brilliant the night before, were dimmed as Dallas drove toward the airport.

He parked the rental car in the lot near the terminal before they headed inside, ready to return to Ranger and fight for custody of J.D. Chandra was prepared for an uphill battle, but anything as precious as that baby was worth whatever it took. By sheer determination alone, she should be allowed to adopt the child she had saved.

As she walked down the concourse with Dallas at her side, her new role as his wife started to sink in. She felt suddenly secure and worked at convincing herself that she and Dallas would be given custody. No parents would love a child more.

From the corner of her eye, she saw Dallas slow near an airport shop, and she wondered if he was going to buy some souvenir of the trip.

"Goddamned son of a bitch!" he growled, stopping short and fishing in his pocket for change. He dropped several coins onto the counter.

Before the startled cashier could ring up the sale, Dallas grabbed a newspaper and snapped it open. There on page one, in grainy black and white, was a picture of J.D.

Baby Abandoned In Colorado Barn, the headline screamed, and in smaller letters, Mother Still Missing As Hundreds Hope To Adopt The Million Dollar Baby.

Chandra's throat went dry. She curled her fingers over Dallas's arms, seeking strength. "How—how did they get that picture?" she whispered, her eyes skimming the newsprint and her legs threatening to give way when the article revealed that the child was living with Sheriff Newell. "How did they get this information?"

"Ranger's a small town," Dallas replied, tight-lipped, a deep flush staining the back of his neck. Never had she seen him more furious. "Gossip runs rampant."

For the first time, Chandra had to face the fact that the odds against them were insurmountable. They were just a couple—a recently married couple—who would stand in line with hundreds of other couples—every one of them as anxious to adopt the baby as she and Dallas were.

"Come on," Dallas said, his voice sounding strangely faraway. "We've got a flight to catch."

Her throat caught, and tears threatened her eyes. *You're just tired,* she told herself, all of her earlier euphoria long gone.

"We haven't lost yet," Dallas reminded her, and he grabbed hold of her elbow and propelled her toward the boarding gate.

"You're right," she said, then shivered. Inside, she knew she was in for the fight of her life.

Chapter Thirteen

So here they were at home—a married couple. They'd driven directly to the cabin and now, after showering and changing, they were preparing to go into town.

Chandra poured herself a cup of coffee and smiled as she poured another for Dallas. It would be easy, she thought, to get into a routine with him, to wake up every morning in his arms and to read the paper, drink coffee and work around the house and outbuildings.

He planned on moving first his clothes and then his furniture as soon as possible. They'd even talked of expanding the cabin, and Dallas wanted to talk to an architect about the remodeling. Things were moving swiftly, but for the first time in years, Chandra felt comfortable depending upon someone besides herself.

She heard him on the stairs, and glanced up to see his handsome face pulled into a frown as he buttoned his shirt.

"I could help you with that," she offered, and he flashed her a slice of a grin.

"You're on."

When he reached the kitchen, she kissed his chest and slipped each button through its hole.

"If you keep this up, I'll never get to work," he said, his eyes lighting with a passionate flame.

"Uh-uh." She finished the shirt and handed him his coffee cup. "Come on outside, I think we should talk."

"About . . . ?"

She braced herself. "Me and what happened in Tennessee."

"You don't have to—"

"Of course I do," she said as he placed a hand on her shoulder. "We've got to start this marriage with a clean slate—no lies, no misunderstandings, no surprises."

Together they walked outside and Chandra felt the morning sun against her back as they leaned over the rail of the fence and watched the horses picking at the dew-laden grass. Sam trotted behind them only to be distracted by a squirrel.

"What happened?" Dallas finally asked, and Chandra decided to unburden herself.

"Medicine was my life," she admitted, thinking of all those grueling years in med school when she had not only worked for hours on end, but had to endure being the butt of too many jokes. Feeling Dallas's eyes upon her, she forced the words about her past from her throat. "I went to school in Philadelphia, then took a position with a hospital in Collier, Tennessee.

"You know about the patient I lost, a seven-year-old boy. His name was Gordy. It . . . it was messy." Her throat clogged momentarily, but she willed herself to go on, to get over the pain. "You saw the newspaper articles, but they didn't explain exactly what happened. I was sued for malpractice by the parents, though they brought him in much too late. They thought he had the flu, and he just got worse and worse. By the time we rushed him to the hospital . . . well, he died of pneumonia within the hour. The parents blamed me." She swallowed hard, looking not at Dallas but concentrating on a swallow as it flew about the barn roof. "There was an investigation, and I was cleared, but...well, I had other personal problems."

"Your marriage."

"Yes," she said with a sigh. "Everything seemed to unravel. So," she finished, trying to force a lightness into her voice, "I ended up here, with a job as a white-water and mountain guide."

"Don't you miss it?" He touched her lightly on the arm, and her heart warmed at the familiarity they'd slipped into.

"What—medicine?"

"The healing."

"Sometimes, but not often. I'm still a doctor," she said. "It wouldn't take much to get licensed here, but I guess I wasn't ready to start practicing again." She felt inexplicably close to tears, and he threw his coffee cup on the ground and took her into his arms.

"Losing a patient is hard, but it happens," he whispered.

"Children shouldn't die."

Gently, he rotated her, forced her to look at him, and Chandra didn't pull away from him as he kissed her lips. "No," he agreed, "no child should ever die, but, unfortunately, it happens. We try our best, and sometimes it isn't good enough." He looked down into her eyes, his own shining in the morning sunlight.

"I couldn't help feeling guilty, that if I would have gotten to him sooner, I could've saved his life."

"How could you have known?"

She shook her head and sighed, resting her cheek against Dallas's chest, feeling his warmth seep into her and hoping some of the old feelings of remorse would disappear. "I was married to Doug at the time, and he couldn't understand why I took it so hard. I wanted out of medicine, at least for a while, and he...he objected. We were making good money. He was a plastic surgeon in Memphis, and he didn't want our life-style to change. He told me that if I quit practicing that I would only be proving that I wasn't cut out to be a doctor, that all of his friends in medical school, the ones who had predicted I couldn't make it, would be proved right.''

"Wonderful guy," Dallas remarked, his voice steely.

"We had our share of problems.''

Dallas kissed her crown. "He was wrong, you know. Wrong about you. My guess is that you were and still are a damned good doctor.''

"Have you ever lost a patient?''

"Too many.''

"A child?''

"There've been a few. And I know what you went through. Each time, you can't help feeling that somehow you should have performed a miracle and saved his life.''

Her throat knotted, and she couldn't swallow. Tears, unwanted, burned behind her eyes. "Yes," she whispered as he pulled her closer, holding her, murmuring into her hair, kissing her cheek. She wouldn't cry! She wouldn't! She'd spent too many years burying the pain and her past. "All those years of school, all those hours of studying, all those nights of no sleep, and I couldn't save one little boy!" Slowly, she disentangled herself and swallowed the lump that seemed determined to lodge in her throat.

"It's over," Dallas promised. "You've got a new start. We've got a new start. So it's time we took the first step and tried to adopt that baby together.''

Chandra smiled through her tears and took Dallas's hand.

Cameras flashed, microphones were thrust in their faces and reporters, en masse, had collected around the Newells' house.

"Is it true you're married?" a woman with flaming red hair asked as Chandra tried to duck past the crowd.

"Yes.''

"And you met Dr. O'Rourke when you brought the baby in—is that right?" another female voice called.

"No comment," Dallas growled.

"Oh, come on, Doctor, give us a break. Tell us a little about the baby. Where do you think he came from? Have you checked with any of the local clinics and found out if a woman in the third trimester never delivered?"

"No," Dallas said.

"You have no idea where the mother is?"

"None." He helped Chandra up the stairs of the Newells' front porch as reporters fired questions nonstop. To keep the crowd at bay, a deputy was posted near the front door, but he let Chandra and Dallas pass, presumably on orders from the sheriff or his wife.

"Isn't it a madhouse out there?" Lenore asked, her eyes shadowed with worry, her face grim.

"I guess it's to be expected," Chandra replied, anxious to see the baby.

"I suppose." But Lenore's face seemed more lined this morning, her lips pinched into a worried pucker. "I've taken in a lot of children in my day, but I've never seen the likes of this," she admitted, parting the lace curtains and sighing at the group of reporters camped in her yard. "And I've quit answering the phone. Seems everyone in the state is interested in adopting little J.D."

Chandra's heart sank like a stone. Even though she held J.D. and gave him a bottle, she felt as if she were losing him, that the cord that had bound them so closely was being unraveled by unseen hands. As she held the bottle, she stared into his perfect little face. She didn't kid herself. Sooner or later, if the media attention surrounding J.D. kept up at a fever pitch, other would-be mothers would be trying to see him and hold him. They would argue that Chandra, just because the child was discovered in her barn, had no more right to be with him than they did. It wouldn't be long before the courts or the Social Services stepped in, and in the interest of fairness, she might not be allowed to see him.

"Has it been this way for long?" Dallas asked Lenore.

"Since before dawn. And the phone has been ringing since about six last night. Someone must've let it slip that the baby's here because before that there was nothing. I was living a normal life. I don't like this, I tell you."

"Neither do I," Dallas replied, and Chandra bit her lip to keep tears from spilling on the baby who would never be hers.

As Chandra settled into a comfortable life with Dallas, the interest in the baby didn't decrease. While she was busy making closet space for Dallas's things, helping him fill out change-of-address forms and planning the addition to the house, her name and picture appeared in newspapers as far away as Phoenix and Sante Fe. At first she was considered a small-time heroine, the woman who had discovered the baby and rushed him to the hospital. Over the next week, her life was opened up and dissected, and all the old headlines appeared.

The story of little Gordy Shore and his death was revived, and her marriage to Doug Pendleton, subsequent divorce and change of name and life-style in Colorado were hashed and rehashed in the newspapers and on the local news. She'd given two interviews, but quit when the questions became, as they always did, much too personal.

It was known that she was trying to adopt the baby, along with hundreds of other applicants, and it had even been speculated that her marriage to Dallas, at first a seeming fairy-tale romance of two people who meet via an abandoned infant then fall in love, was a fraud, a ploy for custody.

"I don't know what I expected," she admitted to Dallas, upon reading a rather scorching article in the *Denver Free Spirit*. "But it wasn't this."

Dallas, who had been polishing the toes of his shoes, rested one foot on the seat of a chair and leaned across the table to stare more closely at her. "Giving up so soon, Mrs. O'Rourke? And here I thought you liked a battle."

"Not when the stakes are so high," she admitted, her stomach in knots. She hazarded a quick glance at him. "And I'm not giving up. Not yet."

"Not as long as there's an ounce of breath in your body, I'd wager," he said, winking at her.

She rolled her eyes, but giggled. The past few days had been as wonderful as they had been gut wrenching. Though she was worried about adopting J.D., her life with Dallas was complicated, but interesting, and their lovemaking was passionate. She couldn't resist him when he kissed her, and she felt a desperation in their lovemaking, as if they each knew that soon it would be over. If they weren't awarded custody of J.D., they would have no reason to stay together. That thought, too, was depressing. Because each day she was with him, she loved him a little more.

Sam whined to go out, and she slung the strap of her canvas purse over her shoulder. "I guess I'd better get to work," she said. "And I'll talk to my attorney today, see what he's come up with."

"I'll walk you," Dallas offered, holding open the door for her as Sam streaked across the yard. The morning was cool, the sky, usually clear, dark with clouds. Even through her jacket, Chandra shivered.

She reached for the handle of the door of her Suburban, but Dallas caught her hand.

"What's up, Doctor?" she asked, turning to face him and seeing his gaze was as sober as the threatening sky.

"I think I've gone about this marriage thing assbackward," Dallas admitted.

"We both have."

"Right. But I decided that we need to set things right. So, I hope this is a start." He reached into his pocket and withdrew a small silver ring, obviously old, with a single diamond surrounded by smaller sapphires.

"Where did you get this?" she whispered as he slipped it over her finger, and the ring, a size or two too big, lolled below her knuckle.

"It was my grandmother's. Harrison's mother. I don't remember much about her—except that she was kind and loving, and the one person in the world who would always stand up for me." He cleared his throat suddenly, and Chandra's heart twisted with pain for the man who had once been such a lonely boy. "She died when I was about eight and she left me this—" he motioned to the ring "—and a little money for college and medical school."

Chandra, her throat thick, her eyes heavy with tears of happiness, touched the ring with the fingers of her other hand.

"You can have it sized," he said. "Or if you'd prefer something new—"

"Oh, no! It's... it's perfect! Thank you!" Moved, she threw her arms around his neck and kissed his throat, drawing in deep breaths filled with his special scent. "We're going to make this work, Doctor," she whispered into his ear. "I just know it!"

Opening the door of the Suburban, she saw the ring wink in the little morning light that permeated the clouds. She wondered vaguely if Jennifer had worn this very ring, and a little jab of jealousy cut through her. But she ignored the pain; Jennifer was history. Chandra, now, was Mrs. Dallas O'Rourke.

She pushed all negative thoughts aside as she drove into town and stopped at Roy Arnette's office. The lawyer was waiting for her, his glasses perched on the end of his nose, his mouth tiny and pinched. "Have you talked to the Newells today?" he asked as she sat down.

"It's only nine in the morning."

Roy sighed. "Then you don't know."

"Know what?" she asked, but she read the trouble in his eyes, and her throat seemed to close in on itself.

"There's a woman. Her name is Gayla Vanwyk. She claims to be the baby's mother."

"But she couldn't be—" Chandra whispered, her world spinning wildly, her heart freezing.

"Maybe not. But the police are interested in her."

"But where did she come from? How did she get here? She could be some kook, for crying out loud, someone who read about J.D. in one of these—" She thumped her hand on a newspaper lying open on Roy's desk. "She could just be after publicity or want a child or God only knows what else!"

"Look, Chandra, I'm only telling you what I know, which is that the police are interested in her enough to have some blood work done on her."

"Oh, God—"

"If she's the natural mother . . ."

Tears jammed her throat, and Chandra blinked hard. "If she is, why did she leave him?" she demanded, outraged.

"If she's the natural mother, this complicates things," Roy said. "She'll have rights."

"She gave those up when she left him!"

"Maybe not, Chandra," he said as gently as possible, and Chandra felt as if her entire world were crumbling.

Dallas! She needed to talk to Dallas. He'd know what to do. "I won't lose him, Roy, I won't!" she cried, though a horrible blackness was seeping into her soul. Again she saw how small her chances of becoming J.D.'s mother actually were. Sobs choked her throat, but she didn't let them erupt. "I want to see her," she said with dead calm.

"You can't. The police are still talking to her."

"I'll wait," she insisted, somehow managing to keep the horrid fear of losing the baby at bay. "But at the first opportunity, I want to talk to that woman!"

"She's definitely postpartum," Dallas said quietly. The bottom dropped out of Chandra's world as she sat slumped into a chair in his office, her heart heavy. "Now we're waiting for the lab to check blood types." He looked tired, his blue eyes dark with worry, his hair uncombed. He rubbed his neck, as if to straighten the kinks, and Chandra was reminded of the first time she'd seen him in the emergency room so few weeks before. He'd been weary then, too, but she'd known that this man was different, special. And now he was as sick with worry as she was. Maybe even more so.

"So she's had a baby," Chandra whispered with a stiff lift of her shoulder as she feigned nonchalance. "That doesn't mean she had *this* baby."

"Very recently."

"Does she look like J.D.?"

He shook his head. "Who can tell? She has black hair, dark eyes. And it doesn't matter, anyway. The boy could look like his father—or someone else in the family."

Chandra's hands were shaking. She clasped them together and saw the ring, Dallas's grandmother's ring, her wedding ring, a symbol of a marriage that, perhaps, was never meant to be. Taking in a shuddering breath, she stared past Dallas to the window where the first drops of rain were slanting over the glass. Thunderheads brewed angrily over the mountains, and the sky was dark as pitch. "I can't believe it. Not after all this . . . She can't just appear and claim the child. . . ."

Dallas rounded his desk and took her hands in his; the stones of the ring pressed into his palm. "Don't tell me you're a quitter after all, Mrs. O'Rourke."

"It seems the odds are against us, aren't they?" Chandra had only to crane her neck to see the newspapers littering Dallas's desk. "That name—the Million Dollar Baby— it's stuck. Did you know that? Some couples are actually in a bidding war to gain custody. What chance do we have?"

Dallas's eyes flickered with sadness. He pressed a kiss against her temple. "We haven't lost yet."

"But it doesn't look good."

"We won't know if she's even possibly the mother until the blood work is analyzed. Even then, we can't be sure. She has no birth certificate—claimed she had him out in the woods near your place. She can't or won't name the father."

Chandra's shoulders slumped. Even if this woman did prove to be a fraud, she was just the first. Woman after woman could claim to be mother of the baby, and sooner or later the real one might show up. If, God willing, she and Dallas were allowed to adopt J.D....

Her heart ripped, and she bit her lip to fight back tears. Dallas was right about one thing, they hadn't lost yet, even though the odds of adopting the child seemed to be getting slimmer by the minute.

Dallas drew her to her feet and wrapped his arms around her, as if he really cared. Her heart nearly crumbled, and she wanted to lean against him, to sob like a baby, to cling to him for his strength, but she wouldn't break down. Instead, she contented herself with resting her head against his chest and listened to the calming rhythm of his heartbeat. God, how she loved him. If he only knew.... But she couldn't tell him. Not yet. She'd seem like some simpering female, depressed and clinging to a man who had no real ties to her.

Gayla Vanwyk wasn't too happy about being in the hospital, that much was certain from the crease in her brow and the pout of her full lips. Dallas guessed her age at twenty-three, give or take a couple of years. She was a beautiful girl, really, with curling black hair that framed a heart-shaped face filled with near-perfect features. Her exotic eyes were deep brown, rimmed with curling ebony lashes and poised above high cheekbones.

She sat in Dr. Trent's office, smoking a cigarette and staring with obvious distrust at the people in the room. Dallas stood near the window and looked down at the parking lot where, wedged between the cars of doctors, nurses, staff and patients, were double-parked vans and cars. Reporters milled about the parking lot and lobby.

"Shouldn't I have my attorney here or somethin'?" Gayla asked, eyeing the men and women who had dealt with the infant.

Dr. Trent, as always soft-spoken, smiled kindly. "This isn't an inquisition, Miss Vanwyk. These are some of the doctors who examined the child when he came into the hospital, and they'd like to explain his conditions to you." He tried to calm her down, to explain that they were only interested in the health of the baby, but she wasn't buying it.

"Look, I've done all I have to," she said, crushing her cigarette in a glass ashtray Trent had scrounged out of his desk. "I know my rights. I want my baby back."

"As soon as the test results are in, we'll forward them to the police and Social Services," Trent said.

"Good. And how long will that take?" She stood up, ending the interview, and deposited her pack of cigarettes into a well-worn purse.

"A day at most, but Social Services—"

"Screw Social Services, I just want my kid."

"You left him," Dallas said, unable to let the conversation end so abruptly.

"Yeah, I had to. No choice."

"Why not?"

"That's personal," she said, narrowing her eyes on him. "And I don't have to talk to you. You're the doctor who wants to adopt him, aren't you? You're married to the woman who found him."

"I just want to get to the truth."

"Well, you got it." She turned on her heel and left the scent of heavy perfume and smoke wafting after her.

"If that's the mother, I don't envy the kid," Dr. Spangler said, fiddling with the buttons on his watch. "Maternal, she's not."

Dallas shoved his hands into the back pockets of his pants. "I don't buy it," he said, his eyes narrowing a little as he considered the woman's story. Even if she was the baby's mother, she seemed more defensive than concerned about the child.

In his own office, he punched out the number of his friend in Denver, the private investigator. Why not check out Miss Vanwyk? If she proved, indeed, to be J.D.'s mother, and the state saw fit to grant her custody, there wasn't much Dallas could do about it. If, however, she wasn't the baby's mother, or he could prove her unfit, then at least the baby would be placed in a home with loving parents—not necessarily with Chandra and him, but with people who loved him.

And what will you and Chandra do? Call the whole thing off? Divorce? Or start over? Living together not for the sake of a child, but because you love each other.

Love? Did he love her already?

Impossible. Love was out of his realm. Or was it? After all, he had given her the ring, a ring he'd never even shown to Jennifer.

At the realization that he'd fallen all too willing a victim to love again, Dallas flung one leg over the corner of his desk and wondered how he could convince Chandra that, with or without the baby, they belonged together. . . .

"Killingsworth Agency," a female voice cooed over the phone, and Dallas snapped his wandering thoughts back to attention. First, he had to find out about the woman claiming to be the baby's mother; next, he'd deal with his marriage.

Three days later, Chandra was a nervous wreck. Certainly blood tests couldn't take so long . . . unless they were testing DNA.

She'd begged Dallas for information, but he claimed he, as a prospective adoptive parent, was being kept as much in the dark as she. It was all she could do not to find Miss Vanwyk and demand answers.

"In due time," Dallas told her. "You can't risk talking to her now. It might jeopardize our chances of adopting the baby."

And so she kept away. But the press didn't let up, and Chandra felt as if her life were being examined through a microscope. As was Gayla Vanwyk's. Chandra's life seemed to be a story right out of the most sensational of the tabloids, and she had trouble sleeping at night. Were it not for Dallas's strong arms on which she had come to depend, she doubted she would be getting any rest at all.

As for work, things were slowing down as summer receded into fall. And though Chandra needed to fill her idle days, Rick wouldn't hear any arguments from her. "Listen, you look like you haven't had a decent night's sleep in two weeks, and we're not busy, anyway. Until all this hubbub about that kid dies down, you take some time off. Consider it paid vacation or a honeymoon or whatever, but you take all the time you need to put your life in order. Listen to someone who knows what he's talking about— this is free advice, Chan. If I would've spent more time working things out with Cindy, she'd probably still be here with the kids and I would still be playing Santa Claus instead of getting Christmas cards from St. Louis."

Never, in the years she'd worked with him, had Chandra heard him complain about the split from the woman who'd borne his children. Though he hadn't married anyone else, hardly even dated, Rick just didn't talk about his past.

Chandra grabbed a rag from behind the register and slapped at a cobweb hanging from the wagon-wheel chandelier. "But I can't just sit around the house and stare at Sam all day," she protested, frowning as she spotted another dangling string of dust.

"Why not? It'd do you some good. You haven't taken any time off since you started working here."

Randy breezed through the door and heard the tail end of their argument. "Hey, you may as well take advantage of Rick's good humor," he said, his eyes twinkling. "I am. I'm gonna find me a woman and a kid and get married and take a few months' paid vacation—"

"Get outta here," Rick said, chuckling to himself. "No, not you, Randy. But you, Chan, do yourself a favor. Get to know that husband of yours."

That husband of mine, she thought ruefully. For how long? Snagging her long denim coat from the peg near the door, she hurried outside and shivered in the cold mountain wind. The first snow of the season had dusted the highest peaks, but here, in the lower valley, raindrops danced in the parking lot, creating shallow puddles that she had to dodge as she made her way to her Suburban. The thought of living without little J.D. was crippling, the thought of living without Dallas devastating. In a few short weeks, they'd become so close, and their marriage, though it hadn't been based on love, had provided, in many ways, the happiest moments of her life—though her parents had been shocked when she'd called them with the news.

"You shouldn't have been so hasty!" her mother had warned. "What do you know about this man?"

Chandra's father had come to her rescue. "Oh, hush, Jill. She's old enough to know what she's doing!"

"And that's what you said when she married Doug!"

Now, remembering the telephone conversation, Chandra smiled at her parents' happy bickering. They'd be lost without each other. They depended upon each other, and, yes, they argued with each other, but she never doubted that their love ran as deep as any ocean and their devotion to each other, as well as to their three daughters, was stronger than any force on earth.

She'd hoped for that same kind of love and devotion in her own marriage to Doug, and it hadn't occurred. But this time...if only Dallas could love her....

She wasn't ready to go home, knowing that there would be more messages from reporters on her answering machine. She drove instead to the hospital, hoping that she could share a cup of coffee with Dallas or just talk to him.

In the parking lot, Chandra encountered reporters, hand-held cameras, microphones and tape recorders. A police cruiser was idling near the entrance, and Chandra recognized the flat, frowning face of Deputy Stan Bodine behind the wheel. Chandra waved at him as she drove to a rear parking lot.

She left her Suburban far from the main doors and dashed through the physician's lot to a side entrance. Inside the hospital, she shook the rain from her hair and rubbed her hands from the cold, then hurried to Dallas's office.

He wasn't in. Dena checked his schedule and relayed that Dallas wasn't due back in the hospital until two, at which time he was to report for his shift in ER.

Chandra visited the nurses in the pediatrics wing, then took the elevator to ER. Dallas hadn't signed in yet. There were a few patients in the waiting room as Chandra started for the door. She was near Alma Lindquist's desk when she heard the voice of a distraught mother.

"But he hasn't taken any liquids. I can't get him to drink, and his temp's been at a hundred and four for a couple of days. The pediatrician says it's just the flu, but I'm worried."

"Who's your pediatrician?" Nurse Lindquist inquired.

"Dr. Sands, and I trust him, but Carl is so sick..."

Chandra couldn't help but overhear the conversation, and she looked at the small boy cradled in his mother's arms. His face was pale, and he could barely keep his eyes open. "Has he had any blood work done?" she asked.

"No, I don't think so," the mother replied, her own face pasty with worry.

"You haven't had a white count?"

"Not that I know of." The mother looked perplexed. "Dr. Sands says there's a virus going around...."

Alma rose from her chair. "Mrs. O'Rourke, this isn't..."

But Chandra didn't hear her. As she looked at the little boy, images of another sick child came to mind. She saw Gordy Shore's listless eyes and pale face, his lethargy palpable.

"Admit this child immediately. Get a white count, and if that's elevated, have his lungs X-rayed." Chandra turned to the mother. "Have there been any other symptoms—vomiting? Diarrhea? Swelling?"

"No, he just barely moves, and he's usually so active," the mother replied, obviously close to tears.

"Don't worry. We'll take care of him."

"Thank God."

"Has Dr. Sands listened to his lungs—"

"Last week," the mother replied.

"Admit this child," Chandra ordered again, but Nurse Lindquist's lips pressed into a stubborn line. Obviously, she wasn't taking any instructions from a woman who held no authority at Riverbend, but Chandra, spying Dallas walking from the stairs, flew past her. "That patient," she said, motioning to the little boy, "is supposed to have the flu, but he hasn't had a white count and..." She rattled off the conversation to Dallas and, thankfully, he listened to her.

"There are other patients," Nurse Lindquist objected as Dallas approached, but he surveyed the waiting room where a few people sat patiently, flipping through ragged magazines.

"Anything life threatening?" he asked.

"No."

"Admit this child—now," he ordered as an ambulance roared to the doors. "And call Dr. Hodges if we need more help." He then led the mother and child back to the examining room.

Pandemonium broke loose as another ambulance, siren screaming, pulled up to the door. Paramedics began wheeling stretchers into the emergency room.

Chandra heard the page calling for every available staff member, and she saw the influx of personnel and equipment. Suddenly, nurses, doctors and volunteers were everywhere as the first of the patients were wheeled into examining rooms.

"Bad accident...truck jackknifed on the freeway..." she heard a paramedic explain to a nurse. "This one needs help, he's lost a lot of blood and his blood pressure has dropped—"

"Put him in room three. Dr. Prescott's on his way."

Chandra didn't even think about the ramifications of what she was doing, but followed Dallas into the examining room, where he was leaning over the boy, a stethoscope to his chest.

"I don't hear anything, but we'll have to see—"

Shannon Pratt stuck her head into the examining room. "Dr. O'Rourke, we need you! Big accident. Multiple victims. We're calling all the staff back to the hospital."

"I can handle this," Chandra said, motioning to the boy, her heart in her throat. "You had blood taken?"

"It's in the lab now."

"I'll take him to X-ray." Chandra met the questions in Dallas's gaze and didn't flinch. A special glimmer passed between them. "They need you out there," she said. Shouts, moans and the sound of rattling equipment and frantic footsteps filtered through the door.

"You're sure about this?" Dallas asked.

"Positive. Come on," she said to the boy as she lifted him into a wheelchair, "let's get some pictures taken...."

The rest of the afternoon passed in a blur. Chandra helped out where she could, but was sent home when the administration caught wind that a doctor not certified in the state was giving advice, if only to other physicians. Though she didn't actually treat anyone, the administration was taking no chances. They didn't even allow her to do volunteer work, for fear that her connection to Dr. O'Rourke, Baby John Doe and Gordy Shore—plus the fact that she was unlicensed—could be grounds for one helluva lawsuit should anything go wrong.

But Chandra was grateful to have been able to help, and she wondered, not for the first time, about becoming licensed in Colorado.

The cabin seemed suddenly lonely and empty. Dallas had told her not to wait up for him, and she felt a despondency she'd never experienced in all the time that she'd lived here.

Several calls had come in while she was out. One had been from a reporter from Los Angeles, another from a married couple from Bend, Oregon, and a third from a lawyer in Des Moines whose clients "would pay big money" for an infant. As if she could or would help them.

Chandra took down the numbers and relayed them to Marian Sedgewick, the social worker, who, to Chandra's dismay, hedged concerning the adoption. She had mentioned that even if Gayla Vanwyk were a fraud, many couples were trying desperately to adopt the child. Though Chandra's petition was given special consideration because of all Chandra's help with the child and obvious love for the baby, there were also good reasons for placing him with someone else.

"Oh, Lord, what a mess." It seemed that the odds of adopting J.D. were impossible. Chandra wanted to cry, but didn't. Even if they couldn't adopt the baby, she and Dallas still had each other. Or did they? Without J.D. would Dallas be willing to try and make this marriage work? She could trick him, of course, by becoming pregnant with his child. He wouldn't divorce her then, not with his feelings on children and family. But could she do it?

No.

She wouldn't base this marriage on lies or trickery, even if it cost her the husband she loved as much as life itself.

Feeling as if the weight of the world rested on her slim shoulders, Chandra walked to the barn and saddled Brandy. The rain had let up a little, and the game little mare was frisky, anxious to stretch her legs as Chandra rode her over the sodden fields surrounding the house. Thoughts of J.D. and Dallas filled her mind, but she refused to be depressed. And just like the afternoon sun that had begun to peer through the dark clouds, her mood lightened.

The smell of rain-washed ground filled her nostrils, and the cool wind raced through her hair. She thought of life without Dallas or J.D. and decided, while her knees were clamped firmly around her mount's withers, that she'd have to tell Dallas that she loved him. She'd always been truthful with him before, and now, even if it meant his rejection, she had to confront him with the simple fact that she'd fallen in love with him. If he laughed in her face, so be it. If he divorced her on the spot, she'd survive. But life would never be the same, and these past few precious days would surely shine as the brightest in her life.

She rode Brandy back to the barn, groomed all the horses, fed and watered the stock, and when she was finished, snapped out the lights. "You could use a bath yourself," she told Sam. "Maybe tomorrow, since I'm a woman of leisure for the next week or so." That thought, too, was depressing. What if she had no husband, no baby, no job? A lump filled her throat, and she scratched Sam's ears. "Well, buddy, we've still got each other, right?"

The big dog loped to the back door.

Chandra couldn't shake her dark mood. She showered, changed and started cooking a huge pot of stew. As the stew simmered, she baked cornbread and found a frozen container of last year's applesauce. Now, no matter what time Dallas arrived home, she'd have a hot meal ready and waiting. *As if that were enough to tie him to you!* What a fool she'd been! And what a mess she'd gotten herself into!

Once the bread was out of the oven, she turned the stew down and grabbed a paperback thriller she'd been trying to read ever since J.D. and Dallas had slammed into her life. But the story didn't interest her and before long she tossed the damned book aside, sitting near the fire and wishing she could predict the future.

She must've dozed, because before she knew it, Sam was barking his fool head off.

Dallas!

Her heart leapt and she wondered if she had the nerve to tell him that she loved him.

As he opened the door, she flung herself into his arms and held him close. Tears filled her eyes at the thought that she could not only lose J.D., but this man, as well.

"What's this?" he asked with a familiar chuckle that touched her heart.

"I'm just glad to see you," she said, embarrassed and sniffing.

His arms held her tight, and he buried his face in her hair. "And I'm glad to see you." He kissed her cheek and held her at arm's length, surveying her. His face drew into a pensive frown at the sight of her tears.

"The accident victims?"

"Most will pull through," he said, sounding as weary as he looked, "but we lost a couple."

"I'm sorry."

"So am I," he said, holding her and sighing in relief or contentment, she didn't know which. She caught a glimpse of naked fear in his eyes, and she wondered what had happened.

"How about a glass of wine?"

"You got one?"

"In a minute." She pulled out a bottle of chardonnay from the refrigerator, found the corkscrew and poured them each a glass. "What will we toast to?" she asked.

"How about to you?" he suggested, releasing the top button of his shirt. "You're a local hero—make that heroine."

"I am? And all this time I thought that the Bob Fillmores of the world would like to tar and feather me in the press."

"Oh, but that's changed. You vindicated yourself," he said with a twinkle in his tired eyes. "Remember the boy you wanted me to treat this afternoon? The boy with the flu. Well, you were right. He has pneumonia. And I think we treated him in time. We pumped him full of antibiotics, and he's starting to respond. Thanks to you. If he'd had to sit around the waiting room..." He shrugged. "Well, it could've been bad."

Chandra felt tears well in her eyes. Vindicated? She hardly thought so. She'd lost Gordy Shore, but this time another life had been spared.

Dallas took a swallow of his wine, then twisted one finger in a lock of her hair, staring at the golden strands as if he were fascinated with her. "You know, even old hardnosed Trent conceded that Riverbend could use another doctor. If you're interested."

"Another Dr. O'Rourke?" she replied, shaking her head, but smiling nonetheless. "Could the world stand it?"

"Could you?" His voice was low and serious.

"I—I don't know." She blinked hard. Practice medicine again? It had been so long. And, in truth, she'd missed it. But she wasn't sure she was ready. "How would you feel about having a doctor for a wife?"

Dallas grinned crookedly, as if he knew something she didn't. He tossed back his wine and set down the glass. "Personally, I'd go for it. I wouldn't mind seeing you every day. In fact, you would certainly perk up the place, but I'm not the only one we have to consider. I don't know how our son would feel about his mother—"

Her wineglass crashed to the floor, shattering and splashing chardonnay all over the floor. Sam jumped to his feet, growling fiercely.

"Our...son?" she repeated hoarsely. Her throat closed and for a few seconds she could hear nothing save the rush of blood through her head. "The baby—is he . . . ?"

Dallas's face split into a wide grin. He took her hand and led her to the stairs where she sank onto the bottom step. "Gayla Vanwyk was lying. She's not J.D.'s mother. She was hired by a couple who wanted a child so badly that they would do anything, including pay her ten thousand dollars to pose as the mother. It might've worked, too. Her blood type was compatible with the child's and since we didn't know the father, it would be hard to disprove her story."

Nothing was making much sense. "Then how—"

"The DNA testing. She balked at that, and Sheriff Newell was already checking her out. I'd already called my friend in Denver—you remember, the private investigator?"

"How could I ever forget?" Chandra said dryly.

"Well, he worked the pieces of the puzzle out and called Sheriff Newell, who confronted Gayla with the truth. She broke down and confessed. She had a baby a few weeks ago, which she sold to another couple, the Hendersons. This was just a way to make a little more cash. Charges are already being considered against the couple that put her up to it."

"But I talked to Marian Sedgewick. There are other people who want the baby—"

"I know. Influential people with money. But when push came to shove, Social Services was worried about a scandal if it turns out that any of the couples who have applied for custody of the Million Dollar Baby have done anything the least bit shady."

"So . . . ?" she prodded, hardly daring to hope, though her silly spirits were rapidly climbing.

"So, until the mother is located, the baby will be put in a permanent foster-care situation, and hopefully those parents will be able to adopt him."

"Meaning us?" she asked. Her breath caught deep in her lungs.

"Meaning us."

Tears ran down her face. "Thank God."

"This means we have to stay married, you know." His steady blue gaze assessed her as he leaned over the stairs, his face so close, she could see the lines of worry near his eyes.

"I wouldn't have it any other way."

"No?"

"Oh, God, Dallas, don't you know how much I love you?" she asked, the words tumbling out in a rasp. "Even if we had lost J.D., I would have wanted to stay married to you. I—I..." Words failed her as she realized he might not feel the same.

But Dallas's blue eyes reflected the depth of his emotions, of his love. He gathered her into his arms. "And here I'd been thinking that you'd leave me if it weren't for the baby," he said, his voice cracking with raw emotion.

"Oh, Dallas. Never!" she cried, taking his face in her hands and kissing him long on the lips. "I just spent the last few hours scheming how to keep you married to me if we lost the baby. No matter what happens, Doctor, you're stuck with me."

"Promise?" he asked, hardly daring to believe her as he folded her into his arms.

"Forever!"

"I'm going to hold you to it, Ms. Hill."

"Mrs. O'Rourke," she corrected with a hearty laugh that seemed to spring from her very soul. She wound her arms around his neck and brushed her lips over his. With or without the baby, she knew she would love this man forever, but the fact that they were to become J.D.'s parents only made their future brighter and happier.

"Come on, *Mrs. O'Rourke,*" he said, lifting her off her feet and carrying her up the stairs. "Let's celebrate."

Epilogue

Deep in sleep, Chandra heard the cry, a pitiful wail that permeated her subconscious. Sam barked, and she was instantly awake.

Dallas mumbled and turned over. "Some father you turned out to be," she muttered, grinning at him just the same. They'd been married over two months and she still felt like a newlywed as each day brought more happiness.

The baby cried again and Chandra smiled. "Coming," she whispered, sliding her feet into slippers and crawling out from the warmth of the bed. She threw on her robe, padded to the bassinet and picked up the squalling infant. "Shh..." she murmured, kissing the down that was his hair. She carried him downstairs and heated a bottle, all the while rocking slowly back and forth, humming and feeling happier than she ever had in her life.

Outside, snow powdered the ground and moonglow cast the icicles and snow with a silvery sheen. As she sat in the rocker near the dying embers in the fireplace, she placed a bottle in her baby's mouth. J.D. suckled hungrily, and Sam circled three times before dropping onto the rug near the hearth.

"Merry Christmas." She heard the words and looked up to see Dallas, his hair rumpled, his eyes still heavy with sleep, looking not too different from the first time she'd seen him in the hospital emergency room.

"Merry Christmas to you, too. Even though it's only Christmas Eve."

"I know, I know." He shuffled down the stairs, clad only in jeans, and plugged in the lights of the Christmas tree. The red, green, blue and yellow bulbs reflected on the windowpanes. "Are you ready for the tribe?" he asked, tossing a mossy length of oak onto the grate before taking J.D. from her arms and feeding his son.

"Your family? Why not?"

"They're loud, opinionated and—"

"I've already met Brian."

"Well, Mom and the girls aren't as bad as he is."

Chandra laughed. "You'll have to put up with mine, too."

"Can you imagine everyone in here?" He looked around the small cabin. The addition wasn't yet finished, and with all the relatives, the room would be cramped. Fortunately, Dallas's family was staying at his condo, as the lease hadn't yet expired, and Chandra's family was going to sleep at the local hotel.

"It'll be perfect."

Dallas, still holding J.D., sat next to the hearth, and Chandra cuddled up next to him. Sam wagged his tail and placed his head in her lap.

"I have an early Christmas present for you," Chandra confided, deciding now was the time to share her secret.

"Can't it wait?"

"Nope. I think you'll want it now."

One dark eyebrow lifted in interest.

"Well, actually, you're not going to receive it until next summer, but it's been ordered."

His face pulled into a frown and she giggled. He must've suspected, for his lips slid into a wide smile. "Don't tell me—"

"That's right, Doctor. We've got a brother or sister for J.D. on the way."

Dallas swallowed hard, and he forgot about the bottle, causing J.D. to cry out.

"Here, let me handle this one," Chandra said, reaching for the baby. "You know, I was worried that someone would come and take this little guy away from us." The baby cuddled close to her breast and yawned.

"Never," Dallas promised. "I don't care how many children we have, J.D. is our first, and I'd walk through hell to keep him with us."

"Would you?" Tears glistened in her eyes.

"You and J.D. and now the new baby are the most important things in my life," he said, his voice husky. He cradled his wife and child close to him. "Nothing will ever change that. And nothing, *nothing,* will ever come between us. I love you, Chandra, and I always will."

The sound of his conviction caused the tears to stream from her eyes. "Come on," he said. "Let's change this guy and put him back to bed."

While the lights of the Christmas tree twinkled and the fire blazed in the grate, Chandra carried J.D. up the stairs. Dallas, holding her, kissed the top of her head. "I've never been this happy in my life," he admitted, and his happiness was the best Christmas present she'd ever received.

* * * * *

Silhouette Special Edition

COMING NEXT MONTH

#745 SILENT SAM'S SALVATION—Myrna Temte *Cowboy Country*
Reluctant rancher Sam Dawson hadn't envisioned a housekeeper like Dani
Smith. Fast-talking, stylish, two kids in tow—Dani swept up so well, she
uncovered his secret . . . proving herself Silent Sam's salvation.

#746 DREAMBOAT OF THE WESTERN WORLD—Tracy Sinclair
Struggling single mother Melissa Fairfield wasn't acting. But when movie
star Granger McMasters gazed upon the graceful, capable woman tending
his garden, he saw the makings of a lifelong love scene. . . .

#747 BEYOND THE NIGHT—Christine Flynn
Mitchell Kincaid was drawn to the thrill of dangerous pastimes. He
thought nothing of taking risks, until Jamie Withers made him face the
biggest risk of all—falling in love. . . .

#748 WHEN SOMEBODY LOVES YOU—Trisha Alexander
Only one thing kept Laura Sebastian and Neil Cantrelle apart: Laura's
engagement—to Neil's brother. Brokenhearted, she struggled not to break
her vow, waiting . . . hoping . . . for mending, magical love to prevail.

#749 OUTCAST WOMAN—Lucy Gordon
Mystical beauty Kirsty Trennon was a woman scorned and alone, until
runaway prisoner Mike Stallard appeared. Both outcasts, they shared
earthly passion; could they clear their names and find heavenly love?

#750 ONE PERFECT ROSE—Emilie Richards
Wealthy executive Jase Millington wanted to give homeless Becca Hanks
everything she needed. But to win the strong, independent Becca's love,
Jase needed to take a lesson in receiving. . . .

AVAILABLE THIS MONTH:

Take 4 bestselling love stories FREE

Plus get a FREE surprise gift!

FREE GIFT OFFER

To receive your free gift, send us the specified number of proofs-of-purchase from any specially marked Free Gift Offer Harlequin or Silhouette book with the Free Gift Certificate properly completed, plus a check or money order (do not send cash) to cover postage and handling payable to Harlequin/Silhouette Free Gift Promotion Offer. We will send you the specified gift.

FREE GIFT CERTIFICATE

ITEM	A. GOLD TONE EARRINGS	B. GOLD TONE BRACELET	C. GOLD TONE NECKLACE
# of proofs-of-purchase required	3	6	9
Postage and Handling	$1.75	$2.25	$2.75
Check one	☐	☐	☐

Name: _____

Address: _____

City: _____ State: _____ Zip Code: _____

Mail this certificate, specified number of proofs-of-purchase and a check or money order for postage and handling to: HARLEQUIN/SILHOUETTE FREE GIFT OFFER 1992, P.O. Box 9057, Buffalo, NY 14269-9057. Requests must be received by July 31, 1992.

PLUS—Every time you submit a completed certificate with the correct number of proofs-of-purchase, you are automatically entered in our MILLION DOLLAR SWEEPSTAKES! No purchase or obligation necessary to enter. See below for alternate means of entry and how to obtain complete sweepstakes rules.

MILLION DOLLAR SWEEPSTAKES
NO PURCHASE OR OBLIGATION NECESSARY TO ENTER

To enter, hand-print (mechanical reproductions are not acceptable) your name and address on a 3"×5" card and mail to Million Dollar Sweepstakes 6097, c/o either P.O. Box 9056, Buffalo, NY 14269-9056 or P.O. Box 621, Fort Erie, Ontario L2A 5X3. Limit: one entry per envelope. Entries must be sent via 1st-class mail. For eligibility, entries must be received no later than March 31, 1994. No liability is assumed for printing errors, lost, late or misdirected entries.

Sweepstakes is open to persons 18 years of age or older. All applicable laws and regulations apply. Sweepstakes offer void wherever prohibited by law. Prizewinners will be determined no later than May 1994. Chances of winning are determined by the number of entries distributed and received. For a copy of the Official Rules governing this sweepstakes offer, send a self-addressed, stamped envelope (WA residents need not affix return postage) to: Million Dollar Sweepstakes Rules, P.O. Box 4733, Blair, NE 68009.

✂ SS2U

ONE PROOF-OF-PURCHASE
To collect your fabulous FREE GIFT you must include the necessary FREE GIFT proofs-of-purchase with a properly completed offer certificate.

(See inside back cover for offer details)